Susannah of the Mounties

Shirley Temple EDITION

Susannah of the Mounties

by MURIEL DENISON

With illustrations from the motion picture
featuring SHIRLEY TEMPLE

RANDOM HOUSE, NEW YORK

To my father
DAVID JAMES GOGGIN
First Superintendent
of Education in the
North West Territories

Contents

Susannah of the Mounties

1. The Telegram

Commissioner John Walsh, commanding officer of the North West Mounted Police in Canada, looked across his desk at the younger officer sitting opposite.

"What's worrying you, Lyons?" he asked in a kindly voice. "You're not a bit like yourself this morning. You look worried. Your mind's only half on these reports. . . ."

The captain hesitated a moment. "I have no right to worry you with personal matters," he began . . . "but . . ." The Commissioner interrupted. "Let me know what's bothering you," he suggested. "I might be able to help."

Captain Lyons took a telegram out of the pocket of his uniform and passed it across the desk. "Would you mind reading this, sir?" he said. "It came this morning."

Spreading out the yellow paper the Commissioner read the following message:

MONTREAL P Q
May 1 1896

CAPT DENNIS LYONS
ADJUTANT NORTH WEST MOUNTED POLICE HDQS
REGINA NORTH WEST TERRITORIES
CANADA

3

JIM AND I SAILING FOR ENGLAND TODAY EN
ROUTE FOR INDIA WHERE JIM HAS COMMISSION
TO PAINT MURAL IN MAHARAJAHS PALACE. IM-
POSSIBLE TO TAKE SUE SO HAVE SHIPPED HER OUT
TO YOU WITH NURSE TO SPEND THE SUMMER.
HOPE TO BE BACK WITHIN SIX MONTHS. A MIL-
LION THANKS FOR LOOKING AFTER SUE WHO HAS
PROMISED TO BE NO TROUBLE. MUCH LOVE
                                                    AILEEN

"Who," asked the Commissioner, looking up, "is Sue? And
why does she need a nurse?"

Captain Lyons flushed. "Sue is my niece, Susannah Winston," he answered. "My sister's only child. Her father is an
artist. Sue is just nine years old. That's why she needs the
nurse."

The Commissioner stood up and turned thoughtfully to the
window overlooking the parade ground of the Barracks. In the
distance a group of red-coated riders were returning to the
stables.

"Do I understand, Lyons, that your sister is sending a child
of nine out here to spend the summer with you?" asked the
Commissioner.

The adjutant nodded. "She's arriving on the Transcontinental tomorrow afternoon, sir."

The Commissioner slowly shook his head. "You'd better
ship her back at once, Dennis," he said. "The bachelor quarters of a Barracks is no place for a little girl."

"I know that, sir," said Captain Lyons.

"And furthermore," continued the Commissioner, "you can't
look after a child and carry on with your own duties at the same

time. I am depending on you for the entire training of the Queen's Jubilee Contingent." He paused a moment and looked sharply at his favorite junior officer. "Do you realize," he said, "that ours will be the first Mounted Police to represent Canada in a royal procession and that we will be up against the picked regiments of the British Empire?"

"I do, indeed, sir," answered the worried captain.

"Then what in the name of thunder do you mean by complicating things with the added responsibility of a child? I tell you, Lyons, she must go somewhere else!"

"But you don't understand, sir," replied the younger officer. "Sue is too young to be sent to boarding school, or to be taken out to India, and I'm her only relative in this country. That's why her mother sent her out to me."

The Commissioner turned back to his desk and sat down. Patiently, he went over the difficulties he and his wife had met in bringing up their own daughter in the Barracks. He explained how impossible it had been to plan for her play-time because there were no other children in the Barracks. It was not long, he said, before she had become a spoiled, tiresome child, wanting her own way in everything; finally she had to be shipped off to school in England. "I had my wife to help me," he continued. "You haven't a wife nor any experience with children."

"But she'll be here only six months, sir," protested the worried adjutant. "After all, no little girl of nine can do herself or anyone else much harm in six months."

"Can't she," answered the Commissioner grimly. "You don't know what little girls of nine can do!"

He stood up. "I don't want to seem unnecessarily hard, Lyons, but I've had experience in matters of this kind and you

haven't . . . I can't give you orders, for this is a personal matter, but I must warn you. The first mischief your niece gets
into, the first time she interferes with your duties, out she goes!"

"I understand, sir, and I assure you that Sue will be no trouble," Captain Lyons answered, but before he could continue
the Commissioner rose and pressed a call bell on his desk. "See
here, Lyons," he said, "I think you had better talk this over with
Mrs. Walsh. She may be able to convince you of what you are
running into."

An orderly entered and saluted. "Captain Lyons and I will
be at my house for the next hour," said the Commissioner.

Silently the two officers left Headquarters and walked along
the short path that led to the first of the row of official resi-
dences, the houses where the officers of the Mounted Police
lived.

"Eliza," called the Commissioner, as he entered his own hall.

"I'm in here, dear," a pleasant voice answered, and the two
men entered the drawing room, a friendly cheery place, filled
with books and flowers and, on this early May day, with logs
crackling in the fireplace. The Commissioner bent over his
wife and kissed her.

"I wish you'd have a talk with Lyons, dear," he said. "I'm
afraid he's in for trouble."

"Whatever in the world are you talking about, John?" said
Mrs. Walsh, laying aside her sewing. "Dennis is never in trouble."

"It looks as if I am now," answered Dennis. "My niece, aged
nine, arrives tomorrow to spend the summer with me."

"How nice," exclaimed Mrs. Walsh.

Captain Lyons shook his head. "The Commissioner feels
that I have enough to do without taking on the care of a child."

"Nonsense," exclaimed Mrs. Walsh, "we'll look after her. Where is she going to sleep?"

The captain groaned. "That's one of the difficulties, Mrs. Walsh. You see, there are already three of us in Bachelor Hall: O'Dare, Hogarth and myself. And there are only four bedrooms. I don't know how I can manage a nurse's bedroom and a nursery. . . ."

"Don't try," said the practical Mrs. Walsh. "Put Sue in the largest bedroom. It will do nicely for a nursery as well. We can curtain off that large landing at the top of the stairs for the nurse to sleep in. She'll be near Sue and yet be able to keep her lamp on if she wants to read."

She rose and turned to her husband. "If you don't need the captain again this afternoon, I'll go over to his house and help him arrange things for his niece."

"I'm coming, too," a gay voice cried, "for I've been listening and I know what's happened." Standing in the doorway was Victoria Walsh, the Commissioner's daughter, fair haired, blue eyed and smiling. "I'd love to help," she continued. "I know just what girls like and there'll be a lot to do."

Commissioner Walsh disappeared into his library, and Captain Lyons, Mrs. Walsh and Vicky went over to Bachelor Hall. It was only a short distance away, farther down the row—a low two-story building with a comfortable drawing room and dining room, kitchen and pantry, a small study for the adjutant himself and, upstairs, four good-sized bedrooms.

"Where does your cook sleep?" asked Mrs. Walsh.

"In Sergeant Whiteside's house. Mrs. Schofield—that's my cook—and his wife are sisters." Captain Lyons smiled. "Hawkins, my old servant, doesn't approve of women." Vicky laughed delightedly.

"Does Hawkins know about Susannah and her nurse?" she asked.

"Not yet," answered Lyons. "And neither do O'Dare or Hogarth. I've no doubt they'll all be a bit surprised."

But if he expected any objections from the two junior officers who shared Bachelor Hall with him, he was greatly mistaken. At that very moment, the two young men themselves came in from duty.

"Dennis has a niece arriving tomorrow afternoon from the East to spend the summer with him," Vicky cried. "Isn't that a surprise?"

"A niece!" exclaimed O'Dare. "Is she pretty? Can she dance?"

"How's her tennis?" asked Hogarth.

Vicky laughed. "His niece is just nine. You'll probably have to teach *her* to dance."

The two young officers plied them with questions and then left for Regina in a high-wheeled yellow dog-cart to buy presents for Susannah. "Gifts to welcome her," cried O'Dare, as he went out.

Captain Lyons led Mrs. Walsh and Vicky upstairs. "This room," he said, opening one of the doors at the head of the stairs, "has been used as a guest room. I thought it might do."

It was a large room with two windows overlooking the parade ground, but dark curtains and heavy walnut furniture gave it a gloomy, cheerless air. Mrs. Walsh shook her head disapprovingly. "This will never do, Dennis," she said. "It's too dark. Let's take down that big double bed and those dark curtains. In the attic at home there is all the furniture from Vicky's own nursery. We'll bring it over, and anything else that would fit in as well. You and Vicky go and rummage in the attic and see what other things you can find. Mrs. Schofield and I will see what can be done here."

Sunlight filtered through the dusty windows of the attic, and there was a faint odor of sweet grass and of lavender and camphor, the sharp tangy smell of saddle soap and the musty perfume of old trunks and papers. From the rafters hung old uniforms and disused saddles, hat-boxes all the way from London, round-topped leather trunks filled with old costumes belonging to Mrs. Walsh, and in one corner a small nursery bed, a little desk and a wicker chair with faded blue cushions.

"Look!" exclaimed Vicky. "There are the very things we're after. Let's see what else there is. Move that screen, Dennis, and we'll have more light."

Half across the window was a tall screen covered with gay pictures. When the captain moved it, sunlight streamed in, touching a dark corner with long fingers of light.

A delighted cry came from Vicky. "Look, my doll's cradle! I'd forgotten all about it." Away in the corner, almost hidden by a huge trunk, was a little wicker cradle. The captain lifted it out into the light; it was lined with pink silk and had net curtains carefully drawn. Beside it was a tiny, nail studded leather box. "That was my grandmother's," said Vicky. "I had it for my doll's clothes. Perhaps your Susannah would like it, too. Let's open all the boxes," she continued. "You never know what you'll find in an attic."

Trunk after trunk was pulled out under her direction, its contents searched, a pile of light blue curtains trimmed with ball fringe rescued from one, a small footstool from another.

Finally Vicky looked up, "I guess that's about all there is, Dennis," she said.

"It's all anyone could ask for," laughed the captain. "Come along! I'll send Hawkins over to carry these across."

Taking the little trunk and doll's cradle with them, they went back to the bachelors' quarters. There they found that Mrs. Walsh had the gloomy curtains down. Assisted by Mrs. Schofield, the white-aproned, motherly cook of Bachelor Hall, she had already managed to transform the room. Instead of brown shadows, sunlight poured in on the red flowered carpet.

While the furniture was being carried over by Hawkins— to whom Captain Lyons had gently broken the news of Sue's arrival—Mrs. Schofield remembered a blue and white quilt she had hidden away, and went off to add it to the nursery. Other things were brought—a chair from Captain Lyons' study, a rug from Mrs. Walsh's, a picture from the hallway—so that when Lieutenants O'Dare and Hogarth arrived back from Regina, Sue's new bedroom was almost ready for her.

The bed was in the corner, the gay pictured screen around the washstand, the wicker chair in the window by the sunshine, the little desk nearby. In the kitchen, Mrs. Schofield was pressing the curtains; in the drawing room Vicky was making a small pincushion; upstairs Mrs. Walsh was finally putting everything to rights.

Into this busy hive, the two junior officers came, loaded with packages. There were crayons and pencils, a slate, a blue porridge bowl and mug, toy horns, a mouth organ and drum, a number of books.

"She'll enjoy reading these," said John Hogarth, laying down a copy of the *Silver Fairy Tales*.

"How much did you read at nine?" asked O'Dare.

"Not much," admitted Hogarth, "but I grew up, and so will Sue. Besides, I shall teach her to read."

"I'll teach her to dance," cried O'Dare.

"I'll teach her to sew," said Mrs. Walsh.

"I'll teach her to laugh," smiled Vicky.

"I'll teach her to cook," said Mrs. Schofield, as she brought in a pile of freshly pressed curtains.

"Come," said Vicky. "We'll hang the curtains now." And she and the two young officers went upstairs, where they could be heard arguing and laughing.

Captain Lyons drew a chair over and sat down beside Mrs. Walsh.

"I wouldn't like the Commissioner to know," he said, "but I am really more worried over Sue's arrival than I'd like to admit. You see, Sue's mother is my only sister." He laughed uneasily. "I didn't tell you," he went on, "that as a child my sister was as wild as a hawk and as obstinate as a mule—and just about the most lovable person I've ever set my eyes on. I haven't seen Susannah since she was a very little baby, but . . ."

"If she is like her mother, we are in for trouble. Is that it, Dennis?" asked the understanding Mrs. Walsh.

"Yes," Lyons nodded his head gravely. "If Sue is like her mother, I'll be nothing but wax in her hands."

Mrs. Walsh laughed. "I wouldn't worry too much, Dennis. We'll help you with her—you'll be all right, and so will Sue."

A red-jacketed figure appeared in the doorway— "Any further orders, sir?"

"None, Hawkins. And thanks for helping out this afternoon."

"Very glad to, sir," replied Hawkins, clipping the words off one by one. "While I don't approve of females as a rule, sir, I hope Miss Sue will find everything to her liking."

"I'm sure she will," answered the captain, wondering what was keeping Hawkins.

"Beggin' your pardon, sir," he said. "I've been wondering if this small present mightn't be in place." He held up a doll made of wood with a carved brown face and shining black eyes. She was wrapped in a brightly colored blanket, and on her back carried a little papoose. "It's an Indian doll, sir, I picked up some time ago, and wondered if it would be all right if I put it in Miss Sue's room."

Captain Lyons beamed with pleasure. "That's very thoughtful of you, Hawkins," he said. "I'm sure it will make Miss Sue very happy. Will you take it up to the nursery?"

A few minutes later Mrs. Walsh and the captain followed. Dennis looked around the room. The curtains had been hung, the bed made, the rugs laid, and in the doll's cradle, the Indian doll was sleeping. She was a funny little doll with a surprised look in her dark eyes, as if she were astonished and pleased to find herself in such comfortable surroundings.

"Her name is Minnie-Pooh-Pooh," said Hogarth gravely, "which Hawkins claims is Woods Indian for 'Happy Laughter.'"

"We must go home and dress, Vicky," said Mrs. Walsh. "We're dining at Government House tonight." And turning for an instant to the grateful captain: "Don't worry about your child, Dennis," she said. "She'll be all right."

Still chatting, they went downstairs and along the Parade. Across the early green of the Barracks Square, a red-coated bugler was facing toward the sunset. Above his head fluttered the Union Jack, and out of the open Barracks doors poured scores of running figures, answering the bugle's call.

The Commissioner joined them. "What smiling faces," he said. "What have you all been doing?"

"Have you forgotten," cried Vicky reproachfully. "We've been getting ready for Sue!"

"You mean, you've been getting ready for trouble," said her father. "And at the very first sign of it, out she goes!"

2. The Journey

Swaying and bumping across the open prairies, the Canadian Pacific Railway Transcontinental Limited sped westward on its long journey from Montreal to Vancouver. In the last sleeping car sat a little girl of nine, staring out of the window with fascinated eyes. She was Susannah Elizabeth Fairfield Winston, the cause of all the Commissioner's worry at the Mounted Police Barracks at Regina. Her red-gold curls were brushed back from her dark blue eyes, and her dress of navy blue challis with a very full tucked skirt came well below her knees. There was a tiny white frill at the neck and a sash of black moiré ribbon around the waist.

Sue pressed her nose closer to the glass. It was, she thought, a very different world from the one she had left behind. Very different from Montreal. There were trees in that lovely city. Trees that shaded the paths in summer and turned all gold and red in the autumn. Here there wasn't a tree to be seen. The whole world was flat. Just the big blue bowl of the sky reaching down until it touched the earth. And the earth was different, too, a lovely purple color that the brakeman had told her came from crocuses. She believed she was going to like the prairies. In Montreal crocuses grew in gardens. Here they were like a carpet. A *most* exciting world, thought Susannah. as she watched a great herd of cattle running across the prairies, with cowboys riding lickety split beside them.

A brakeman came through the car, and Sue stopped him.

"Do you know where the conductor is?"

He smiled at her. "Sure, he's up front somewhere. Anything the matter, Missy?"

"Nothing is the matter," said Sue, "except he promised to take me through the train before we reached Regina."

"You'll have plenty of time yet," said the brakeman. "Why, Regina is almost a whole day away."

"But you'll tell him I was asking, won't you?"

"Sure, I will," he answered. "He'll be along soon."

Sue sat back in her seat and thought about the past week. First there had been the excitement in Daddy's studio when the telegram came from India, her mother's little shrieks of delight, much hurried packing, and a great to-do about a nurse for Sue. Sue had thought there couldn't be so many nurses in the world. Mummy had been very fussy about them, Sue remembered, and finally Daddy had stopped cleaning his paint brushes and had said, "Leave this to me, Aileen. We can't take a year to choose a nurse. I'll show you how to do it." Sue giggled as she remembered Daddy passing down the line of some seven or eight nurses. Finally he had stopped at one, looked at some papers called references and had told her to stay.

"Her name's Matilda Devlin. She's Irish, clean as a whistle, and has excellent references," he said, "and she'll laugh with our girl while we're away." And he went back to cleaning his brushes. Sue's daddy considered laughing a very important matter, like the proper food and lots of sleep.

So that night Matilda Devlin and herself had gone to bed in the strange berth of a train, something she had seen but never been on before. She remembered how both parents had kissed her goodbye, all smiles and tears, how her pretty mother had told her to be good and always to behave like a little lady. But her father had given her a small knitted purse with a whole quarter in it. She felt in her pocket. The purse was still there, and inside was the shining silver quarter. She had shown it to the conductor who had admired it greatly and had told her that before she reached Regina he would take her through the train.

Sue looked out at the shimmering prairies again and remembered the conductor. She hadn't seen him since the early morning.

A sound came from the berth opposite, with its long heavy green curtains tightly drawn.

Poor Nannie, thought Sue, and slipping off her seat, disappeared through the curtains. "Does your head still ache, Nannie?" she asked.

In the dim light of the berth her nurse lay moaning softly. "Sure, it aches fit to split."

"Can I do anything for you, Nannie?" Sue asked. "Would you like a cup of tea?"

But Matilda Devlin shook her head feebly. "Just leave me be," she said, and turned her face away. "There's nothing anyone can do."

Sue reached over her and took a bundle out of the berth and returned to the seat across the aisle. The bundle turned out to be her favorite doll, one Madame La Tour, a beautiful wax creature, with fair hair and blue eyes like Sue's own. She was dressed in the height of fashion and was, Sue thought, very "elegant" which was one of Sue's favorite words, learned at the dressmaker's just before leaving Montreal.

Madame La Tour's traveling costume consisted of a red cashmere dress, with a vest of creamy silk ending in a ruche around the neck. Over this was worn a sumptuous red velvet coat with silk-braid trimming. On her head was a small bonnet of the velvet, with a spotted veil drawn tightly over the nose. A velvet muff completed this dazzling ensemble, and Sue contemplated her with complete satisfaction.

"Let's go adventuring," said Sue to Madame La Tour. "Let's go and find the conductor."

Tucking her doll under her arm, she started down the aisle. But on opening the door, Sue found that what had been easy with the conductor holding fast was difficult all by herself. The cars were coupled together but the platforms were not enclosed, and a strong wind blew between them. To cross from one car to another, she saw, would need both hands and she would have to hang on very tight.

"I can't leave you behind, Madame La Tour," she said, "and I haven't three hands. I'm in what Daddy calls a very nasty fix."

But once Sue started out "adventuring" she never turned back. So she studied the problem. How could she use her two hands and carry Madame La Tour as well? She laughed then and untied her sash. Knotting it about Madame La Tour, she retied the sash around her waist and pushed the doll around until she hung in a most surprising fashion down her back. Sue gave a little jump and wriggle, but Madame La Tour stayed in position. "Good," said Sue, and tugged the door open. Reaching out to the iron railing and holding it firmly, she pushed herself hand over hand across the swaying platforms. The wind was blowing hard between the cars, and she was breathless when she got inside again, but it was an adventure, Sue thought.

The train was a long one and everyone smiled at her as she passed with Madame La Tour bobbing out behind. There was nothing interesting to see in the various cars. They were all like her own with green or red plush seats, until she reached a different kind of car with wicker seats and the strangest people in it. It was a Colonist car, reserved for emigrants and settlers going West to take up new farms.

In one seat an old woman slept noisily. She had a skirt that Sue thought must be a mile around. Sue drew nearer and examined her dress. The full skirt was plain, and so was the tight fitting bodice, except for the loveliest embroideries stitched in wool—roses, violets and daisies—and on the old woman's head was a small shawl, tied under her chin. The shawl had gay flowers on it, too. She opened her eyes and smiled. Sue asked her if she had seen the conductor. The woman answered her in a strange language, one that Sue had never heard before. An old priest in a faded rusty robe called her to him. "She is a Doukabor," he said, "coming out to visit her son in Regina. Do you know what a Doukabor is?"

Sue shook her head.

"The Doukabors come from Russia, and even little girls dress as she does over there. The Doukabors are a kind people and good farmers. What are you doing in this car, little one?"

"I'm looking for the conductor," said Sue, curtseying.

Down the aisle, sitting around an iron stove, was a group of four men, black haired with dark shining eyes. Two of them held little guitar-shaped instruments which they were strumming quietly. As Sue went nearer they burst into song again, a gay song that made her want to dance. When they finished Sue clapped her hands delightedly.

"More," she cried. "More!"

One of the men rose and bowed gravely. Sue curtseyed in her best manner, as she did when important company came to the studio in Montreal.

"I can sing, too," said Sue, "in French and in English. Shall I sing for you?" Once more the leader bowed. Sue laid Madame La Tour on the table and placing her hands behind her back, began a little song. A song all French Canadian children know from babyhood:

> Alouette,
> Gentille Alouette,
> Alouette, je te plumerai.

The two men softly followed her with their guitars as she sang, and when the tune became familiar, played louder:

> Alouette,
> Gentille Alouette.

Sue repeated the refrain a second time and the old priest added his voice. Soon others joined the little group of singers. A soldier came through. The old Doukabor woman nodded her head happily. Sue thought all this much more exciting than Montreal, for everyone was singing and the car was full of happy voices.

The song ended, everyone gave her presents. The old priest pressed a large brazil nut into her hand; the Doukabor woman a bright ribbon; the soldier a red and white sugar stick. Sue put them carefully in the pocket of her dress.

Just then the conductor came through the car. He seemed surprised to find Sue there. Taking her by the hand, he led her away from these pleasant people and back through the long train to her own car. It was empty except for Nannie

moaning in her berth and a tall, dark, good-looking young
man staring out of the window.

"I wonder if you would keep an eye on this little lady,"
the conductor said to the young man. "Her nurse is ill, and
she'll get hurt wandering through the train alone."

"Put her right down there, conductor," he said, patting the
seat beside him. "I'll see she doesn't wander."

Sue placed Madame La Tour on the seat opposite and
climbed up beside the young man. He had, she thought, the
friendliest smile she had ever seen.

"My name is Susannah Elizabeth Fairfield Winston, and
I'm nine and a quarter years old. Now it's your turn. What's
your name?"

"James Andrew Patrick Angus Montague Douglas, and I'm
twenty-seven and five-twelfths years old."

"What an awful lot of names," said Sue. "What do you call
yourself?"

"I haven't quite decided yet," said the young man, "but
suppose you call me Monty. How's that?"

Sue tried it. "Monty." Then "I like it," she said. "Tell me
more. Where are you going?"

"To Regina," he answered.

"Not truly," said Sue delightedly. "Why, that's where I'm
going. You see, I'm going out to join the Mounties. My Uncle
Dennis is a captain there, and I'm going to live with him."

"I'm going to be a Mountie, too," said her new friend unexpectedly. "At least, I hope I am."

"Don't you know?" asked Sue.

"Not quite," he answered.

"Why not?"

"Well," he explained, "you have to be awfully good to join

the Mounties. You must be tall and strong and well built, and if someone else is taller or stronger or better built than I am, I'll be left out in the cold."

Sue couldn't bear that and said so. "Why are you going to join the Mounties?" she asked.

"Oh, for many reasons," he answered.

"Tell me," coaxed Sue.

"First, I have no home." He seemed very cheerful about it, Sue thought.

"You could come and live with Uncle Dennis and me," she offered.

Monty laughed. "I don't think Uncle Dennis would like that, Sue."

"Where was your home?"

"Scotland."

"Why did you leave it?"

"Oh, Susannah, I'm afraid I was a bad boy!"

"Were you!" said Sue. This was something she could understand, for she was always being called BAD or a tomboy or a hoyden; and the word "bad" seemed to be always associated with pleasant things such as painting the floor with her father's best oil paints or putting rice in Mummy's bed.

"Were you very bad?" repeated Sue. "Tell me more."

"Well, I have a large ferocious aunt," he said, "who wants me to do as I am told, and when I don't she won't give me any pocket money, so I've come away to earn my own pocket money."

"You don't sound so very bad to me," said Sue. "What's her name?"

"Aunt Charlotte."

"Aunt Charlotte," repeated Sue. "Well, if I ever meet her

I'll tell her I think you're very nice and how my daddy gave me pocket money, even though he does think I'm bad most all the time." Sue brought out the little knitted purse and showed Monty her beautiful shining quarter.

"You see," she explained, "my Nannie was sent along to look after me but I've had to look after her. I dressed myself for the first time this morning. I wonder if my Uncle Dennis will like me," she continued. "Do you think he will?"

"I'm positive of it," said her new friend, Monty.

She told him, too, of how she had to go to Regina because India was too hot for little girls, and how her nurse had a dreadful headache and was practically useless.

The dining-car steward came through the train.

"First call for luncheon," he cried.

Monty looked down at her. "How are you going to get your luncheon with your Nannie laid up?" he asked.

Sue was wondering that same thing herself, for it had been hours since the conductor had taken her in to breakfast.

"How would you like to have it with me?" he asked.

Sue almost bounced off the seat with relief, but she wasn't too relieved to ask, "Can I have ice cream AND cake?"

Monty smiled down at her. "Certainly, but hadn't you better ask your Nannie first if I may take you?"

In a flurry Sue disappeared behind the curtains of the berth, to emerge with freshly brushed curls and permission to go to lunch with the young man she now thought of as her most important friend.

The dining car was always a dazzling sight to Sue, with its little tables, shining silver and glass, and Negro waiters with white coats and sparkling teeth. Monty let her order her own food and his. It was, she thought, a very perfect day. He didn't finish all his ice-cream, she noticed, but that, he explained, was because he was F.R.U.T.B.

"What is that?" Sue asked. "Is it Doukabor language?"

He laughed. "No, that means Full Right Up To Busting."

It took her a little time to memorize the letters F.R.U.T.B.; but all the way back to the Pullman with Monty she chanted the magic symbols to herself and then curled up on the seat beside him.

Click-click went the train over the rail joints. Monty softly sang to her about a little boy who built "Castles in the Air," and Sue drifted off to sleep.

"Regina next," called the conductor. "Regina next. All passengers for Regina."

Sue sat up with a start. "I must dress Madame La Tour," she said, "and see about Nannie." Nannie was still very limp and quite unable to help Sue, so she trotted back to Monty again, holding coat, hat, gloves and collar.

"Nannie," she explained, "is yellow like a duck's foot and says she's fit to die. I'll never get her dressed in time for Regina."

Monty called the conductor who, after questioning, gave a slightly more cheerful account of Sue's nurse.

"She can dress herself all right," he said, "but she declares she hasn't the strength to pack and look after the little girl." Sue protested. "I can dress myself and pack, too. At least, pretty well." Monty bent over her.

"When Nannie goes to the washroom," he said, "let's surprise her by having all the packing done before she comes back."

A few minutes later Matilda crept past them with her hair in kid curlers, a beflowered flannel gown tightly wrapped around her and a sponge bag over her arm. The conductor looked at her with disfavor. "Why did they choose her for you?" he asked Sue.

"Daddy said she was Irish and would laugh with me," answered Sue.

"Well, she won't," said the conductor. "She's the mournful Irish and when the Irish mourn, they mourn worse than any other kind. She'll never laugh with you, Missy. You'll have to make your own laughter."

Nannie vanished into the washroom and the two men and Sue pulled back the curtains and started packing. Sue found it the most exciting kind of packing. Instead of tissue paper being folded between the clothes, Monty and the conductor stuffed things into the leather bags any old way, and when the bags didn't close, the conductor, who was fat, sat on them until the clasps clicked together easily.

When the conductor next called Regina, the three of them were ready; Monty and Sue very important and smiling, Nannie wan and white in her elaborate uniform but, Sue noticed, "quite alive."

With shrieking brakes, the train slowed to a standstill. Out of the window Sue could see people on a crowded platform.

"I wonder," she said eagerly, "which is Uncle Dennis?"

"I wonder," echoed Monty as he swung her off the train to the station platform, while the practically useless Matilda followed close behind.

3. The Arrival

Sue looked out over the crowded platform. There were horses and carriages, and much excitement and bustle: trunks being taken off the train, gay welcomes, laughter, a voice crying, "Make way for Her Majesty's Mails," and everyone moving aside while the mail bags were carried through the crowds to the baggage car, and then the clanging of the engine's bell, her friend the conductor calling, "ALL ABOARD, ALL . . . . . LL ABOARD," the brakeman waving his hat at her, and a shriek from the engine as the flier moved slowly away. But the talking and the laughter did not stop and no one moved as the train pulled out. They stood watching until it disappeared in a trail of smoke.

This was the second station Sue had seen, and it was full of the strangest people, quite different from the station in Montreal. There everyone had looked more or less like her parents. Here—well, Sue found it a little frightening. She tightened her hand around Monty's and felt very small indeed.

"What's the matter, Sue?" asked Monty. "Feeling scared?"

"Only a little bit," said Sue bravely. "Do you see my Uncle Dennis anywhere?"

Monty shook his head. "What does he look like?"

25

"I don't know," answered Sue. "Do you suppose he doesn't know I'm coming?"

Monty laughed. "Not a bit of it. Let's look around and see if we can find him."

A bent old woman with long black hair brushed past them. Behind her followed a tall man with a brown face, wrinkled like old leather and with hair worn in braids over his shoulders. Both were wrapped in soiled, colored blankets, and on their feet were beaded moccasins.

"Indians," whispered Monty. Sue thought she had never seen anyone so straight or tall, or move so slowly as the grave-faced Indian. A knot of bronzed men in flannel shirts and wearing broad-brimmed hats laughed together in a corner. There were women in pretty dresses and frilly capes with little beribboned hats just like her mother's, a padre, a knot of ranchers, all in riding clothes, a grizzled old man, a cowboy smacking his lariat against his leather chaps. Everyone was talking, laughing, busy. No one paying any attention to Monty, Matilda or herself.

Sue's heart beat faster. What if Uncle Dennis didn't come? She remembered again the studio in Montreal, her laughing mother whose hair always seemed faintly perfumed. Sue felt she would remember that perfume all her life. She wished she could have it near her now. In the distance the train was only a faint blur. The crowd turned their faces from the West and started to move slowly off the platform.

Still no Uncle Dennis but Sue's ears caught a new sound: the jangle of spurs, the steady trot trot of marching horses, a sharp command, and around the corner of the station swung a detachment of the North West Mounted Police in all the glory of their scarlet and gold uniforms.

"Look, Monty!" cried Sue. "Look, RED COATS!"

He nodded. "Mounties from the Barracks, Sue, where you are going." He moved over and spoke to one of the scarlet-coated men. "Can you tell me anything about Captain Lyons?" he asked. The Mountie smiled. "There he is now," he said and pointed to a carriage with two horses rapidly approaching. But Sue hardly heard him. She was delightedly watching the mass of gay brave scarlet as the detachment moved away.

"Do you think I could ever have a red coat like that?" she asked Monty.

"I don't know," he replied. "Those coats belong to the Force and you have to work very hard to get one of them."

"Then I'll work and work and work!" said Sue, "for I want a red coat more than anything else in all the world."

The carriage stopped at the platform and two men got out, both in uniform: one very tall and dark with blue eyes and the straightest back and broadest shoulders she had ever seen. The other was older, with grizzled hair and a waxed military moustache.

"They are very small at nine, sir," Sue heard the second one say. "You can hardly see them." The tall man laughed. "If she's anything like her mother, Hawkins, we'll hear her before we see her," he said. Then he caught sight of Monty with Sue and moved forward hesitantly.

"I'm looking for a little girl about the same age as your own," he said to Monty. "Do you happen to know whether she got off the train?"

Monty laughed. "This is not my little girl," he said. "This is Susannah Winston, and I think you must be Captain Lyons."

The tall man bowed. "I am. And is this really Sue?"

"It's really Sue," Monty said.

Sue looked up. "Are you my Uncle Dennis?" she asked.
He nodded and taking her hand, turned back to Monty who
introduced himself.

"I am Angus Montague," he said. "Sue's nurse was ill and
I helped them both off the train." He presented Matilda
Devlin, a picture of woe behind them.

"Hawkins." The older man stepped briskly up to Captain
Lyons' side. "Will you take Miss Sue's nurse to the carriage?
See about the luggage, and we'll follow."

"Yes, sir," said Hawkins, saluting. He beckoned to Matilda,
who seemed to recover rapidly at the sight of his red coat.

"I'm taking Sue to the Barracks," Captain Lyons said. "Can
I give you a lift anywhere?"

Monty bowed. "No, thank you. I've come to Regina on
business that I must attend to immediately." The two men
shook hands. Sue looked around her. The platform was almost
empty. She couldn't see Matilda anywhere, the conductor was
gone, the brakeman, and now Monty was going, too. She loosened her hold on her uncle's hand and clung to Monty. "Don't
go away. Please come with us," she implored. "I shall miss you
dreadfully."

Monty looked down at her in surprise. "I thought you said
you were coming out to join the Mounties," he said. "Mounties don't cry and they always do what they are told." Waving
his hand, he disappeared around the corner of the station. And
for the first time since they had left Montreal, Sue felt very
much alone.

"Come along, Sue," said her Uncle Dennis. "We're going
to the Barracks."

On the far side of the station, double and single buckboards, dog-carts, farm wagons, open victorias and covered two-wheel carts were trying to get away amid the cheerful whoops and yells of a party of ranchers who were showing off by "bucking" their horses. No one seemed alarmed, Sue noticed, and everyone was very gay, but she held Madame La Tour tight for fear of harm, and pressed closer to her uncle's arm.

Matilda was sitting beside Hawkins in the front seat of a little carriage, covered with a fringed canopy. The horses, two beautiful bays, were smallish and they fretted at their bits and pawed the ground restlessly. Uncle Dennis helped her into the back seat and got in beside her.

She looked at him more closely as they started off. His uniform was dark blue and there was braid on the cuffs and shoulder straps, gold insignia on the narrow collar. Very tight blue trousers and high shining black boots. A little cap was worn on the side of his head. It was quite perfect, Sue thought, but a trifle dull in comparison with the uniform of scarlet and gold worn by Constable Hawkins sitting so straight in front of her.

She touched her uncle's arm. "When do we see Regina?" she asked.

Her uncle laughed. "This *is* Regina," he answered.

"Only this little bit," said Sue, astonished.

"Only this little bit."

"But it isn't pretty," she said, "and it is so little."

"Never mind," he answered. "It will grow and grow, faster than you."

"But where is the Barracks?" she asked. Her Uncle Dennis pointed toward the west where the Barracks lay hidden in a cloud of gold. "Over there," he said, "about three miles away."

They left Regina behind, crossed the railway tracks and drove along a winding prairie trail. Sue sniffed the air rap-

turously. "Nice smells," she said. The crocuses were deep
purple when you were close to them, and underneath violets
lifted their heads through the fluffy grass that Uncle Dennis
called prairie wool—"because it's soft," he explained, "and
easier for the ponies to eat than the tall grass that comes later."

Clip, clop, clip, clop. A party of riders swept past, waving
and laughing. The people, she noticed, were all eager, as if in
search of something they had almost found. Sue suddenly
bounced in her seat and pointed to the sidewalks.

"They're on stilts," she cried. "They're on stilts! I've never
seen sidewalks on stilts before."

True enough, the sidewalks were built high off the ground
in places, just as if they were on stilts. Her uncle explained
that they were built that way so that they wouldn't be flooded
in wet weather. "In the spring," he said, "the little sloughs
are full of water, and if a sidewalk was laid flat it would be
under water and make walking impossible."

"What is a slough?" asked Sue.

"A slough," said her uncle, "is a slight hollow in the earth
that fills with water in the spring and wet weather and becomes
marshy and wet, a sort of bog."

There was a squeak from the seat in front and Matilda
turned around. "Did you say bog?" she asked.

"I did."

"Sure, my home was built on a bog in Ireland," she said.
"It was the loveliest place, full of black peat. Please forgive my
interrupting, sir, but you don't know how I miss my own country."

"You will find plenty of old-country people in the Barracks,"
said the captain kindly. "I wouldn't weep over it, if I were
you."

But Matilda loved weeping and continued to sniffle to her-self. Sue looked at her with strong disfavor. "We'd better not mention bogs again," she said, and her uncle agreed.

The ponies trotted on. "Will we never get to the Barracks?" Sue asked.

Her uncle drew her up against his shoulder. "See," he said. She followed the direction of his arm. Before them lay a group of low red-roofed buildings, surrounded by a high wooden fence. "That's *NOT* the Barracks!" she exclaimed. He nod-ded.

"But I thought a Barracks was for soldiers and was big and made of stone. I saw the Barracks at Quebec once. It was a very grand place. Can *this* be the Barracks, and are there any soldiers?"

"This *is* the Barracks," her uncle answered quietly. "And it's the men inside the Barracks that make it grand, Sue, not the buildings." They drove through open gates. The carriage stopped for a brief moment. A red-coated constable saluted smartly. A few yards further on another sprang to attention. Somewhere a bugle blew. Sue blinked her eyes. "What's that?" she asked.

"Mess," said her uncle. "You go to your meals here when the bugle calls."

Running across the parade ground in front of her there seemed to be millions of red-coated soldiers, all hurrying into a large white building. Briskly the horses trotted around the large white-fenced square of ground that she later came to know as "the Parade," and stopped at one of the low two-storied houses.

"Here we are, Sue," said her Uncle Dennis, getting out. "This is your new home. I hope you will be happy here."

"I hope so, too," said Sue, but she couldn't help wondering why Uncle Dennis seemed so serious about his welcome.

The front door opened as she and Madame La Tour went up the path. Inside the door were two tall young men in uniforms like her uncle's, and in the background a rosy cheeked woman in blue with a white apron. They were all smiling and waiting.

Uncle Dennis introduced her. "Sue, this is Mr. O'Dare and Mr. Hogarth and Mrs. Schofield, my housekeeper." Sue curtseyed gravely. Mr. O'Dare bowed very low indeed. "You'd better call me Michael," he said, "for I see we are going to be friends."

"I'd like to," said Sue, returning his smile. "Are you a Mountie?"

"I am," he said. "Are you going to join?"

But Mrs. Schofield was already hurrying her upstairs, along with Matilda.

"The captain wishes to have tea with her before he goes back to H.Q.," she explained to Matilda, "so get out another dress for her. I'll wash her and brush her hair."

Sue looked around the bedroom. "Is this my room?" she asked. "Is this little desk for me? Is the chair? Are those my bugles on the wall? Is that my drum?" And while they changed her dress she examined her books, the little trunk for her doll's clothes, and lastly came upon the cradle. She squealed with delight as she lifted the Indian doll. "That's a present from Mr. Hawkins," said Mrs. Schofield, and a moment later, Hawkins himself appeared at the door.

"The captain sent me up to know if there was anything wrong?" he said. "We could hear Miss Sue downstairs."

"Good grief," laughed Mrs. Schofield. "He'll soon get used

to hearing this child screaming, for mark my words, Mr. Hawkins, Miss Sue is a screamer. Aren't you, my duck?" And with a final brush to her shining curls, Mrs. Schofield released Sue with a warm hug and kiss.

Holding the Indian doll aloft, Sue flung herself on Hawkins. "You gave her to me," she cried. "You gave her to me. Thank you very much, Hawkins. What's her name and where did you find her?"

"I found her in Regina," said Hawkins, looking rather shamefaced, "and her name is Minnie-Pooh-Pooh."

"What's her baby's name?" asked Sue.

"That's her Papoose," said Hawkins, loosening Minnie-Pooh-Pooh's baby from her back, "and her name is Minotah."

"Minnie-Pooh-Pooh, Minotah," repeated Sue. "What do they mean?"

"Well, Minnie-Pooh-Pooh means 'Happy Laughter,' and Minotah is Indian for sweetheart."

The sound of a bugle call played on the piano downstairs made Hawkins turn. "Call to Mess," he said. "That's for you, Miss Sue."

At a little table, Sue, Madame La Tour and Minnie-Pooh-Pooh and her Papoose had their evening meal. Over her apple-sauce and brown bread Sue talked to the two young officers. They were the youngest officers in the Force. Michael O'Dare was very gay, and she liked his red hair, merry blue eye and funny little moustache. John Hogarth was lively, too, with dark hair and a quick way of moving. Everything, in fact, was altogether delightful and she couldn't understand why her uncle seemed worried and kept looking at her so anxiously when the two young officers teased her and made her laugh until she screamed.

When he left for a mysterious place called H.Q. John and Michael taught her to play Mess on the piano with one finger. Later she sang *Alouette* for them. But they knew it, too, and lifted her up on the piano and while she sang the verses, they joined her in the refrain until the very house seemed to enter into their happy song. After that Michael taught her the first steps of an Irish jig while John Hogarth played a tune called *The Pretty Maid Milking Her Cow*.

It was all thrilling, and when they topped off the evening by playing leapfrog until the whole room was untidy and a picture fell off the wall, without anyone once telling her to stop screaming, Sue felt Montreal a poor spot and the Barracks far better than she could have dreamed.

But at eight o'clock Matilda came for her, and she was carried off to bed. She didn't like the idea much and said so, but when she was undressed and bathed and tucked into bed with Minnie-Pooh-Pooh beside her and Madame La Tour elegantly asleep in her own little cradle, Sue thought over the events of the day and found them very satisfactory.

She had lost her friend Monty, it was true, but he had promised to come and see her soon. And she had made other friends: her Uncle Dennis and John and Michael; Hawkins and Mrs. Schofield; Minnie-Pooh-Pooh and Minotah; and she had a new dream to cherish, the dream of some day having a Mountie's red coat of her very own to wear.

And so, tucking Minnie-Pooh-Pooh closer to her, Sue drifted off to sleep with the sounds of the First Post in her ears.

4. The Inspection

It was a strange wakening the next morning. At first Sue couldn't remember where she was. Her room was full of misty grey shadows that finally broke into pools of light. She could see patches of sky through the open windows, and there was a soft chatter of birds. A little wind stirred the curtains. She sniffed. There seemed to be something sparkling in the air around her, some feeling of restlessness, as if the wind were marching. Sue smiled at the idea of the wind marching, and cuddled back against her pillow. The sky was all blue now. Clear across the morning's promise sounded the notes of a bugle. Sue had never heard anything half so beautiful.

"You've got to get up, You've got to get up," it seemed to cry. For a moment there was silence, as if everyone were turning over for another snooze. And then somewhere across the Parade a door banged, a voice called, other voices answered. There was a sound of running feet, of whistling. In the distance a horse whinnied. In the house a door closed softly. She held her breath and turning back the covers crept out of her bed and tiptoed to the open window.

Across the parade ground, she could see the red coats of the Force scurrying to and fro. Another bugle sounded. More men came tumbling out of the buildings opposite, and lined up in

rows. A third bugle, and the men disappeared into another
building.

Save for the birds and the sound of horses' feet, all noise
ceased.. Sue turned away from the window. She loved her
carpet with the great red roses running over it, and the gay
screen around the washstand with its colored pictures of children, dogs, little lambs and elegant ladies in long dresses. She
tried drawing pictures on the slate she found in the little desk.
A fourth bugle sounded.

"Bugles," she said to herself, "mean business. I'll go and ask
Uncle Dennis what kind of business!"

She opened her door very softly and crept out in the hall.
"Sue," a voice whispered. She looked up, and saw Michael
O'Dare in his striped dressing gown, his red hair all on end,
his face unwashed but his blue eyes smiling at her.

"What do you want, Sue?"

"Bugles," said Sue. "Lots of bugles. What do they mean?"

"They mean—

"Get up. Get washed.

"Get shaved. Get dressed.

"Get your breakfast.

"Get your men.

"Get your horse.

"Get your gun."

"What a lot of getchas," said Sue. He nodded.

"Wash your face and get into a dressing gown and I'll take
you down to breakfast with me. I've early duty, so we must
hurry."

Sue hurried back to her room. Behind the big screen stood
a large walnut washstand with a marble top. On it was a set of

white china, but when she tried to lift the water jug, she found
it too heavy. Sue smiled. She knew this was a chance for what
Daddy called a "lick and a promise." Dipping the end of the
towel in the water jug, she hastily wiped it over her face. With
her dressing gown clutched about her and with Minnie-Pooh-
Pooh in her hand she went out and found Michael waiting for
her.

In the dining room the breakfast table was already laid and
Mrs. Schofield, full of smiles and bustle, gave her oatmeal
while Hawkins looked after Michael. No one asked her where
Matilda was and why her hair wasn't brushed, no one told her
to stop talking or not to speak with her mouth full.

"Who is the man on Parade that scolds the men?" she asked.

"How do you know he does?" asked Michael.

"I heard him after the second bugle," Sue answered. "He
barked at them, but no one minded."

"*That* was Sergeant Whiteside. Would you like to meet him,
Sue?"

Sue nodded. "Very much." Another bugle sounded.

Michael rose. "See, Hawkins," he said, "if you're not needed
this morning, you might show Miss Sue over the Barracks.
Tell the captain I mentioned it." He pushed back his chair
and saluting Sue, left hurriedly.

"Are you a sergeant?" Sue asked Hawkins, as he poured her
a glass of milk.

"No, Miss Sue. I'm the captain's batman."

"What's a batman?" asked Sue.

"A batman is an officer's body servant. Every officer has
one."

"What does he do?"

Hawkins coughed importantly. "He cleans his boots, polishes his buttons, makes his bed, serves him at table, brings him his mail, cleans his side arms, presses his uniforms. . . ."

A feeble voice broke in.

"Miss Sue, you *are* naughty." Sue and Hawkins turned. In the doorway was Matilda, dressed in crisp blue and white uniform and bristling with annoyance from the top of her stiff cap to the soles of her buttoned boots.

"What will the captain say to your eating breakfast all unwashed and not dressed?"

Sue giggled. "He'll say like the first bugle—

> "You've got to get up,
> You've got to get up."

Hawkins and Mrs. Schofield who were clearing the table laughed, but Sue knew they were laughing at Matilda for being late herself, so she didn't mind when Matilda took her upstairs to pull the snarls out of her curls and scrub her with soap.

She finished her breakfast with Uncle Dennis, who still wore that anxious expression when he looked at her. She wondered why, but was too busy listening to the plans for the day to interrupt. Hawkins had repeated Michael's message. At ten o'clock Sue was to be taken over the Barracks and shown everything. "You'd better teach her the duties of a new recruit," smiled Uncle Dennis.

"Yes, sir," said Hawkins.

Promptly at ten, Matilda and Sue set off in the company of Hawkins. Matilda looked very well, Sue thought, but it was Hawkins who delighted her the most. She had heard him tell Mrs. Schofield that he was "going off for a bit to spruce up," and if this was "sprucing up" Sue wished she might forever walk with so dazzling a creature. Six feet one in his stocking feet, Constable Hawkins was resplendent in tight fitting trousers of dark blue with yellow stripes down the side, black riding boots and a scarlet tunic buttoned down the front with shining buttons. On his head was the famous pill-box with its band of gold, tilted to the right side and kept in place by a black patent leather strap worn between the chin and lower lip.

"La, Mr. Hawkins," said Matilda in admiring tones, "I'm sure I've never walked out before with so fine a gentleman."

"You're not walking out with me," snapped Hawkins, who seemed to have taken a dislike to Matilda. "You're accompanying Miss Sue on an inspection of the Barracks." Sue slipped her hand into his and felt very important.

The Barracks was built in the form of a square with the parade ground in the middle. A road divided the Parade from the buildings, which were all painted white with red roofs. At opposite sides of the Square were two large houses, one the Commissioner's and the other the Assistant Commissioner's residence. The officers' houses were smaller, but all had tiny green lawns about them. Around the Parade were young trees—the only trees Sue had seen since she arrived—and they seemed very small. But Hawkins explained they hadn't been planted very long and some day would be quite as big as the trees in Montreal.

The parade ground was used for inspection, for orders, for everything that Hawkins could think of. It was empty just then, and they went on to the entrance gate of the Barracks. Here, in a small box-like house called a Sentry Box, stood the guard, and Sue learned that when anyone approached he was challenged and had to stop and explain his business.

"What is a challenge?" asked Sue.

"Let's go outside for a moment and then come back," said Hawkins, "and we'll see."

They passed out of the gate without question and before them stretched the prairies. Wide unbroken plains of crocus-studded grass. Nothing but prairies; no sound except the stamp of horses' feet behind them, the notes of the bugle again.

They returned and with Sue leading, passed through the wide open gate.

"Who goes there!" cried the red-coated Constable.

"Give your name," whispered Hawkins.

"Susannah Elizabeth Fairfield Winston," said Sue shakily, for she was a bit frightened at the ringing tones of the guard.

"Tell him your business," whispered Hawkins again.

"I am inspecting the Barracks," said Sue. Her eyes lifted to the guard's and she saw he was smiling at her. "And I'm taking my nurse and Constable Hawkins."

"Pass, Miss Winston and party," cried the guard, saluting smartly.

Sue felt very proud as she skipped along beside Hawkins who explained that the building beside the entrance gate was the Guard House, where there was always an officer of the day. It was very exciting having Hawkins present her as "Miss Winston." The Guard House was where prisoners were brought and where orders were posted, but they could hear horses' feet nearer now and Sue tugged at Hawkins' hand.

The stables lay back of the men's sleeping and living quarters. Each stable had stalls on either side, with a window in each stall. Great double doors at either end of the stables were open. Sue gave a delighted sniff. There was a nice mixture of hay, leather, and freshly polished bits of blacking. Matilda gave a little squeak of terror.

"I'm afraid of horses," she said. "Oh, Miss Sue, don't go near those great beasts."

Sue held tighter to Hawkins who marched into the stable with her. Smith, the stable orderly, who was the only small man in the Force, came forward.

"Miss Winston would like to inspect the horses," Hawkins said to him.

"Right you are, ma'am," said Smith smiling. And Sue walked down the stable and listened to the good points of each horse.

Nellie was the best hunter, Bob a real rogue, Hawk-eye the most nervous, Lady the gentlest; and so on until they came to a huge chestnut, Ginger, the Commissioner's own horse. Sue was so interested in Ginger that Smith went into the stall and brought him out. He was seventeen hands high, Smith explained, as gentle as a lamb and brave as a lion. His chestnut coat gleamed as he nibbled sugar from Hawkins' hand, and he stood quite still while Smith blackened his hoofs as if they were boots. This finished, Smith asked Sue if she would like to put Ginger back in his stall. She nodded, full of happy terror at the honor, yet not quite knowing what to do.

"Come around here." Sue obeyed and taking the halter in her left hand and with Smith beside her, marched into the dark stall. But a tug on the halter made her realize that Ginger hadn't moved.

"Get up there, old boy," said Smith.

"Get up there, old boy," repeated Sue, giving the halter a tug. Ginger followed. It was very frightening, Sue thought, as she heard the big horse follow her and felt his breath on the back of her neck. But Smith smiled at her again and knotted the halter to the stall.

"Get over," he said, for Ginger filled the stall, and he slapped the horse on his flank. Ginger moved over a little.

"Now you," said Smith, motioning to her to do the same.

"Get over," roared Sue, imitating Smith, and then walked out of the stall, flushed with excitement.

"I thought horses kicked," she said.

"No horse'll kick," said Smith, "unless you treat it dirty. If you treat it gentle, it'll treat you gentle, and that's your first lesson in horse flesh, Miss Sue."

From the stables Sue visited the tailor's shop, the little chapel, the store rooms and the Riding School, where she saw Sergeant Whiteside. He was standing in the centre of the Riding School and barking orders at an odd dozen men who were riding their horses in a ring around him.

Hawkins explained that all recruits had to be taught to ride, first bareback and then with saddles, before they rode in company with the others. "And you can take it from me, Miss Sue, by the time Sergeant Whiteside is through with you, you could ride a horse standing on your head."

"Oh," tittered Matilda, rolling her eyes in mock terror, "I shouldn't like to ride on my head."

Sue wasn't sure, but she thought she heard Hawkins tell her that she hadn't any head and therefore needn't worry. Sue felt the same way about Matilda, but hadn't dared say so.

The Riding School was a large building outside of the Barracks square and the floor was covered with sawdust. Sue couldn't make out what the sergeant was saying to the men, he was talking so quietly, but suddenly the horses started walking around in single file. "Trot," roared the sergeant; the horses trotted. The men looked very uncomfortable as they rode by without saddles or stirrups.

"Canter"—they seemed to enjoy the easy lope better.

"Gallop"—the horses raced by, but as they passed one rider tumbled off at Sue's feet. The rest laughed and the horse galloped on as if he still carried his rider. The recruit scrambled to his feet.

The sergeant roared out at him, "What do you mean, falling off that horse?"

"I lost my balance, Sergeant."

"You may never lose your balance in this Force. Back to your horse."

"You see," said Hawkins. "You can make mistakes anywhere else, Miss Sue, but not in the Force."

The sun was growing hotter now as they passed around the far side of the Parade, toward the Commissioner's house. Beside it was that mysterious building called H.Q., which Sue had heard about the evening before. She found that H.Q., stood for Headquarters, or the Commissioner's office, and Hawkins solemnly explained that no one ever went there except on business.

And then, as if the morning hadn't been complete, Sue saw the band march into the Parade, red coats vivid in the sun, instruments gleaming; and higher and more thrilling than the birds, the music of the *British Grenadiers* rose on the prairie air. Sue felt as if her heart must burst. It was so gay, so joyous, so triumphant.

> "And a row, tow, tow, tow, tow, tow,
> For the British Grenadiers,"

sang Hawkins softly beside her. There was a great clatter of
hoofs, a flashing of buckles and bits and spurs, and at a fast
trot a company of the Force rode by, with Uncle Dennis at
their head. He joined the inspection party a few minutes later
and listened to Sue's delighted story of her morning's adventures.

"Come along, Sue," he said. "I'm going to take you on a
most important call and I want you to be on your very best behavior." Just as if she hadn't been all morning, thought Sue.

"We are going to call on Commissioner and Mrs. Walsh,"
he said impressively. "Commissioner Walsh is the Commanding Officer of the North West Mounted Police or, as you call
them, 'The Mounties.' He is the finest officer in the world
and I am very fortunate to be under his command. I want you
to do your best for me now, Sue." Opening the gate, they went
up the walk to the Commissioner's house.

Mrs. Walsh was in the drawing room and Sue curtseyed
deeply to her. When the Commissioner entered, she curtseyed
again, but no one paid much attention to her and she examined the Commissioner shyly. He was very tall, she thought,
and very stern, with bright blue eyes; rather frightening in
spite of the tiny smiling wrinkles around his eyes. His beard
was clipped short in military fashion and his voice inclined to
harshness. He smiled again, this time at Sue.

"Well, Susannah," he said, "what are you thinking of?"

Sue smiled back at him. "I was wondering," she said, "how
soon I could join the Force and when I'd get my red coat." The
Commissioner laughed. "You have to be six feet in height,
over eighteen years of age, able to read and write either
the French or English language, weigh a hundred-and-sixty
pounds, and be strong as a horse."

Sue sighed gustily. It seemed a large order for someone who didn't weigh even one hundred pounds. She decided then and there to start learning the duties of a member of the Force.

They went in to luncheon, and Sue felt quite grand sitting at the Commissioner's right hand. But the conversation baffled her. It was all about a Queen who was very old and how her Uncle Dennis would have extra work to do for the Queen as well as his regular work. By the time dessert arrived, Sue gave up trying to understand what it was all about and examined the Commissioner again. There was no doubt in her mind but that he was terrifying. It wouldn't be good for you if you tried to fool him, she decided, and yet somehow she wasn't really afraid of him. She thought she'd go and see for herself what that place called "H.Q." looked like inside.

5. Sue Joins the Force

Sue was very curious about the Queen. "What Queen?" she asked Uncle Dennis, when they were back in their own house. Uncle Dennis looked shocked.

"When one speaks of the Queen, Sue, one only means our Queen."

"Yes," said Sue, "but who is she?"

"Victoria the Good, Queen of Great Britain and Ireland, Empress of India, and the Dominions beyond the Seas," answered Uncle Dennis in the same tones with which the sentry had cried "Who goes there!"

"My gracious," said Sue, "I did hear about her last summer. We had firecrackers and sky rockets on her birthday."

"She was only seventeen, Sue, when she became Queen of England," said Uncle Dennis. "That was nearly sixty years ago, Sue, and now she is an old, old lady, very frail and tired, for no other Queen has ever reigned so long. No other Queen could have made England the mighty Empire that it is. The Indians call her the 'Great White Mother.' And here," Uncle Dennis continued, "is where you and I come in.

"Next year the whole world is to do honor to her most gracious Majesty. On June 22, 1897, there will be a Jubilee service at St. Paul's in London."

52

"What's a Jubilee?" asked Sue.

"A Jubilee is a time of great rejoicing, and as an Empire we are rejoicing that our good Queen has reigned so long and so well. Every colony or dominion in the Empire is sending troops to march in the royal procession in London from Buckingham Palace to St. Paul's. The North West Mounted Police Force are sending a contingent of picked men. Besides my regular duties, I have to train the contingent. You see, Sue, our men must be better than any others there."

Sue nodded. "But where do I come in? Do I go over with you?"

Captain Lyons laughed. "I'm afraid not, Sue; only members of the Force."

"Then can't I join the Force now? I could learn to be a soldier," she pleaded, both hands on her uncle's knees. "I could help you perhaps."

"You can help me now," he said, "by being a good soldier and following orders."

The door opened and in came Michael O'Dare and John Hogarth. They listened to the day's adventures and agreed with Uncle Dennis that if she wanted to join the Force, she must have military training and place herself under orders like a good recruit.

"Then you can train her," said Uncle Dennis, "I'm due at H.Q."

The two young men looked at her and laughed. Sue laughed back. They were so gay and quite gorgeous, she thought, in their blue uniforms with frogs and high boots.

"What do I do first?" she asked.

"Well," said Michael, "we'll first turn this room into a recruiting office."

A table was placed in the middle of the room and the two young officers sat down at it. Hawkins was stationed at the door. "Now, Sue, you go outside and knock," said Michael O'Dare.

Sue knocked once. Hawkins answered, "Who goes there?"

"It's me and I want to join the North West Mounted Police Force," said Sue in a gruff voice, as much like the Commissioner's as she could make it.

Hawkins opened the door. "Come in," he barked. "Sit down on that bench over there." The bench was Uncle Dennis' best sofa, and Sue walked over to it with as long strides as she could manage.

"A new recruit, sir," said Hawkins, saluting the officers.

"What's he look like?" asked O'Dare. "Up to standard?"

"A little under weight, sir, but he looks as if he'd be very intelligent."

"Bring him in and let's have a look at him," Hawkins motioned; Sue stepped up to the table.

"Name?" frowned Michael.

"Susannah Elizabeth Fairfield Winston."

"Age?"

Sue heard Hawkins who stood behind her whisper, "eighteen." "Eighteen," she repeated, and then faltered, "at least I will be."

"Why do you want to join the Force?" asked John Hogarth.

"Because I want to go to England with Uncle Dennis and see the Queen and because I want to wear a red coat."

Michael made his voice very gruff. "Well, well. These are hardly reasons for joining the Force. If you join the Force it must be to preserve law and order in Her Most Gracious Majesty's North West Territories."

"Yes, sir," said Sue, properly impressed.

Michael solemnly continued: "The medical officer will now examine you to see if you are physically fit."

"This way," said Hawkins, gravely leading Sue into the dining room.

John Hogarth arrived and cleared his throat noisily. "I am the medical officer," he said. And with Hawkins' help he put Sue on the table and found her to be six feet in height, eighteen years of age, weight one hundred and sixty pounds, eyesight perfect (will probably see too much, he added) and with lungs and heart in excellent condition. "Take this man back to the Recruiting Officer," he said to Hawkins, "I shall advise his acceptance."

Importantly Sue advanced to the table again.

"Recruit Winston, you have been found physically fit. Can you read and write in the English and French languages?"

"I can read a bit in English," she answered, "and I can sing in French and dance in Irish."

"Excellent qualifications," said Michael O'Dare in a deep voice. "We will now administer the oath of allegiance."

Standing in front of the three men, Sue raised her right hand and repeated after Michael the oath every member of the Force took on joining,

"I, Susannah Elizabeth Fairfield Winston, solemnly swear that I will faithfully, diligently and impartially execute and perform the duties required of me as a member of the North West Mounted Police Force, and will well and truly obey all lawful orders and instructions which I shall receive as such, without fear, favor, or affection of or toward any person. So help me God."

Sue felt very solemn as she said the last words and the three men looked very solemn, too. Then Michael asked her if she knew her duties as a recruit. Sue shook her head and he explained that she must be punctual, obey orders without question, and be neat and tidy always. Every day they would call her out on Parade, and after inspection give her her orders for the day.

"But how shall I know when's Parade?" asked Sue.

"By the bugle call," answered Michael.

"Now then, Recruit Winston, have you any questions to ask?"

"Yes," said Sue. "When do I get my uniform?"

"Ah," said Michael. "Not until you have a good conduct sheet and you've ridden with the Commissioner."

That seemed a very long way off to Sue. She had no horse, she couldn't ride, and she knew how hard it was to be good according to grownup standards. What had often been just an adventure to her had turned out to be a crime in the eyes of Matilda. It was all very puzzling. But remembering Matilda, she smiled again.

"A recruit doesn't need a nurse," she said. "Let's send Matilda back to Montreal."

Lieutenant Hogarth shook his head. "Matilda's your batman," he said. "You'll need her."

"But I don't want her," said Sue.

Lieutenant O'Dare stood up. "Recruit Winston, are you questioning the orders of your officer?"

There was a dreadful silence in the room. All three men were looking at her very sternly. "I was just explaining," began Sue.

"A good recruit obeys orders," said O'Dare. "He never questions them."

"I'll do better next time," said Sue in a small voice, for she felt very small and very silly.

"Very good, Recruit Winston. Now we'll teach you the bugle calls."

By the time Mrs. Schofield brought in the silver tea tray, Sue had learned to play Reveille and Lights Out on the piano —with only one finger, it is true—and had learned how to salute smartly.

There was buttered toast for tea and little sponge cakes, a glass of milk for Sue, but three cups on the tray. "Who is the third cup for?" asked Lieutenant O'Dare.

"Miss Vicky," answered Mrs. Schofield. "She telephoned and I was to tell you that she is coming to take Miss Sue for a drive."

"Three cheers," said John Hogarth, pulling down his coat and straightening his collar. "Sue, you are now about to meet the pride of the Force—Victoria Frances Walsh."

"Who's she?"

"The Commissioner's daughter," answered John.

"Shall I tell her I'm a soldier now?" asked Sue, feeling she should add something to the importance of the moment.

Michael swung around. "You're not a soldier, Sue," he said. "You are a member of the North West Mounted Police."

"Soldiers wear red coats," protested Sue, "and the Force wears red coats."

"But it's different," he told her. "Soldiers are for war, for fighting. We are police. We are here to keep the peace, to make the prairies safe for people to come and build new homes. And we are here to protect the Indians too, so that bad white men may not steal from them. We are here, Sue, to see that law and order rule. We are not here to fight."

"But I thought police always wore blue," said Sue, wishing she could understand.

"They do," said Michael, "almost all the world over. But long ago, when the first British regiments came to Canada they wore red coats; and the Indians learned that where there was a red coat, there was kindness, medicine, gifts, friends. Red stood for all that was good in the white man. And after a time the Indians learned that red meant justice, too . . . that if a Redcoat was called to decide a point in a quarrel, the Redcoat decided for right, without fear or favor.

"So years ago when they were first forming the Force, the Indians asked that the men wear red coats, saying, 'We know that the soldiers of our Great White Mother wear red coats and are our friends.' So now, Sue, wherever the red coat is seen, and it can be seen a long way off, it is a warning to both strong and weak, honest and dishonest that the rule of law prevails."

"I see," said Sue, "I see."

But there was a laughing voice in the hall, and through the doorway came a lovely lady, tall and slim, with golden hair tucked in little curls under her hat. She was dressed in a suit of soft cornflower blue, the color of her sparkling eyes. The revers and vest of the coat were tan and it was fastened with large silver buttons. Huge leg o' mutton sleeves ended. above soft driving gloves of fawn.

"Where is Sue?" she cried. "I've come to take her for a drive."

"I'm here," said Sue, curtseying, "and I'd love to go driving, Miss Vicky."

Matilda was waiting on the stairs with hat and gloves, and with the help of the two officers, Hawkins, and an orderly, they were finally settled in the yellow buckboard. Miss Vicky shook the reins lightly, chirruped like a bird to her horse, and they were off around the parade ground, out through the gates and across the prairies.

On the way to Regina, Sue learned that Miss Vicky was just home from school in England, had only just grown up, and had before her return to Canada been "presented." The tones in which Miss Vicky said the word "presented" told Sue that here was something quite out of the ordinary, like being sixty years a Queen or taking the oath of allegiance.

"What," she asked, "is being presented?" And Vicky told her it was the grandest thing that could happen to a young lady.

"It's great fun," continued Miss Vicky. "You get into your carriage and drive to Buckingham Palace. The streets are lined with people to see you pass and everyone is very gay. When you get to the Palace you are taken to the dressing room to see if your gown is correct, and then you wait until your name is called. Then you take your place in the line and follow until you reach the Throne. You make your curtsey and afterwards you go to a party where everyone comes to see you in all your finery. It's very thrilling, Sue." As if in memory of that exciting day, Miss Vicky shook her reins and chirruped again to her horse.

"Do you think I could be presented some day?" asked Sue. "I should like very much to see the Queen."

But Miss Vicky was passing over the railway tracks and was giving all her attention to her horse. Far away they heard the shriek of the locomotive bringing in the Transcontinental.

After collecting a parcel at the Rectory, doing some shopping and leaving a note with the Judge's wife, they turned the horse toward the Barracks again. By this time Sue knew

all about Miss Vicky's return from England, how she loved
dancing and riding and tennis, how her father had only that
morning given her a beautiful horse of her own to ride. Well
content with their world, the two young ladies drove home
toward the Barracks.

But much as Sue liked the idea of going to court, her decision to become a Mountie was far more important, and when
she saw a red-coated figure in the distance, swinging along the
narrow sidewalk, her interest was aroused. As they came
nearer, she realized that the red coat belonged to a Mountie;
that the swing of the shoulders was familiar. She wondered
where she had seen it before.

"Stop, stop," she suddenly screamed. "It's Monty, it's
Monty! Oh, please, Miss Vicky, stop!!"

Startled, Miss Vicky reined in her horse, but before the carriage stopped, Sue was scrambling out over the wheel and running across the prairie grass to where, unconscious of the commotion he was causing, her friend Monty of the train journey
strode along the sidewalk.

"Oh, Monty, it's me, Sue," she cried. "You've joined the
Force, and you look beautiful. Come quickly. Here's Miss
Vicky."

Miss Vicky had drawn up along the sidewalk and was waiting for them. But when Sue dragged him over, chattering like
a magpie of her doings, Monty behaved in the strangest
fashion. Saluting, he said, "I shall see you some other day,
Sue," and lifted her in.

"But come and drive with us now," Sue cried. "Come and
drive with us now."

Monty shook his head, saluted again and swung back to the
sidewalk. Miss Vicky drove quickly past him.

"Whatever's happened," said Sue crossly. "He was so nice to me on the train. Now he hardly speaks to me. He didn't speak to you at all. Why wouldn't he drive with us?"

"He can't," said Miss Vicky. "It's against regulations."

"Couldn't you speak to him?" asked Sue.

"Oh, that would never do," Miss Vicky answered primly.

"I think it's very silly," said Sue. "He's as nice a man as Uncle Dennis and much more fun, and he's much nicer than your father, too. He's so . . ." Sue paused for the right word. "He's so friendly."

"I know," said Miss Vicky, "but these are regulations, Sue, and whether we like them or not we have to obey them. Father is friendly, too," she continued, "but you see, he has a lot to do."

Miss Vicky looked down at the bright head beside her. "And he has you to bother him, too, Sue," she said slowly. "You see, when I was little, I was a very spoiled and naughty child. I caused everyone a great deal of worry and Father is afraid that you will do the same and interfere with your uncle's work."

"No I won't, Miss Vicky," said Sue. "I took a vow this afternoon when I joined the Force to be good and obey all lawful orders, but I still think no regulation should keep you from talking to a nice man like Monty—and I'm going to find him again as soon as ever I can!"

6. Sue Visits Headquarters

A door banged downstairs. A bugle call rang out across the Parade. A butterfly, golden as the day, drifted in the open window. Sue watched it with sleepy eyes. Far away there sounded the beat of a drum and Sue was wide awake, and remembering with concern the events of the past week.

Michael and John had only paraded her twice. The first time she had been very prompt and so had they. The second time they had overslept and had been so hurried that they hadn't even noticed her shoes weren't polished. Since then they had forgotten all about it.

There had been the morning, too, when she slipped into the Sentry box behind the guard's back, while he challenged an approaching carriage. Sue remembered what a fuss he had made when she wouldn't move. Finally he and the sergeant had bribed her to leave with sugar sticks.

Another day she had run away from Matilda and sought refuge in the stables. There was no one there when she arrived and all she had done was cry "Move over" to a large black horse, in the way Smith had taught her. She didn't know that the horse was a wild one, tied in a stall for the first time that day, and Smith returned just in time to save her from its lash-

ing heels. Smith had been dreadfully cross with her and made
her sit still on an empty box until Matilda came for her.

Matilda was so silly, too, always misunderstanding orders
and running after Hawkins, declaring Sue was lost when she
was only hiding behind a door. Sue sighed and wriggled her
toes. It seemed as if she was always getting into trouble. The
high windy whistle of a freight train across the prairies caught
her ear.

Trains, thought Sue. Trains brought back Montreal and
the long trip out, her vanished friend Monty and his promise
to see her "some other day." She wished she could see him
now; he'd understand.

"Some other day." Why not today? Turning back the
quilt, Sue ran to the door. "Matilda," she cried. "Matilda, do
get up! We've very important things to do."

Breakfast over, Sue, with Matilda starched and stiff beside
her, set out on her hunt for Monty. She tried the Guard House
first.

"You can't go in there," said Matilda.

"Why not?" asked Sue, climbing the steps.

"It's only a place for prisoners," protested Matilda feebly.

Sue peered in the open door. The Guard Room was a
shadowy place, empty save for a table, a half dozen chairs
against the wall, and a high, old-fashioned desk where a sergeant stood with a great book open before him. A monster inkwell and a pen lay beside it.

"Can only prisoners come in here?" she asked.

"Do you want to lay a charge?" he said.

Sue entered. "What's a charge?"

"Well," said the sergeant. "Suppose your house had been
robbed and you knew who did it; you would come to me and

'prefer a charge.' I would listen to your story, decide what was best to do, get an order, go out and find my man and bring him in here. When I brought him in, I would enter his name in this book, along with the details of his crime and arrest, and then lock up the man until further orders."

"Show me the book," coaxed Sue. The sergeant lifted her up. The open page of the big book was clear and white, only the date and year were written on it.

"Where are the crimes?" she asked.

"There are none today," he answered. "There were none yesterday, and," turning back the pages, "only a little one the day before."

"But what's the sense of a great big book if you don't write more in it?" she asked.

The laughter of the sergeant surprised her. "Ah, you've got the wrong idea," he said. "The less writing in this book, the better the Force is doing its job. If there wasn't a single entry in it from cover to cover, the Police would be doing a perfect job on the prairies. What counts, Miss Sue, is not the arrests we make, *but the arrests we don't have to make.*"

Sue hoped she understood what the sergeant was trying to tell her, but she wasn't altogether sure.

"How do you mean?" she asked.

"Well, it's like this," he explained. "The Force is here to take care of people, and when you take care of people you don't just take care of crimes. You help them. See, if you had a farm twenty or thirty miles away from here and you were all alone out there, we'd call upon you every little while and see if you were all right. If you were a Doukabor and couldn't speak English and were planting the wrong kind of crops, we'd tell you what to plant. We'd find out if your children were going to school, or if you needed a doctor. If you were an Indian and were drinking firewater, we'd warn you to behave. We're here to guide and protect the settlers. That's our job."

"Then could you help me," said Sue, much impressed with all she had heard.

"Sure. What do you want?"

"I want to find a new recruit called Monty."

The sergeant shook his head. "Can't you tell me anything more about him. What's he look like?"

"He's as big as you are," she said, "and very dark."

. The sergeant touched a bell. There was a sound of scrambling feet, of chairs being pushed back; and then from a door at the back of the Guard Room, four constables entered. Slim, erect, bronzed from the prairie sun, they came stiffly to attention.

"Do any of you boys know of a new recruit called Monty? He's about my size and dark." Not one of them had ever heard of him. The sergeant turned back to Sue. "Can't you tell us anything more about him?"

"Yes," said Sue. "He has a most elegant way of speaking, and a nice smile."

But they knew of no new recruit that fitted Sue's description. Just then Matilda's complaining voice broke in.

"How much longer do I have to wait out here?"

"I must go," said Sue. "Thank you very much," and she saluted smartly. To her delight, they returned her salute, and as she went down the steps, one of them called to her.

"Try Sergeant Whiteside at the Riding School," he said. "He might know."

Through the gate and out across the prairies they went to the Riding School. They could hear Sergeant Whiteside as they approached . . . *Trot* . . . *Canterrr* . . . *Gallop* . . . and the thud of the horses' feet. They waited in the doorway until the sergeant was free. Sue told her story all over again.

"Do I know a recruit called Monty? I do not, Miss Sue, and no one ever has a nice smile when I'm teaching him to ride. They're too busy sticking to their horse to smile. You'd better try Smith at the stables. He might know."

Back across the prairies, and out of the blinding sun into the cool brown shadows of the stable they trudged. But Smith didn't know of anyone answering the description, and like Matilda, he was inclined to doubt whether Sue's friend had ever joined the Force.

"But I saw him," said Sue, "and he looked very grand in his red coat."

"Well, if I were you," advised Smith, "and I wanted to find a man as bad as you do, I'd go straight to Headquarters."

"I will," answered Sue, for she had set her heart on finding Monty, and it seemed to her a very sensible idea to go straight to the Commissioner.

Out into the sun again and around the Parade, Sue led the protesting Matilda. "Sure, Miss Sue, if you walk without your hat you'll get sunburned and the captain won't like it. Put your hat on again, Miss Sue." But Sue shook her head and walked faster. She liked the feel of the sun hot on her head and the way the breeze lifted the thick curls on her neck; she liked the feeling of importance that the hunt for Monty gave her.

When they reached Headquarters, she turned to Matilda. "I am going in to see the Commissioner," she said. "You needn't wait." Before Matilda could complain, Sue went up the path leading to Headquarters, the Commissioner's office.

There was a tiny lilac tree by the door, red geraniums outlined the path and the knocker on the door gleamed brightly. But Sue knew you didn't knock. She had watched others go right in. Pushing open the door, she stepped into a long, narrow waiting room with a table down the centre. There were chairs around it, windows at either end of the room, and on the wall were pictures and maps.

At a flat topped desk on her left a young constable sat writing.

"Hello! What can I do for you?" he asked.

"I want to see the Commissioner."

"Name, please," said the young constable, with a smile.

"Sue Winston." She came over to the desk and leaned on it. "How soon can I see him?" she asked. "It's very important."

"I'm afraid you'll have to wait, Miss Sue. Will you have a chair?"

"Thank you," said Sue, sitting down at the long table. There was a big book on it but the pictures on the wall looked more interesting. She got up and walked around the room. The maps, she thought, were dull, but the framed photographs of the Force quite exciting, even though some of them looked rather like Father Christmas with their beards and moustaches.

There was only one photograph of a man without a uniform. This puzzled her. "Who can he be?" she asked the constable. "He hasn't a uniform."

"That," he replied, "is Sir John A. Macdonald who founded the Force."

"Why doesn't he wear a uniform?" pressed Sue.

"Well, you see, he wasn't a member of the Force, Miss Sue. He was only the Prime Minister of Canada."

"The poor man," said Sue. "And who is this?" She pointed to the next picture.

"That is the Father of the Force. Superintendent Griesbach, the first man to enlist."

Sue looked at the picture for a long time. "He looks very nice," she said, "and he has a most gorgeous moustache, hasn't he—all fluffy and droopy? Now, Hawkins' moustache is long and droopy, but very stiff."

"How do you know?" asked the constable.

"Because he told me. He uses a pomade that comes from France, and if you use a little and twirl the ends between your fingers and your thumb, your moustache is practically rigid all day." Sue felt very proud to be able to pass on this valuable information to the constable, and then realized that he had neither moustache nor beard.

"Why haven't you a moustache?" she asked.

The young constable walked over to his desk and took out a little book and turned the pages.

"'The Recruit's Manual,'" he said, "states that 'All individuals of the Force can please themselves as to wearing whiskers, moustaches or beard, but those who prefer to shave must do so daily.' You see, Miss Sue, you can do as you please about your face, provided it is clean and shaved."

"Yes," said Sue. "Does Uncle Dennis know about that book you read from? His moustache is like a tooth brush."

"Yes," replied the constable. "Your uncle knows about this book. It is given to each member of the Force when he joins. It must be produced at Kit Inspection, and it gives you complete instructions as to your behavior in every particular, every moment of your life in the Force."

"*Every* moment?" questioned Sue.

"Well, almost every moment."

"And if it didn't tell you something, what would you do?"

"I'd use my head."

"Well, would that book tell you what to do if I asked for a piece of paper and a pencil?" asked Sue.

"It does."

"Show me," urged Sue.

The constable leafed over the pages; "Here we are . . . 'At all times strive to promote good feeling and respect for the Force.' And there's your paper and pencil, Miss Sue. What do you want them for?"

"To draw pictures," she answered, and going over to the table amused herself drawing pictures of Hawkins, Matilda, Smith and even the Commissioner, but she had trouble with his beard. Sue lifted the cover of the big book. There were pictures of men inside. She carried it over to the constable's desk.

"Tell me," she asked. "What is this book about?"

"Can't you read?" he questioned.

"A little bit," said Sue.

"Well, try," he said. "What's this say on the cover?"

"MEN WANTED," she spelt.

"Well, that's what it's about," he said, opening the book. "These men are wanted by the Force because they have broken the laws of the prairies."

"Can't you find them?" asked Sue.

"We haven't found them yet, but we will. You see, we keep this book with their pictures in it and we constables memorize the face and description of each bad man. We don't always get them at first, but sooner or later we do."

"Are they very bad men?" asked Sue, awed by the thought of a whole book filled with bad men.

"Some are. Now this man is wanted for selling firewater to

the Indians. He doesn't look bad, Miss Sue, but he's a holy
terror. He went over the Border when he heard we were on
the lookout for him, but he'll be back and we'll get him."

"What's firewater?" asked Sue.

"Whiskey, bad whiskey. It burns the Indians' throats, drives
'em crazy and starts 'em fighting. We won't allow it."

"They don't all look bad," continued Sue, turning the pages.

"I'll find you some wild ones," said the constable obligingly.
"See here."

"My goodness gracious," Sue agreed. "He does look *very*
bad."

The constable nodded. "Yes, sir! He's a tough one, as bad
as they come. Killed one of our men a couple of years ago and
been in hiding ever since. We all know his face all right, and
the first time one of us lays an eye on him, it will be all up with
him."

Sue looked at the face on the page. It was a large print of a
dark, round-faced man with small black eyes, thick hair and a
surly expression.

"Oh, I shouldn't like to meet him," said Sue. "He couldn't
look worse. What's his name?"

"Joe Labiche," answered the constable, still looking at the
picture. "He's half Indian, half French, a bad mixture."

"I can speak French," said Sue. "*Je suis une 'tite rascalle.*
And I know a French song."

Just then a bell rang, and hastily pulling down his tunic, the
young constable disappeared into the Commissioner's office.

Sue compared the picture of Joe Labiche in the book with
the one on the notice board hanging on the wall. The bigger
the picture, the worse he looked, she thought, and picking up
her pencil, proceeded to give Joe Labiche in the book a pair of

heavy military moustaches. The effect was startling. The surly expression vanished, the evil look of the man disappeared.

"My goodness!" said Sue, with a delighted giggle. "WON'T the constable be surprised." But she was not entirely satisfied with the result of her work. Ink would help, she thought, and carrying the inkwell from the desk to the table she carefully outlined her drawing with the pen.

A door closed behind her, but she was too absorbed to notice that there were two men in the room, or that one of them was Uncle Dennis. But she heard his voice, and he sounded very annoyed.

"What are you doing in here, Sue?" he asked sharply.

"I've come to see the Commissioner on important business," Sue answered. "*Look* at Joe Labiche!"

Her uncle bent over the table. "What have you been doing!" he exclaimed.

"I'm just inking him in," said Sue proudly. "I'm almost through. You wouldn't know him now, would you?" she asked the young constable, who looked as if he wanted to laugh, but her Uncle Dennis seemed very angry.

"This is shocking, Sue," he said. "You have no business to be in here, and you have no right to touch anything." As if there were anything wrong in just adding a moustache to a man's face, thought Sue.

But at that moment the Commissioner's door opened. "Good morning, Susannah," he said, "did you want to see me?"

Sue slipped off her chair. "Oh, yes, Commissioner Walsh," she said. "Could I please ask you a very special question?" Uncle Dennis looked annoyed and the Commissioner didn't seem too pleased either, but he asked her to come in. The office was bare, like the waiting room, and sitting on the opposite side of the desk she told him about her vanished friend Monty.

"I think we can find him," he said. "Let's see, he is tall and dark, has a nice smile, an elegant way of speaking, and his name is Monty. Right?"

Sue nodded. The Commissioner took out a file marked "Recruits" and went through a pile of papers. He shook his head. "There is no one here of that name," he said, "and there are dozens that are tall and dark. And there is no mention of a nice smile. Can you tell me anything more about him?"

Sue thought a moment. "Yes," she said. "He has an Aunt Charlotte at home in Scotland and she won't give him any pocket money so he came out to join the Force."

He went over the file again. "Is this your man, Sue?" he said, handing her a photograph. "Angus Montague?"

"That's Monty," she cried delightedly, "but I thought he had a lot of other names."

"That's all the names he has here," said the Commissioner.

Captain Lyons protested, "You're very kind, sir, but you mustn't allow Sue to take up any more of your time."

The Commissioner rose. "Well, Susannah," he said. "You know your recruit's name now. Your uncle will be able to find him for you."

Gravely he shook hands and with Uncle Dennis pushing her smartly before him, Sue was hurried through the waiting room and out onto the sidewalk.

To Sue it had been an entirely satisfactory morning, with victory at the end. She wanted to start in search of Monty at once, of course, but a glance at her uncle's face told her that she had better wait until after luncheon at least. He was flushed and he carried his head higher than ever and looked very grim. "And all," murmured Sue, "because I put moustaches on Joe Labiche."

7. Sue Finds Monty

Luncheon was a very silent meal; the most silent Sue remembered having for a long, long time. She did her best to make her uncle talk to her but nothing seemed to have the least effect; neither dropping her spoon nor asking for a second helping of rice pudding, which was a sure way of pleasing her mother. Uncle Dennis didn't even notice.

Finally, when he pushed back his chair and said, "Come along, Sue, I'd like to speak to you in my study," she knew she was in for a bad time. He reminded her of the day the Staff Sergeant had found the unpolished button on a recruit's tunic. The Staff Sergeant had roared and grown red in the face, but Uncle Dennis was grim and quiet. She wondered if she didn't prefer the sergeant's way of being cross.

"Sue," said her uncle, when the study door closed behind them, "I suppose you know that you have behaved very badly."

"But Uncle Dennis . . ." Sue began.

"Now let me do the talking. There are some things you cannot do, Sue, and going to the Commissioner's office is one of them. He's a very busy man, but what is more important he doesn't approve of . . ."

But before her uncle could tell her what it was the Commissioner didn't approve of, there was a knock on the door and

75

Hawkins stepped in, looking almost as unhappy as Sue felt herself.

"Beg pardon, sir," he said, "but could I have a word with you? It's important."

"Certainly, Hawkins. What is it?"

"I'm leaving, sir. I'm leaving this afternoon for the Duck Lake Post, sir."

"You're what?" cried her uncle, and Sue found out then that he could roar every bit as well as the Staff Sergeant. "What do you mean, Hawkins? Leaving for Duck Lake? What's this all about?"

"It's that female, Matilda, sir. I'm sorry, sir, but I can't stand her any longer. She makes a fool of me, running after me before the entire Force calling, 'Oh, Mr. Hawkins, Mr. Hawkins, could you help me find Miss Sue?' "

Sue held her breath and hoped he would go on imitating Matilda, he did it so perfectly, but her uncle broke in: "What's this about Duck Lake? I've signed no transfer."

"No, sir, you haven't," agreed Hawkins. "But you did tell me that you'd not stand in my way anytime I wanted to see more of the country."

Captain Lyons sighed. "That's true, Hawkins. Are you going to hold me to my promise?"

"I must, sir," said Hawkins miserably. "I'm no use to either man or beast with that nurse around."

"But what about my niece?"

"I don't like leaving Miss Sue, sir. She's all right. It's only that, being lively, she runs all over the Barracks."

Captain Lyons stood up. "Hawkins, you can't leave me. You know how important this year is."

But Hawkins was determined. "I've seen to everything," he said. "I've a recruit ready to take my place."

The captain shook his head. "What does a recruit know about a batman's duties?" he asked. "And how could any stranger coming in here keep a hand on this household?"

"This one could, sir," Hawkins replied. "He's cut above the average. Not only knows how to care for horses but knows all an officer's needs as well."

Sue was very interested in the conversation. Here was her friend Hawkins telling her Uncle Dennis that Matilda was practically useless—something she had always known herself. She laid a hand on her uncle's knee.

"Let Matilda go, Uncle Dennis," she said. "Then there wouldn't be any trouble and I could have a lovely time with Hawkins."

Captain Lyons turned. "I had forgotten you were here, Sue," he said sharply. "Go into the drawing room and wait until I send for you."

Gracious, thought Sue, things *are* happening, and opened the study door. What was in the hall in front of her? She blinked her eyes. Was she dreaming? Could it be true? She took a step forward. *It was true!* Standing very straight in his scarlet tunic, a young recruit smiled down at her.

"Monty!" she screamed, "Monty! MONTY!"

"Quiet, Sue," he warned. "Quiet!"

But quiet was beyond Sue's understanding. She ran back to the study. "Uncle Dennis," she cried, "he's here. Monty's here. You can let Hawkins go and Matilda, too. Monty'll take care of me."

But Monty remained standing in the hall, and halfway be-

tween the two men Sue stopped, startled that no one shared
her excitement.

"What's this man's name?" asked Captain Lyons.

"Montague, sir, Angus Montague."

"Montague!" called Captain Lyons.

"Yes, sir," and Sue watched her friend enter and salute
smartly. She loved the way Monty answered "Yes, sir," he
sounded so elegant.

"I understand from Hawkins that you already know why he
is leaving for Duck Lake this afternoon."

"Yes, sir."

"You also realize that your duties here will be somewhat out
of the ordinary, requiring tact and patience."

"Yes, sir."

"And he can play with me," broke in Sue.

Her uncle turned. "Go into the drawing room, Sue," he
said. "I'll see you later." There was something in her uncle's voice that made her leave without further question, but
she had to go through the hall to reach the drawing room, and
no one had told her that she couldn't go *very* slowly through
the hall. . . . Besides, she could hear what was going on in
the study if she took a long time to reach the drawing room.
She examined the curtain over the study door and listened to
her uncle.

"I am anxious that my niece be happy and interested," he
said, "but I have so little time that I'll have to depend on you
to keep an eye on her."

"That shouldn't be difficult, sir," replied Monty, "and I don't
think the nurse will bother me."

She heard Hawkins moan softly. "I've warned him, sir," he
said. "He can't say he didn't know."

Sue giggled and then smothered the giggle in the curtain, but not fast enough.

"Excuse me, sir," she heard Monty say. The next moment she felt two strong hands clutch her and she was whirled out of the curtain. It was Monty!

"First lesson, Sue," he said. "Good recruits do not snoop! Off to the drawing room with you."

Astonished, Sue trotted off to the drawing room, but not before she heard her uncle say, "Does she always behave like that for you?" and Monty's answer, "Why not, sir."

Sue sat down. This whole day was turning out quite differently from what she had expected. There was a sound at the door and Hawkins came in.

"I'm off to get my kit together," he said. "Be sure you do what Monty tells you. He's a good sort and knows all the things you should know—things I can't tell you about, for I never knew them."

"Won't you ever come back?" asked Sue.

"Yes," said Hawkins sourly. "When that female is gone."

"Tell me," Sue coaxed. "Where did you find Monty?"

"Over in Block C, Miss Sue, and when he heard me talking about going to Duck Lake, he came along and said, 'Hawkins,' he said, just like that, 'Hawkins, I'd like that berth of yours, if you're leaving.' And before I knew it, Miss Sue, I had him here." Hawkins paused. "Or, I wonder, Miss Sue, did he bring me here?" Hawkins thought for a minute and then gloomily got up. "Times have changed," he said, "when a female drives me out of the captain's house."

A few minutes later Captain Lyons' voice sounded in the hall. "All right, Monty, you're in charge." A door banged and Sue saw her uncle go down the path and across the Parade.

"Susannah," called Monty's cheerful voice. "Susannah, your uncle tells me you are to show me the house, where his things are kept, introduce me to Mrs. Schofield and generally make yourself useful. Where shall we begin?"

"Oh, let me show you to Mrs. Schofield first," cried Sue. "I've told her such a lot about you." And with her fingers hanging on to his tunic, she ushered Monty into the pantry where Mrs. Schofield was mixing gingerbread. "Here's Monty," she said. "He's come to take Hawkins' place."

Mrs. Schofield smiled. "We'll miss Mr. Hawkins," she said to Monty, "but I'm sure we'll do our best to make you happy, and . . ." Her cheerful smile faded. "Come in, Matilda," she said crossly.

In the doorway Matilda stood with her head a little to one side. "How do you do?" she said with a silly smile.

"Very well, thank you," answered Monty briskly. "Able to get out every day. How about you?"

"I like getting out every day, too," simpered Matilda, "but this is a strange wild country and I don't like going out alone."

"Too bad about you," said Monty. "It looks as if you'll have to spend the rest of your life indoors. Why wasn't Miss Sue's hair brushed before luncheon?"

"I'm sure I don't know, sir," said Matilda.

"Why is she wearing a crumpled dress now?"

"I didn't finish the ironing!" faltered Matilda.

"Then get about your ironing now," said Monty, "and don't waste time talking." Slowly Matilda disappeared into the basement laundry.

Mrs. Schofield nodded her head approvingly. "That's what the poor girl needs, Mr. Monty. A strong hand over her.

She's a silly thing, but she has a kindly heart. I've no doubt you'll manage her."

Promising to come back later for gingerbread, they went to Sue's room where she showed him her treasures—the desk, the books, the little cradle, and last of all her greatest treasure, Minnie-Pooh-Pooh, the small brown Indian doll. They visited the bedrooms of her uncle, Michael and John.

Monty inspected their uniforms and boots, their buttons. "All one hundred percent perfect," he said. "It'll keep me busy matching Hawkins' skill."

"What do you mean?" asked Sue.

"I mean, that I will brush their uniforms, clean their buttons, polish their boots, and do everything Hawkins did for them. You see, Sue, I've had my training as stable orderly, as block orderly, and now I take my turn as batman."

"What's a block orderly?"

"It's mid-June," said Monty, "and you have been here seven weeks and don't know what a block orderly is?"

Sue shook her head.

"I thought you'd joined the Force."

"Yes," said Sue, "and I took my vows but Michael and John never have much time to train me. I'm not a very good recruit."

"Too bad," said Monty. "All that time wasted. Well, I'll tell you what we'll do, Sue. We'll start your regular training this afternoon and keep it up every day. Have you a bulletin board?"

Sue shook her head. "I don't know what you mean."

So Mrs. Schofield produced the cover of a cardboard box and under Monty's instructions covered it with strong white paper. At the top of it, with the coloured crayons that Michael had given Sue, Monty drew a buffalo head, surrounded by maple leaves. Underneath the head was a ribbon inscribed with the motto, *"Maintiens le Droit."*

"Maintain the Right, is what it means," he explained to Sue. "It's the motto of the Force. And this is your bulletin board. We'll hang it on the foot of your bed. On it we'll post all orders. Now for the first week of training, I think we'll make you block orderly."

"Yes," said Sue, "but what does a block orderly do?"

"Well," said Monty, "I had to sweep and dust the recreation rooms, the halls, etc., of Block C. But as you're not quite as big as I am, we'll make you pick-up orderly. Anything left on a chair or the floor, you're to pick up and put away in its proper place. If you do this so well that there are no complaints laid, you'll then become pony orderly."

"What's that?"

"Same as stable orderly."

"Will I have to go over to see Smith and help him water the horses every day," cried Sue, who thought this sounded too good to be true.

"No," said Monty, with a twinkle, "but you'll have to look after your own pony."

"But I haven't any pony," said Sue, puzzled at Monty's smile.

"No, you might have some day if you show you can be a good recruit," answered Monty.

But Sue didn't quite understand. That she would ever have a pony seemed unbelievable!

"What more?" she asked. Training as a recruit with Monty promised to be really exciting.

"You must examine your orders every morning," he said, "and make sure you have not missed anything. Then you will parade before me for appearance. The condition of your hair and hands, your clothes, are of first importance, for this Force is the smartest in the world. Every week your work will change until you are a completely trained recruit."

"When that happens, do I get a red coat?" Sue asked, "and do I go to London with the Jubilee men?"

"Oh, I couldn't tell you about that," said Monty. "That's in the Commissioner's hands. If you satisfy him, you go. If you don't, you stay at home—and that counts for all of us."

"The Commissioner'll take me," said Sue confidently. "I am a great friend of his. I went to see him this morning."

"Yes," said Monty. "I heard you went to see him and damaged Government property."

"I never damaged any property," said Sue. "I only drew moustaches on Joe Labiche, the bad man."

"Still, that picture was Government property," said Monty, in a grave voice, but with a smile on his lips.

Sue smiled with him, but as they went downstairs for gingerbread, he talked to her of the Force, how busy the Commissioner and her uncle were and how she must do nothing to worry them.

"You remember my Aunt Charlotte?" he asked. Sue nodded. "Well, she said something that fits here, only she said it to me when I was a very little boy. It was this, Sue. Children should be seen and . . ."

"NOT HEARD!" shouted Sue. "I know. Daddy says that to me."

"Well," said Monty, with a twinkle, "you and I are recruits, Sue, and until we are full fledged constables, we had better be seen but not heard. That is, if we want to go to London town."

Sue nodded. "I understand," she said. "What next?"

"Bugle calls. How many are there?"

"Four," said Sue proudly. "Reveille, you got to get up. Parade, you got to line up. Mess, come and get your dinner, and First Post, it's time for me to go to sleep."

"Not enough, Sue, there are sixteen," Monty answered laughing, "and they go like this." Clearly and briskly Monty played them for her on the piano, played them until she had memorized another—"stables."

Mrs. Schofield appeared at the door. "Matilda's just carried up the laundry," she said. "There will be a fresh dress for Miss Sue to put on before her supper."

"Up you go!" said Monty.

While Matilda was changing her dress and brushing her hair, Monty played the bugle call to supper. Over and over, Sue heard it, softly, crisply, loudly. Over and over, until she stood before him saluting gravely. He returned the salute, but even saluting was different now. When Michael showed her how to salute, they were all very merry over it. But with Monty it was different. "When you salute," he said, "it must be with snap, precision, grace."

They had supper together out on the little porch, and he told her of a recruit's daily training.

"We learn to care for our horses, sick or well, to groom them, take care of the stables, to use a rifle and a revolver, some military law, and of course foot and arm drill, first aid, and most of all, to handle people in the kindest, friendliest way."

"Do you get paid a lot of money?" asked Sue, for it seemed to her that no one could ever sleep or play with all that work to do.

"We get fifty cents a day, and we sleep on a board with only a blanket over it."

She looked at him. "On a board!" she said. "Truly?"

"Yes. We fold a blanket over the board and cover ourselves with another. It's not as bad as it sounds."

"I think it sounds dreadful," said Sue. "I shouldn't like it at all. And doesn't your head hurt remembering all these things?" she asked. "I'm just bursting with the things I have learned to-day."

With a great clatter and noise, Michael and John came in. "Hawkins," they called. "Hawkins!"

"He's gone," cried Sue. "He's gone and Monty's here. Come and see!"

The two lieutenants came in from duty and for a breathless half hour had tea, heard of the day's happenings, learned how Monty had put Matilda in her place, and with the help of Monty got themselves into full dress and drove away in fine feather to dine at Government House. Sue helped Monty as they left. She picked up their clothes while he brushed and polished and made things tidy.

Finally he wrote out her General Orders, and when Matilda turned out the light, Sue's bulletin board was at the foot of her bed, already posted with things for her to do.

Far away through the blue twilight Sue heard voices a long time later. It sounded as if her uncle and Monty were coming up the stairs. The door opened, and through her eyelashes she could see them cross the room to her bed. She closed her eyes tightly.

"I think she's sleeping," she heard her uncle say.

"I think she's foxing, sir," answered Monty.

Sue laughed at that. "I'm wide awake," she said.

"Sit up, Sue," her Uncle Dennis said, holding out what seemed to be a shining golden star. "This is what we wear on

our helmets. It's the crest of the Force, but it can only be held by good conduct."

Sue looked at it breathlessly. It was exactly the same as the crest Monty had drawn at the top of her bulletin board. She traced the motto with her finger. "Maintain the Right!" she said.

"It's yours," said her uncle, "as long as your conduct satisfies your commanding officer." Sue took a long breath. "But you lose it," he warned, "for bad conduct. Understand?"

She nodded.

"Good night, Recruit Winston."

"Good night," said Sue softly.

The door closed. In the darkness she touched the golden crest again. Was there more to being a recruit than just a red coat and shining spurs, she wondered.

8. Beppo, the Pony

Sue looked anxiously around her room. Had she remembered everything? She thought she had better go over her orders again and make sure.

"I've hung up my nightie," she told herself, "and emptied the waste paper basket, tidied my desk, and I've got a clean hankie. I think I'm all right, but I wish Monty'd come."

It hadn't been hard to be good all week. There had been so many things to do. Since Monty came, all kinds of delightful things had happened. She had learned that salt and vinegar took tarnish off buttons, but that a mysterious thing called elbow grease was needed to make the buttons shine again; Monty had taught her how to play *Old Black Joe* on the mouth organ; and she and Matilda had driven into Regina with Monty to collect some parcels for Uncle Dennis. There had been a rainy day, too, but that had been quite pleasant, helping Mrs. Schofield make a cake, and after luncheon making toffee with Matilda. Michael had taught her another jig. Once there had been a tea party when everybody came to tea and, all dressed up in her white dress, she passed cakes in a little silver basket.

She went over to the bulletin board and counted the daily orders. Six for the morning. That was all right, for she had dressed Madame La Tour and Minnie-Pooh-Pooh quite early.

She hadn't a crime, she thought, as she looked at the snowy page, not even a little one. "Monty should let me wear my crest today," she thought.

"Sue," a voice called from below. "Susannah."

Sue ran to the window. Standing below her on the grass was Miss Vicky.

"Would you like to come for a drive, Sue?" she called.

"Oh, yes, Miss Vicky. When?"

"Right away, Sue."

"I haven't been inspected, Miss Vicky. I can't come till Parade's over."

"Never mind Parade this morning, Sue. I'll fix it up with your uncle. I'll be back in five minutes." And Miss Vicky disappeared around the corner of the house.

What *shall* I do, wondered Sue. The shining golden crest could only be worn if she had a good conduct sheet at the end of her first week of training. She wanted to go out with Miss Vicky most dreadfully, but if she left the house without inspection there would be a mark against her. Matilda was downstairs in the laundry, Mrs. Schofield in the kitchen. There was no one to advise her, but her orders were clear. She was not to leave her room until Parade was over. She touched the crest pinned to the top of the bulletin board. Would Monty never come?

"Sue!" It was Miss Vicky's voice again. Sue ran over to the window but didn't dare to look out. She knew if she did, that she would run right downstairs. "I can't come," she cried. "I can't come. Oh please, Miss Vicky, wait!"

There was no answer from Miss Vicky—just the sound of horses' feet and much laughter. She looked at the crest again and at the sunlight streaming across the floor. Where *was* Monty?

Across the sounds below she could hear feet coming up the stairs. The door opened and Monty came in. Sue hoped her commanding officer didn't see the tears of impatience in her eyes as she returned his salute; and never had she heard a sweeter word than his "Dismissed" at the end of inspection.

"Get your hat, quick," he said. "We're going driving with Miss Vicky."

"You, too, Monty?"

"Yes, Sue, and here is your reward!"

He pinned the crest on her dress near her shoulder— "Where decorations are worn," he said, "and this is given for good conduct, Recruit Winston!" Together they raced down the stairs.

In front of the house Miss Vicky sat waiting in a high two-wheeled yellow cart with two horses, hitched one in front of the other. An orderly was standing at the lead horse's head. Sue had never seen anything so smart.

"What do you call it?" she asked, as Monty lifted her up beside Miss Vicky.

"A dog-cart, and the horses are being driven tandem," Miss Vicky answered.

Monty looked at them both. "Captain Lyons gave me orders to accompany you," he said.

Miss Vicky nodded. He swung himself up beside her, the orderly let go the head of the lead horse, and around the Parade they dashed, out through the gates and onto a prairie trail leading, so far as Sue could see, to where the blue sky touched the earth, flaming now with the deep red of the prairie rose.

"This," said Sue, "is the loveliest morning I've ever known."
She sniffed the breeze which blew back her curls, stirred the
ribbons in Miss Vicky's broad brimmed hat, and set the horses
to tossing their heads.

"Where are we going?" she asked.

"To see an old, old friend of mine," said Miss Vicky, "a man
who has known me since I was a baby. His name is Chief
Laughing Cloud."

"Not an *Indian!*" exclaimed Sue, unable to believe her ears.

"Yes. I haven't seen him since I returned to Canada and this
is a visit of ceremony. You must be very polite, Sue."

"Yes," said Sue, wriggling with excitement. "Do I salute
or curtsey?"

"I'd curtsey," said Miss Vicky, "and if you are good you shall
help Big Chief choose a pony for you!"

"A pony! For me!" cried Sue joyously. "TRULY! I can't
believe it. I just *can't* believe it."

Miss Vicky laughed. "It's true," she said. "You've been so
good all week that last night your uncle asked me to buy you
a pony so that you might learn to ride and become an even
better recruit."

She went on to explain that when she had been little, Big
Chief had given her her first pony and that twice a year he had
visited the Barracks to see how she was getting on with her
riding. She told them, too, of how the horses supplied for the
Force to ride were bred by farmers and had to be of a certain
height and weight, but that for personal use the Force bought
their horses through Indians of good repute.

Miss Vicky shook the reins. "Twice a year," she continued,
"they drive their wild horses down to a corral near the Barracks,
and the best of them are weeded out, sold to us and broken for

saddle and harness. It's an exciting time," she said; but Sue interrupted. An awful thought had come to her. "Does Matilda get a pony, too?" she asked anxiously. She couldn't understand why Miss Vicky and Monty laughed. If they'd had the responsibility of Matilda all the way from Montreal they wouldn't think it so funny to have to take care of her.

"No," said Miss Vicky. "No," said Monty, "Matilda does not get a pony." And they laughed again.

But Sue no longer heard them. A pony of her own with shining coat like those in front of her now. A pony with a mane that would blow in the wind when she rode him lickety-split across the prairies as she had seen the cowboys do. A pony that would take sugar from her hand with soft velvet lips, and wear a bridle and a shining bit and a saddle that would creak as she sprang to his back. A pony of her very own! Sue felt as if her heart would burst.

Monty touched her arm. "Look," he said.

The prairie land was dipping slightly, and before Sue lay an Indian camp, a long way off against the sky, but she could hear the faint sound of a dog barking, the whinny of a horse. There were figures moving, too, and the wind brought the scent of wood smoke to mingle with the perfume of the roses.

As they drew near, she could see the tepees. Cone-shaped with birch poles sticking out of the narrow tops, and brightly colored in reds and blues and yellows. She counted. There were over ten of them, some larger than others, and all very close together. Behind them, drawn up in a half circle, were tepee carts and wagons, and in front a smouldering fire, with pots and pans half buried in the hot ashes.

Miss Vicky slowed the horses down to a walk. There was much scurrying to and fro in the camp; Sue could see buffalo rugs shaken and spread out in front of the tepees. And then from the largest tepee she saw the figure of a man appear.

"Can it be Laughing Cloud?" she asked.

Miss Vicky didn't answer but pulled in the horses. A young Indian ran out and caught the rein of the leader. Monty helped Miss Vicky down and then swung Sue to her feet.

Coming slowly toward them was the Indian Chief. Behind him followed braves and children and two young Indian squaws. Miss Vicky moved forward.

The chief raised his right arm in the air, hand open and palm facing them. Miss Vicky did the same, and then she laughed, the laugh of an old friend greeting another, and shook hands with him. Sue listened. What was it Laughing Cloud was saying?

"Welcome, Daughter of the Great Shamoganis," * he said in a deep voice. "Welcome. Three snows have passed since your shining head lightened these lands. Tell me of the Great White Mother. Is it well with her?"

"It is well," answered Miss Vicky. "She is old with years and her back is bent, but she cares for her people still."

Laughing Cloud pointed toward Sue and Monty. "These, these people, they are friends?" he asked.

"Friends of mine," she answered, and beckoned them to advance. Sue came forward and dropped a curtsey while Monty saluted.

Laughing Cloud looked at Sue. "Whose child?" he asked.

Vicky explained. "I have come," she said, "to buy a pony for her like the one you gave me long ago." While they talked about the kind of pony, Sue looked around her.

Laughing Cloud was the tallest man she had ever seen, with

* Shamoganis is Cree Indian for the North West Mounted Police.

his head carried high as an emperor's. His brown face was stern, and his beady black eyes looked at Miss Vicky without blinking—like a bird's, Sue thought. His black hair was parted and worn in two long plaits over his shoulders. At the back of his head he wore two eagle feathers. A pair of trousers and a loose shirt of buckskin falling to his hips were gaily decorated with dyed porcupine quills and beads and much buckskin fringe. Around him he held a yellow blanket with a gay design in blues and reds. Moccasins covered his feet. Sue thought he was a perfect Big Chief.

The braves around him looked very much the same. The squaws were wrinkled and bent and seemed much older than the braves. One carried on her back a moss bag lined with squirrel skin. In it was a tiny brown baby. The children were like their parents in every way except for one, a boy older than herself. He wore no blanket and had his hair cut quite short.

A buckboard drove into the camp and a tired-looking man with the black suit and white collar of the missionary, climbed out of it, followed by a little girl.

"Ah, Vicky," he said, "it does my eyes good to see you again."

The little girl was about Sue's age, but shy and, like her father, shabbily dressed in worn clothes. Monty explained. "He is Mr. Holmes, the traveling missionary," he said, "and goes from one camp to the other, always with his little girl."

Laughing Cloud was leading them around the camp now. Sue saw that the tepees were covered with skins, all of them dyed bright colors in strange patterns. Inside there were great piles of blankets and buffalo robes; there were tin cups and plates; and Sue noticed that the women and girls wore necklaces of beads. At the end of the row of tepees a snow-white canvas tent caught her eye.

"What can that be?" she asked, for the tent had a cross on it.

Mr. Holmes heard her and turned back. "This tent," he said gently, opening the flap of the tent, "is the English Church on the prairies, ministering to whomever comes. It is my home, my church, my first-aid hospital, whether you break your head or your heart," he said cheerily.

Sue looked in. Two stretchers, a folding table, two small tin trunks, a leather bag.

"It's very little to hold so much," she said, feeling vaguely that the little white tent held something more than just the camping outfit, something bigger than just the walls of the tent.

"What's your name?" said Sue to the little girl.

"Jane," she answered.

"Can you ride?" asked Sue.

Jane nodded.

"Well," said Sue importantly, "this morning I'm getting my first pony. I expect I will be riding with you very soon."

The little girl stared at her silently. Sue wondered if Miss Vicky was ever going to stop talking to the Big Chief and if she had forgotten about her pony. She moved forward.

"Where's my pony?" she said, interrupting.

Big Chief looked down at her and muttered something in his own tongue.

"What's he say?" she asked Mr. Holmes.

"He says," interpreted Mr. Holmes, "that little hawks should not beat their wings when great hawks rest."

"And that," said Monty, "means children should be seen . . ."

"And not heard," said Sue crossly. "I know, but I want my pony."

The little Indian boy with the shorter hair came over to her. "I show you horses," he said. "Come with me."

"What's your name?" asked Sue.

"Buffalo Child Running Horse. What's yours?"

"Susannah Elizabeth Fairfield Winston," answered Sue, for she had no intention of letting this Indian boy think he had a longer name than hers.

"Too much name," the boy answered.

"You've got too much yourself," said Sue. "Where are the horses?"

"My Father Big Chief," said the boy. "I'm Little Chief."

"All right, Little Chief, you can call me Sue," she answered. And with Jane following and Monty keeping an eye on them in the distance, Sue and Little Chief went down the sloping ground to where some fifty ponies were enclosed in a corral. Little Chief ducked under the birch poles and went among the ponies fearlessly. He jumped on the back of one and with sharp shrill cries and waving his arms, he gradually separated half a dozen of the smaller ponies into a corner of the corral.

Sue looked them over eagerly. Somewhere in this corner was her very own horse. She wished she knew which. She liked the fat black one best. He had a white star on his forehead and a roguish look in his eye.

"When they are small, prairie ponies are called shagannapi," said Little Chief. "When they are bigger they are called horses."

Laughing Cloud and Miss Vicky were very near now. Monty was smiling at her and there was much discussion about the ponies in the corner of the corral. Laughing Cloud liked the black pony; Miss Vicky, the piebald with the long mane. Monty liked none of them.

"Why not?" asked Miss Vicky. "What's wrong with them?"

"Nothing," said Monty, "except that Sue is not going to be a little girl much longer. She should have a larger pony and learn to ride properly like any good recruit."

Sue could have hugged him for that. He knew just how she felt, but she wished he could also know how impatient she was. Would they never decide? Monty called Little Chief, and together they picked out a beautiful little biscuit-colored horse. They took it out of the corral, and Little Chief rode it up and down, up and down. He walked it, trotted it, cantered it, and galloped it. Finally Monty put up a small jump of a birch pole on two upturned pails. Lying low on the horse's neck, and without a saddle, only a halter, Little Chief flew over the barrier.

"This," said Monty to Miss Vicky, "is the horse that Sue should have. It has a beautiful gait, is well mannered and yet spirited." Laughing Cloud agreed, Little Chief agreed, Mr. Holmes agreed, and there was soft laughter and clappings of approval from the rest of the Camp, waiting back on the edge of the sloping ground.

Miss Vicky smiled down at Sue. "He's yours if you'd like him," she said.

"Like him!" said Sue, unable to believe that at last she had her pony. "Like him! Oh, Miss Vicky, you are an angel. Oh, Monty, Oh, Big Chief, Little Chief, *every*body!"

But Monty and Little Chief were placing a bridle on the pony and wiping off his back with a cloth. Monty called her, and she raced back to him. Little Chief held the bridle and Monty lifted her up on the pony's back and held her there while he led the pony up and down.

"What's his name?" she asked.

"My first pony's name was Beppo," said Monty. "Would you like to call him Beppo?"

"His name *is* Beppo," said Sue, "forever more." She felt so grand that she almost felt sorry for the rest of the world that they couldn't be Sue Winston riding her first pony on the western prairies with a hot sun overhead.

"Come, dear," called Miss Vicky. "We must go. Come and say goodbye."

Monty lifted her off her horse, and she ran over to where Miss Vicky stood beside Big Chief.

"Now, Laughing Cloud," said Miss Vicky, "you must tell me what this pony costs."

Big Chief waved her away. "When you were five snows old," he said, "I gave you your first pony. For twenty snows the Shamoganis have protected us, as the feathers protect the bird from the frosts of winter. Speak no more of payment."

"I am very grateful, Big Chief," she said. "My father will be very grateful to you, too. Some day he will come and thank you himself."

Sue liked the way they spoke to each other. They were so dignified. But as they turned away from the corral, she saw Beppo back among the ponies again.

"Am I not going to ride Beppo home?" she asked.

"Not today," Monty said.

"But I want to ride him home. He's my pony."

"Quiet, Sue!" Monty's voice was stern. "You don't know how to ride, you have no saddle and no habit. You can't ride the pony today."

"I will ride my pony," she answered, stamping her foot. "Miss Vicky, Monty says I can't ride my pony. You'll let me, won't you?"

But strangely enough, Miss Vicky agreed with Monty. "Not today, Sue," she said, "and please don't behave like a silly child."

"I'm not a child," Sue flashed back. "I'm a recruit. I won't be called a child, and I won't drive home. I'm going to ride."

"You're going to drive home," said Monty, "and unless you behave yourself you'll get C.B. when you return."

"What's C.B.?" asked Sue, quieted for a moment by the new military term.

"It means Confined to Barracks," said Monty grimly, "and confined to Barracks means no riding or driving."

Sue pushed her hair back from her hot face. She didn't like the idea of C.B., but on the other hand she knew that if she made enough fuss she would get her own way—at least, she always had in the studio in Montreal. She stole a look at Monty. She wasn't so sure she could get her own way with him, but she was tired of being good; she was tired of hearing Matilda telling her to behave like a little lady. She was tired of hearing of how she mustn't disturb her uncle or the Commissioner. She thought it all very silly, as if what she did could upset the Barracks. She wanted to ride her pony, and she was *going* to ride her pony!

With a gnarled brown finger, Laughing Cloud touched her mass of red-gold curls; his beady black eyes were disapproving.

"She has the head of a golden swan," he said, "but she stings like a bumblebee."

From behind the squaws, Little Chief and Jane were laughing and beckoning to her.

"Come over here," called Little Chief.

"We've something to show you," added Jane and there was a fresh burst of laughter from them both.

"What is it?" Sue asked sulkily. They led her round behind the tepees and there was the strangest sight she had ever seen. An old horse stood there and over its shoulders were crossed two long poles, which dragged far out on the ground behind. A little hammock made of skins was stretched between these poles, just behind the horse's tail.

"Want to go for a drive?" asked Jane.

Sue nodded. Little Chief swung himself up on the horse and Jane helped Sue into the hammock. Slowly the horse moved off, with the hammock swaying gently and then without any warning Little Chief dug his heels into the ribs of the horse who galloped down the slope and around the corral, with Sue bouncing up and down like a rubber ball. Finally they drew up in front of the dog-cart where the whole camp was now waiting for the ceremonial farewells.

Sue tumbled out of the hammock. She was breathless and very cross. "What are you laughing at," she demanded, "and what is that thing, anyway?" she asked, looking at the queer contraption she'd been riding in.

"That's a travois," Jane answered. "It's built to carry babies."

"What'd you put me in it for then?"

"Because you're a cry baby," said Little Chief.

Laughing Cloud lifted his hand. "Little Hawk will not weep again," he said. "She now knows that laughter wins more friends than tears."

9. The Habit and Saddle

All the way home Sue dreamed of how nice it would be to live in an Indian encampment; to ride all day with Little Chief; hunt gophers with him and catch badgers, too. She had never seen a badger, but in Miss Vicky's room there was a rug, soft gold in color, with white markings that Sue thought most lovely. Perhaps Little Chief would help her find a badger. She intended to ask him when she saw him again, for he had told her as they left that he would come with his father when they brought Beppo to the Barracks.

"You're coming in to luncheon with me," said Miss Vicky, as they drove through the gates.

Sue looked up at Monty. "May I?" she asked.

He shook his head. "You don't deserve to, Sue," he began.

Miss Vicky interrupted. "Forgive her this time," she said. "After all, it is only once in your life that you choose your first pony."

"All right," Monty answered, "but remember, Sue! No good recruit ever kicks up a fuss."

"I never will again," Sue promised.

Mrs. Walsh was waiting for them on the verandah. "What kind of a morning did you have?" she asked in her friendly, comfortable voice.

Sue told her all that had happened, about Beppo and Little Chief and Jane and even about the ride in the travois. "But what I really want to do," she explained, "is ride with the Commissioner, go to the Jubilee, wear a red coat and race over the prairies with Little Chief."

Mrs. Walsh nodded. "I know," she said, "but you'll have to take your training first. You'll like it better when you've learned to ride." She took Sue inside. "Come along upstairs with me," she went on. "I've something to show you."

They went up to Mrs. Walsh's bedroom, and there box after box was lifted down from a big cupboard. Sue wondered what in the world they could be looking for, but at last they opened a flat yellow box, marked:

Stone, Mason and Stone
Habit Makers
to
H.R.H.
The Princess of Wales.

Out of the folds of tissue paper, Mrs. Walsh lifted a bottle-green skirt; next came breeches and then leggings and a little jacket.

"What is it?" asked Sue.

"It's Vicky's riding habit," Mrs. Walsh answered, "the first habit she ever had."

"It's very pretty," said Sue.

"She was such a nice little girl," Mrs. Walsh added. "And now . . ."

"Now there's much more of me to be nice," said Miss Vicky, who had come into the room without either of them noticing her. "You wouldn't have me small again for anything, Mother. Besides, if I were, there would be no habit for Sue."

"Pull your dress off," she said to Sue. "We'll try this on."

"For me?" said Sue, excitedly, as she tugged at the buttons on her dress. "To ride Beppo in?" Getting into a habit, she found, was a most complicated business. First you put on tight fitting breeches that came below the knee and laced there with leather thongs. Then you put on gaiters made of the same material, bottle-green broadcloth. These fitted over the foot with a leather strap to hold them in place and buttoned up the side with what seemed to be millions of buttons. Over this went the funniest skirt Sue had ever seen. It was long on one side and short on the other, and when it was hooked around her waist the long side was looped up to a button so that she could walk without tripping. Lastly there came a little green jacket, buttoned all the way up the front with round cloth buttons.

Miss Vicky tilted the big pier glass so that Sue could see herself full length. "I look almost grown up," said Sue. "Don't I?"

"Almost," Mrs. Walsh agreed. But Miss Vicky was in despair.

"Look, Mother," she said. "It's so big for her that she could slip out of it."

"Nonsense," answered Mrs. Walsh, "take her over to the Regimental Tailor and he'll take darts in it. The skirt is all right. It's only the jacket that needs altering. It will look very nice. We'll have to get her a hat and a crop."

"But, Mother, what about a saddle?" asked Miss Vicky.

"What about it," said Mrs. Walsh. "Your first saddle is in the attic. You and Sue go up and hunt for it, while I put these things away."

Up the attic stairs they scrambled and hunted through the trunks and boxes, the old wardrobes, opening drawers and emptying bags. But there was no saddle; some broken bridles on the floor near the window, a set of pony harness, but that was all.

"Mother," cried Miss Vicky, "are you sure the saddle is up here?"

"Quite sure, my dear. It's in a box, all wrapped up in old flannel," Mrs. Walsh called from the bottom of the stairs. ·

Back they went and started all over again. On the top tray of a trunk they found a box containing Miss Vicky's christening robe, and both of them giggled as they compared the length of it with the size Miss Vicky had grown to be; "But it isn't the saddle," said Miss Vicky, and side by side they went downstairs, one as disappointed as the other, to tell Mrs. Walsh about their unsuccessful hunt.

"Ring the bell beside you, Sue," she said. "Dawson might know where it is."

Dawson did know. "Why, yes, madam," he said. "The Commissioner had it sent to the harness room when Miss Vicky went to England. He was afraid the leather would rot if it was left up in the hot attic."

"Couldn't we go to the harness room now?" asked Sue, fingering the buttons on her habit. With a saddle waiting just across the Parade, Sue couldn't understand why anyone should want to eat. Luncheon now seemed a great nuisance.

But Mrs. Walsh sat her down beside the Commissioner. Sue saluted him when he came in, but he didn't return her salute, and it was plain to see that he was in a fine fury about something. Mrs. Walsh treated him as if he were a baby, Sue thought, instead of the Commissioner of the Force. He complained that the soup wasn't hot enough, growled about the way the men rode, told them all that the Force was slovenly, and barked at Sue when she asked him what the word meant.

When Sue asked him if he knew that she was going to the Jubilee with him, he was very tart and told her that that would be something for him to decide, that the Force was a place for men, not irresponsible children. Sue thought that a pretty mean remark, but she went bravely on and told him she had a pony of her own now and could go riding over the prairies whenever she wanted to. She'd go to Regina all by herself, too, she said. That seemed to make the Commissioner even more angry and he told her she was never, never to ride alone!

"Never?" asked Sue.

"Never," he replied.

"Why not?"

"Because I say so," was his answer, and Sue thought it a very stupid one.

"If you are through, Vicky," interrupted Mrs. Walsh, "you and Sue had better go over to the harness room and see if you can find the saddle, and then take her on to the tailor and tell him to take in the jacket. I'll see that Matilda joins you there."

Hopping and skipping about Miss Vicky, Sue went around the Parade. Everyone smiled at her as she passed, and Sue knew it was because they liked her green habit, though she felt they would like it better when she was riding Beppo.

Monty was waiting for them and took them through the carriage shed, a most exciting place, with all sorts of carriages, buckboards and dog-carts, and a very grand Victoria barouche, and sleighs and toboggans.

It was dim and cool and in places a bit wet, for an orderly was washing and dusting the carriages, shining the carriage lamps and polishing the silver trimmings on the barouche. Sue thought it would be a lovely place to play games on a wet day, only she couldn't quite see Matilda playing hide and seek with her. She would complain, Sue felt sure, and be afraid of getting her uniform dusty.

In the harness room there seemed to be millions of saddles and bridles and harness and chains and bits, all kinds of cleaning materials, and on a shelf some silver cups; but there was no sign of Miss Vicky's saddle. Sue grew more anxious as they searched. No one seemed to remember it being there, and she heard Monty tell Miss Vicky that the other saddles were too large for her to use. Smith, the stable orderly, looked in the door. Sue asked him anxiously if he had ever heard of the saddle?

Smith thought for a long time; so long that Sue wondered if he'd ever speak. Suddenly, he whistled. "You come with me," he said.

Back into the carriage shed, wriggling in between the winter sleighs stored away close together, she followed the little orderly, and away in the corner behind the closed sleigh that Mrs. Walsh used in the winter time, there was a tiny wicker pony cart just big enough for two. On the floor, wrapped up in sacking, was a knobbly bundle. Smith winked at her. "There you are," he said, lifting it out. "There's your saddle, Miss Sue. I just remembered Hawkins was Harness-Room Orderly when Miss Vicky went to England, and he put all her things together."

They unwrapped the sacking. For years it had lain there in the carriage shed and the leather was dull and a bit hard, but to Sue it was the most beautiful little saddle in the world. Triumphantly they carried it back to the harness room. Monty examined it.

"It only needs new webbing in the girth band," he said, "and a cleaning and it will be as good as new. I'll see to it while you are having your habit fitted, and by the time you are home it will be waiting for you. All good recruits know how to clean their saddles," he continued. "You shall start this afternoon."

He carried the saddle across to the tailor shop, a fascinating place, with broad shelves and bolts of scarlet and blue cloth against the wall; between the windows in an open chest there were lengths of gold lace and galloon, cards of brass buttons. Round boxes held dozens of helmets and pill boxes. There were tunics hanging on a rack, that were evidently in for repair, and in the centre of the room was a wooden horse—at least, that was what the tailor called it. It looked like a large wooden sausage with four very long wooden legs. It had a tail of bright red flannel, and on it Monty strapped Sue's little saddle. The tailor stood her up on his cutting table, while he pinned up her skirt.

"That's a very funny kind of a horse," said Sue.

"It's a tailor's horse," said the tailor, with his mouth full of pins. "The jacket needs to be taken in at least two inches under the arms," he said to Miss Vicky, "and the skirt shortened; otherwise it's perfect. I'll send it over this afternoon."

He lifted Sue off the table and placed her on the saddle to adjust the skirt. Sue found she had to loosen the button at the side and let the skirt down the full length, so that when she sat in the saddle with her knee over the pommel and her left foot in the stirrup, the skirt hung straight and square.

Matilda fluttered in the door. "Mrs. Walsh told me to report here at half-past two," she said.

"But where are Miss Sue's things?" asked Miss Vicky.

"Oh, I forgot them," Matilda answered. "I'm very sorry."

"Go to Mrs. Walsh and pick them up," said Miss Vicky, "and bring them back here."

"You see," said Sue. "I have to look after her instead of her looking after me. She forgets everything."

"If I could have Miss Sue's habit now," interrupted the tailor, "I could start to work at once and let her have it about five."

Miss Vicky loosened the jacket. "Give me something to wrap around her until her nurse returns," she said. "I have to go now, but, Sue, you're to wait here until Matilda comes back. And that means you're not to leave."

Sue nodded. She liked the tailor, who had a funny way of whistling between his teeth. When the others left, she would get him to teach her how he did it.

Monty unstrapped the saddle, and Miss Vicky took off the habit and wrapped Sue in a blanket and left her sitting on the tailor's table.

"Show me how to whistle," she coaxed when they were alone. But no amount of trying helped her. She could not whistle with the same lovely squeak. At last he told her why.

"It's the way your teeth are formed," he explained. "You see, Miss Sue, I've a space between my teeth and this whistle is peculiar to me." He looked very proud as he said that, and true enough he had a space between his two front teeth. Seeing her disappointment, he picked a piece of grass from the outside and, placing it between her fingers, taught her how to make a lovely piercing shriek, and then left her to go back to his machines in an inner room. For a time she was content to go on practising.

Through the window she could see the Parade. She counted two bugles and still Matilda did not come. That's at least half

an hour, Sue reminded herself, for the bugles blew every fifteen
minutes in the day.

From her uncle's house Monty appeared, carrying her saddle
and walking in the direction of the Guard House. Sue knew
what that meant. Monty was angry with her. He had told her
she was to clean her saddle, but not finding her at home when
he returned, was taking it away, perhaps forever. He didn't
know that she wasn't disobedient, but just that Matilda hadn't
brought back her clothes.

Would Matilda never come? There was no sign of her and
she couldn't run bundled up in this big blanket, but she must
reach Monty before he disappeared with the saddle.

On the rack nearby were three tunics, freshly pressed and
repaired. She pulled down the nearest. In the inner room the
tailor's machine was humming loudly.

Dropping the blanket, she slipped into the coat, which
dragged on the ground behind her, and was out the door and
full tilt across the Parade, calling to Monty, "Wait, please
wait."

She found running very difficult in the long tunic but she
scrabbled it up in front and did the best she could, her small
feet twinkling busily. She could see Monty disappearing with
her saddle, the saddle that had almost been lost forever. "Wait,"
she cried, then realizing that her cries weren't being heard, and
remembering her newly found accomplishment, she stood still
and snatching up a piece of grass, blew as hard as she could.

Even Sue was surprised at the noise that followed. Monty
stopped and looked toward her. The sergeant at the Guard
House ran down the steps. Heads popped out the windows
of the dormitories. But Sue noticed none of these things. She
didn't even notice the Commissioner crossing the Parade with

two important visitors and Uncle Dennis and Michael in attendance. All she could think of was Monty and her anxiety to catch him as soon as possible.

"Please, Monty! Wait!" she called and, forgetting all about the long coat she was wearing, plunged forward, tripped and sprawled full length at the Commissioner's feet.

My goodness—what a commotion! Everything happened at once.

"Sue, what are you doing," cried her Uncle Dennis.

"I'll take her, sir," called Michael.

"Has the child hurt herself?" exclaimed one of the visitors.

But above all the other voices, Sue heard one angrier and louder than the rest. It was the Commissioner. "What in thunder is she doing in my best tunic," he roared. Almost at the same moment, Sue found herself in Monty's arms, and then the sound of laughter, soft feminine laughter. It seemed to her to be the only pleasant thing in all the world which now contained only men's angry faces. And then for all too short a time to be believed, everyone talked at once. Even Sue realized that she had made a mistake. For it seemed that she had stolen the Commissioner's coat from the tailor's shop, had almost ruined it, and had made herself and everyone else ridiculous.

How anyone could be quite as bad as they said she was Sue couldn't understand. She wished they would stop talking, for she was afraid she was going to cry, and no one seemed to hear her when she said, "I'm sorry." But the laughter continued, and it came from across the Parade. From the shelter of Monty's arm she could see Miss Vicky's blue parasol. Monty saluted and carried her away.

Sue stole a look at him. He looked very cross, but he was shaking all over, the way Sue often shook when she tried not to laugh out loud. Over her shoulder she saw Matilda with an armful of clothes following them. She sighed and kissed Monty on the ear nearest her, but he seemed to be very unimpressed.

"Please don't scold her," pleaded Miss Vicky, when Monty put her down in the Commissioner's garden. "It wasn't altogether her fault. Matilda kept her waiting a very long time. I discovered her still talking to Dawson not five minutes ago."

But something told Sue that this time Miss Vicky's pleading wouldn't help her. This time, she knew, she was really in for trouble.

10. Sue Learns to Ride

Sue wondered if the afternoon would ever come. Laughing Cloud had sent word that he would bring Beppo to the Riding School at three o'clock. It was not yet even luncheon time. She went upstairs again and looked at her habit laid out upon the bed with the black shoes shining beside it, and fingered the little gold-headed crop that Miss Vicky had given her.

She looked mournfully at the bulletin board. All that black writing on the nice clean white paper was her list of crimes. Somehow she didn't think she would ever forget them.

1—She had been ordered to remain in the Tailor's Shop until her clothes were brought to her. She had not done so.
This Was Disobedience
2—She had stolen the Commissioner's coat.
This Was Theft
3—She had appeared on the Parade improperly clothed.
This Was Disorderly Conduct
4—She had resisted arrest.
This Was Conduct Prejudicial to Discipline
5—She had stamped her foot when the sentence of C.B. had been passed upon her.
This Was Insubordination

Sue shivered. She couldn't bear to remember that dreadful scene. Uncle Dennis sitting at the table with Michael and John on either side of him. Monty waiting in silence to present her, and Matilda sniffling in the background. At first she thought it was a game, but not even Michael had smiled at her when she told them that she thought the Commissioner was an old crab to get so angry with her for running across the Parade.

She wished she hadn't stamped her foot, for instead of C.B. being only from afternoon until breakfast today, they had lengthened it to luncheon today. *And* worst of all, Monty had removed her golden crest in front of everyone. It was on top of the bulletin board now. She wondered if she could ever win it back. With so many lovely things to do, it was strange that so many of them were wrong.

No one had spoken to her after she was sent to her room for C.B., and even Minnie-Pooh-Pooh's bright eyes seemed to turn away from her. No one came to kiss her good night. Matilda just brought her a tray and then undressed her and put her to bed. She cried a little when it grew dark and no one could see her, for it seemed as if she was always wrong; and then she had heard the door creak ever so softly.

"Sue," a voice had said, "don't speak. It's John. I just came to tuck you up."

Sue had told John then how she felt about it all. He was most understanding, but warned her that he was disobeying orders, too, and that she must never tell he had come in. "You know, Sue, we may seem very strict, but it's all so important. If we are silly and never stop to think, your uncle has to leave his duties to look after us instead of doing his own work, and that bothers the Commissioner. All you need do is think a bit more before you jump. See?" John had pushed her hair back off her hot face and turned her pillow. It was easier to go to sleep after that.

The beginning of the day had been dreadful. Everyone had said good-morning to her as if she were a stranger. No one, not even John, had smiled at her. But after breakfast things had brightened a bit. Mrs. Schofield had covered her up in one of her own aprons and taken her out to Monty who was waiting on the back verandah. A strange Monty, in khaki slacks and an old shirt. He had a tin of saddle soap in his hands, and on the table in front of him was her saddle.

Carefully he showed her how to wipe all dust off first, then with moistened rag to cover the saddle with the creamy soap and rub it in. "You'll need lots of elbow grease," he had said, "for not until the leather is soft, is the saddle finished."

She had worked like a beaver at it. Every little while Mrs. Schofield would come out and give a rub, too. Once Matilda tried to help her, but Sue pushed her aside quickly. Even at cleaning a saddle Matilda seemed to be no use. There were a few spots on the leather that wouldn't come out, and Sue showed them to Mrs. Schofield.

"Yes, I know," the cook answered. "But I tell you, my dear, men know most things, but they don't know about the value of a bit of spit in cleaning. I spit on my finger like this and rub it hard on the spot, and it seems to help." Sue had tried spit whenever Monty wasn't around. She thought she would go down again and see if there was even a spot of dust left.

Before he left for Parade Monty told her that her C.B. would be up at three o'clock. "You and Matilda are to leave here at half-past two and go straight to the Drill Hall and wait there until I come."

With a last look at her habit, Sue went down to the back

verandah. There it was, a dark leather saddle, shining and soft, the way Monty had said it should be when finished.

"Mrs. Schofield," she asked, "do you think three o'clock will ever come?"

"Of course it will," said Mrs. Schofield cheerfully. "How would you like to have your luncheon out here on the back porch today? You can keep an eye on your saddle at the same time."

Mrs. Schofield was a very understanding person, Sue thought, when her tray came out to her. "Chicken!" she exclaimed.

"Yes, Mr. Monty thought you ought to have your luncheon early when you were to be riding this afternoon." And Mrs. Schofield looked as important as Sue felt.

Two o'clock did come finally and up in her room Matilda brushed Sue's hair until it lay smooth and shining close to her head. Sometimes Sue thought there was too much hair brushing in the world. The gaiters were buttoned, the skirt adjusted with the long end looped up at the side, the jacket fastened. Sue took her crop off the bed and ran into her uncle's bedroom. There in the long mirror she could see herself from head to toe and she liked what she saw. The bottle-green habit fitted her perfectly and her curls brushed close to her head looked like a little golden cap.

"Come along, Matilda," she said. "If we walk slowly we'll get there just in time." With Mrs. Schofield to wish her luck, they set off for the Drill Hall and her first riding lesson.

Soberly Sue walked around the Parade. She didn't feel like crossing it with what had happened yesterday so fresh in her mind, but her spirits began to revive as she passed the Guard House and the big sergeant came out to tell her how nice she looked and to admire her crop. On past the little chapel they went and out across the prairie where roses stretched for miles, then into the Drill Hall where Monty was waiting with her saddle on a rack beside him.

They saluted each other. "Have I long to wait?" asked Sue.

Monty pointed through the wide doors. Against the blue of the sky three horses showed, two of them with riders, one without. "Is that Beppo?" Sue asked. Monty nodded and smiled, and Sue knew from his smile that yesterday was forgiven. Now she could see Laughing Cloud's blanket hanging loosely from his shoulders and Little Chief leading Beppo. With a sudden spurt, the three horses raced toward the Drill Hall and drew up with a fine flourish outside the doors.

Taking the lead rein from Little Chief, Laughing Cloud rode forward and held up his hand in the greeting of friendship.

"Ride, O Daughter of the Shamoganis," he said. "Ride with the wind and the rain. Ride with the sun, but until your hairs are white as the swan's, ride only on the plains."

Sue took the halter and gave Big Chief her very best salute. Monty explained what Big Chief had said. "It is safe for you to ride in all weather, provided you only ride on the prairies where you can see your home wherever you turn. In the hills you would be lost very soon."

Monty and Little Chief were putting the bridle and the saddle on Beppo. "Now," said Monty, "first you speak to your horse. Pat him and let him see what kind of a person is going up on his back."

Sue followed Monty and stood straight in front of Beppo and rubbed his nose.

"Next," said Monty, "you must learn to mount." He showed her how to gather her reins in her left hand, to rest her right hand on the saddle, place her left foot lightly on his hand and then at the word "Up," to spring to the saddle. She found she was pretty clumsy at first, and tried at least a dozen times before she did it with style.

"Now, Sue," Monty said, fixing her skirt so the folds fell properly, "straighten your back. Your eyes must always look between your horse's ears. Look far enough ahead so that if you see a hole or a ditch you will guide your horse around it. Your horse is something for you to take care of. And, Sue, a good rider doesn't use a crop. He doesn't need it. It's for ornament only."

He led her up and down, up and down, and then they went into the Drill Hall. "We're going to trot now," said Monty. Sue found that very breath-taking and bumpy. She almost fell off once and Monty stopped to tell her that she couldn't fall off if she kept her knees pressed tightly against the saddle.

"My goodness, but I joggle," she said. Her hair was loose and she was breathless, but she didn't know how anyone could be so happy. Riding had promised to be good fun, but it was much better than it promised.

Laughing Cloud, who was watching her, spoke to Monty, and Little Chief disappeared, only to return with Smith and a horse for Monty. Smith was very pleased with Sue's riding and told her so. Monty mounted his large black horse and with a leading rein, led Beppo out onto the prairies. Laughing Cloud joined him and the three rode for a few minutes along the trail. Sue was a bit scared as the two big horses moved close to her.

"I'm so far down," she said, "and you're so high up."

Laughing Cloud smiled at her, and Sue was surprised to find what a nice smile he had. "Little hawks need not fear the wind while great hawks hover near," he said.

They turned home and there, in front of the Drill Hall to see her ride proudly in, was Mr. Holmes with Jane and Miss Vicky. Everyone seemed so happy. Miss Vicky had come to ask Laughing Cloud to pay the Commissioner a visit; Mr. Holmes had brought Jane because she wanted to see Sue ride; Little Chief had come to lead the pony; and Smith was there because of Sue. But Monty told her to stay on her pony, and she rode proudly into the stable where the Commissioner's horse, Ginger, was kept.

"Now," said Monty, as he lifted her off Beppo, "you must learn how to care for your horse." She found she must first tie her horse with a loose halter and then remove the saddle. That was hard work, for the saddle was held on by a girth pulled very tight, but with the help of Smith she managed and hung the saddle up on a low peg nearby that Smith had built for that very purpose. Smith gave her a cloth and standing up on a box she wiped down the neck and back and flanks of Beppo who was hot, and then led him into a stall and with Smith's help took the bridle off and fastened his halter.

"Thank you, Beppo," said Sue. "You are a darling horse." Beppo nodded his head as if he quite agreed.

Jane was waiting for her with Little Chief, when she came out. Mr. Holmes had gone with Miss Vicky and Laughing Cloud to see the Commissioner. Monty took the children outside the stable and while they rested in the long grass, he told Sue that she must never water her horse for fully half an hour after riding, that she must tie him securely but always so that his head was free, that she must not ask her horse to do what she would not do herself, that all good recruits saw to their horses' needs before they thought of their own.

"Yes, sir," said Sue, the way Monty did when speaking to Uncle Dennis.

"Miss Sue." It was Smith's voice calling her from the stable. "Come and see what I've got here."

Sue ran through the stables, followed by Jane and Little Chief. Standing in front of the door was the little wicker pony-cart Smith and she had found together yesterday. It was spick and span and shining, and in the shafts stood Beppo with light brown harness.

"For me?" asked Sue. "Really and truly for me?"

"Why not?" said Smith, and he told them how he had taken the pony-cart out yesterday, cleaned it, and remembering that Miss Vicky had once used it, had asked her about the harness. Miss Vicky had found it under the window in the attic, and Smith mended it, put it on Beppo, and now Sue had a pony and carriage all her own! "Hop in, Miss Sue," he said. "I'll take you around the Parade."

The seats were lengthwise and it really held only two people. But Smith was small and so was Sue, and they sped around the Parade in great style. Back at the stable Smith handed over the reins to Little Chief and by sitting close Sue found room for Jane, too.

Round and round the Parade, Beppo trotted and while Little Chief taught Sue how to drive, he told them tales of his Indian ancestors and of how to hunt bears, make pemmican and even snare gophers. Sue learned from Jane that her mother had died when she was a baby, that she and her father traveled from camp to camp where he was missionary and interpreter, that the tent was her only home.

"Where do you keep your dolls?" Sue asked.

"I haven't any," Jane answered. Sue felt unhappy. Jane was poorly dressed and there was a hungry look in her eyes when Sue asked her about her dolls.

Little Chief drew up in front of the stables. "Take nurse home now," he said.

"All alone!" said Sue. "By myself?" He nodded. With sighs of fear as to what might happen if the pony ran away, Matilda got in beside her, and Sue drove slowly around the Parade home. But when Matilda got out, Sue sat still. Beppo didn't move, and she was glad. She wanted to think a bit. She had a pony and a saddle and a cart and Minnie-Pooh-Pooh.

A constable passed. "Would you hold my horse a minute while I get something inside?" asked Sue. He took the reins.

In the door and up the stairs Sue raced. There was Madame La Tour, sound asleep in her cradle and very lovely. Sue lifted her and put on her red velvet coat, bonnet and veil. "I'll have to hurry," she said to herself, "or I'll never do it."

Carefully she placed Madame La Tour beside her on the seat and then started on the great adventure of driving herself *alone* for the first time. She shook her reins the way she had seen Miss Vicky do, and chirruped. Beppo moved away at a slow pace, and then a little faster until he was trotting briskly as she reached the stable.

Laughing Cloud was there with Little Chief, both of them mounted and ready to leave. Mr. Holmes was in the dusty buckboard with Jane beside him.

Laughing Cloud made her a long speech in Indian, and Mr. Holmes told her what it meant. "He thinks you have good courage like the Shamoganis," he said, "but that you are like the young hawk, greedy; you reach for things before you can use them. He bids you learn to use your wings before you try to fly. And he gives you an Indian name, Sue; Little Golden Hawk."

Sue liked that. She was not only a recruit but belonged to

an Indian tribe. She held up her hand in the greeting of friends.

"Goodbye, Sue," called Jane. But Little Golden Hawk rushed forward. "For you, Jane," she said, and reaching over the dusty wheel, she held up Madame La Tour.

Jane's eyes opened wider and wider as her arms clasped the velvet bundle. "For my very own?" she asked.

"Yes," said Sue, "and her name's Madame La Tour."

What was it Hawkins had said Minnie-Pooh-Pooh meant? She tried to remember. Happy Laughter—yes, that was it. And it was with Happy Laughter in her ears that Sue watched her new friends turn their horses toward the west.

11. On a Prairie Patrol

W hat do I do next?" asked Sue.

"You place it round the hole," answered Little Chief, "like this." Kneeling, he traced a tiny trench with a stiff blade of grass around the dust of a gopher hole. Taking the string noose from Sue he dropped it into the trench.

"Now," he said, "you take the end and lie like this." He lay flat on the ground, facing the hilly side of the gopher hole. "When he comes up, he always looks out the flat side of his hole . . . then pull like lightning, and you got him!"

Little Chief fixed a noose for Jane and for himself, and all three lay flat on their tummies and waited. High above them a meadow lark, grey plumed and yellow breasted, sang its prairie song. There was no other sound in all the world.

Sue held her breath and watched the gopher hole. She hoped she could pull like lightning. Her hands were stronger, she knew, than they were a few weeks before; quicker, too; and Monty and Sergeant Whiteside had been teaching her how to use her eyes. Now, when she was riding, she knew that if the deep bluish grey of the grass was touched with green, marsh ground lay underneath the greenness. Marsh ground was bad footing for her pony, and Sue would guide Beppo away from such danger. She had learned, too, to watch for bare patches in

131

grass. They were very hard to see, but such places always meant badger holes where a pony could catch his foot and trip, perhaps break a leg.

Sue wished a gopher would come up. There were so many when she rode along this trail, popping up and looking at her as she passed. Now, when she was lying here with the hot sun baking her back there wasn't even one in sight. A bumble-bee droned by, hunting for sweets in the wild peas that had followed the roses.

A tiny grey head flashed into sight in front of her.

"Pull like lightning," said Sue to herself, and pulled. The string was taut, and Sue had to hold tightly, for the noose had disappeared down the gopher hole.

"I've got him," she shouted.

Quicker than lightning, Little Chief was at her side. His brown hand helped her pull. The string tightened and slacked away. Little Chief put his hand down the hole and slowly brought it out.

"Good hunter," he said. In his hand was the tiny grey gopher with its shining black eyes. Around its tummy was the noose.

"Where'll we put it?" asked Sue.

"Up in the box beside Matilda," he answered, and the three of them ran over to where Matilda, in the shade of an um-brella, was sitting reading. The box was covered with wire screening and lined with fresh grass. Little Chief dropped the gopher in, and they went back to their hunting. Between them they caught five more, big fat ones. Sue found it took a very quick hand and all one's attention. But she noosed the last, and dragged it out of the hole and picked it up in her own hands.

"Look," she said. "It's so tiny!"

"It's a baby," said Little Chief. "You let him go."

"Why?" asked Sue.

"A good hunter never keeps a baby animal," answered Little Chief.

"Why not?" asked Sue, for she liked the little gopher and could feel its tiny heart beating against her hand.

"Before the White Man came," said Little Chief, "here ran the buffalo. Here was meat in plenty, robes for cover in the winter snows, hides for the making of tepees. But the White Man wanted all. He took cow and bull buffalo alike. He took the baby, too. Now there are no more buffalo. By the time I am chief, none will roam the prairie."

Sue kissed the little gopher's head. It was soft as down. "Where'll I put it?" she asked.

"Kneel," he answered, "and open your hand. It will run away by itself."

Sue knelt and placing her hand upon the ground, opened it gently. The tiny creature trembled as if not sure that he was free, and slowly crept off her hand onto the grass. The grass was something he knew. With a frisk of his tail, he disappeared down the hole.

The three hunters joined Matilda, who had a large pile of sandwiches, a tin of cookies and a jar of lemonade beside her. It was fun to feed the gophers crumbs and listen to them chatter and see them scrabble at the wire netting. Fun to picnic out there in the soft wind instead of sitting at a table.

A rumble of wheels in the west came to them. Two Indians, driving a cart full of poles, drew up a little distance away. They started driving stakes into the ground, outlining a square of ground.

"What are they doing?" Sue asked.

"Making a corral," Little Chief explained. "Next week we drive the wild horses down and the Shamoganis come and choose which they will buy. The horses are kept inside the corral and my father and two others bring their tepees and camp beside them until the sales are made."

The Indians placed their poles between the stakes and bound them, leaving a wide opening which Little Chief explained would be closed when the horses were driven in.

"Who drives them down?" asked Sue.

"I do," said Little Chief proudly.

Jane laughed. "You mean, you help drive them down," she said. "It takes six riders, Sue," she explained, "to keep the wild horses in line for a corral, and they have to ride very hard and fast. I know," said Jane, as Little Chief tried to interrupt, "for I have seen them every year."

"If Little Chief can drive wild horses, why can't I?" asked Sue.

"Because you're a girl," he answered. "And I'm a better rider."

"I'll show you whether you are or not," said Sue. "The first time you bring your pony down here I'll race you."

"Well, you'll lose," said Jane, "for he is a good rider, but he's not the best rider and he can't drive wild horses alone."

"Jane," a voice called. "Little Chief. Come along." Mr. Holmes was waiting on the trail in his buckboard. He had left the two children with Sue in the morning while he went in to Regina for supplies. They carried over the precious box of gophers and showed them to him and then he drove off with Jane, promising to come soon again.

Sue carried her gophers home to show to Uncle Dennis and changed into her habit. Monty was always very busy now and

Sue had to meet him at the Riding School, for this afternoon he had promised to take her out with him on a prairie patrol if her riding lesson was a success.

She could see Beppo waiting at the Riding School, hear him whinny as he saw her coming across the prairie. He's asking for his sugar, thought Sue, and felt in her pocket for the two lumps she always carried—one for a greeting, and one for farewell. Sue knew if she forgot or pretended that she had forgotten, he would follow and nudge her gently with his velvet nose. Sue skipped a step or two; it was so lovely to have one's own horse.

She could never think of the hours in the Riding School as lessons. They were too exciting. From the very first day when Sergeant Whiteside had put a long white lead rein on Beppo and had roared at her in the same way he did to the recruits, she had loved it. It had not been long before she could manage Beppo easily, but "sticking on your horse and racing it is not riding," the sergeant had told her. "What you need is style." That had been hard. Never to forget to carry her head up, her back straight, to hold her reins lightly and yet firmly enough to pull her horse up if it stumbled. At times her head had been sore with remembering.

"Here you are, Miss Sue," called Sergeant Whiteside. "Up you get." And he held out his hand for her to mount. Inside the Riding School, the recruits were resting their horses. Down the centre a small jump had been placed. She went through the regular routine. Around the Riding School first at different speeds. "Head up, chin in," roared the sergeant. Around she came again. "Reins too short," he called. "Give your horse neck room. Gallop!"

"Halt!" Sue reined in Beppo. "Very good, Miss Sue. Now

you're going to learn to jump. You see that barrier?" he pointed
to the pole across the centre of the Riding School. Ride your
horse around twice, at an easy gallop. The second time, ride
him right at the jump. Let your arms follow your reins and
let the horse do the rest. Only DON'T forget to keep your
knees tight against the saddle. Off you go!"

My goodness, thought Sue, this IS exciting. Twice around
the ring, and once up the centre to the jump. She tried to remember all the sergeant had said, but Beppo was too quick. She
suddenly felt him lift himself, and then she left Beppo. Her
crop left her, everything left her, and she landed in the soft
ground of the drill hall with a thud.

"Gracious, Sergeant," she said, "whatever did I do?"

"You disobeyed orders," said the sergeant. "You got off your
horse without permission." Sue picked herself up and looked
at him. He was smiling, though his voice sounded stern.

"Can I try again?" she asked, and caught Beppo's rein.

Over and over the jump she went. Over and over again she
nearly fell off, but the last time, when she held her knees tight
against the saddle, she managed to arrive on the other side of
the jump without having to fling her arms around Beppo's
neck, a thing Sergeant Whiteside disliked intensely.

Monty came over and helped her tie Beppo to a post. "We'll
rest awhile," he said, "and then start out on our patrol."

Sue brushed her habit and fed Beppo sugar while Monty
told her of the prairie patrol.

"We just drop in and ask how things are going," he said.
"Often a man can't leave his farm or ranch and needs help or
advice which the Police try to give. People are so far apart that
sometimes the Mounties are the only touch they have with the
outside world for months. Come along, Sue, we'll go."

Sergeant Whiteside came outside as they started away. "Elbows in," he cried. "Elbows in, Miss Sue."

"I wish I could remember to keep my elbows in," said Sue to Monty. "I always seem to ride with them stuck out."

"You'll learn," said Monty, and at an easy canter they rode away, scattering gophers back into their holes as they passed, stirring up nesting birds, breaking down the long grasses, easing their horses now and then to watch the tawny tiger lilies sway in the wind.

Sue had never ridden away from the Barracks before, and to her this was a great adventure. She had driven Beppo into Regina along with Matilda in the pony-cart. That was safe and easy, for the road was the only one between Regina and the Barracks, and she couldn't get off it, even if she tried. The only thing she had to be careful about was crossing the railway track, but as you could see the train for miles and hear it, too, there was little danger. Everything was much pleasanter since she had had Beppo. She even liked Matilda, but Sue felt she'd never be really content until she had ridden with the Commissioner and had a red coat. She had worn her crest for weeks now, and her bulletin board held only a tiny crime or two.

"Monty," she asked, "how long do you think it will be before I can ride with the Commissioner?"

"I don't know, Sue." Monty reined in his horse. "You have to be awfully good before you can ride with him."

"Have you ridden with him yet?"

"No," he replied, "but I hope to soon."

"And then will you stop being a recruit?"

"Yes," he answered. "I shall become a sub-constable, and then, I hope, a constable and so on."

"Until you're the Commissioner?" asked Sue.

"Well, I could do it that way," said Monty, "but I doubt if I ever get that far. Let's try a canter, Sue!"

Sue wondered why everyone put her off when she talked of riding with the Commissioner.

A little house appeared on the prairie. "This is the nearest farm to Regina," said Monty, as they came up to it. It was the smallest house Sue had ever seen, just one room, and built of unpainted boards and patched here and there with broken shingles. Two rain barrels stood under the slope of the roof. A tired woman in a sunbonnet and cotton dress came out and pointed to where her husband was ploughing behind a fair-sized barn.

"I'd go with you," she said, "only I'm just kneading my bread and I daren't leave it." Her voice had no life in it, Sue thought, but when Monty asked her husband if he needed help of any kind, the man shook his head. "We're all right," he said, signing the Patrol Book which was kept as a record of visits made by the Force, "but it's lonely. We don't mind the hard work, but we miss our friends. England seems a long way off at times. But we'll make out all right." He bent down and lifted a handful of earth. "Look at that soil," he said, showing it to Monty and Sue. "Rich black beautiful earth that will grow wheat such as the world has never known." He smiled at Sue. "Come this way again," he said. "It does our hearts good to see young ones."

"Are you tired, Sue?" asked Monty, as they rode into the sunset, leaving the farm behind them. Sue shook her head. "Then let's gallop a bit."

Over the prairies, gold with the light of the setting sun, they raced. The faint fragrance of the sweet grass was in the air, the cool of the evening on their faces. Sue knew that Monty was watching her and she held her head up and her chin in. She even remembered her elbows. Monty's horse was a big one, and he trotted easily to Beppo's canter, but Sue kept the pace until they halted at the Barracks gates.

"Pass!" cried the sentry.

Michael was coming in as they reached home, and he lifted her off Beppo's back. "How's she coming, Monty?" he asked.

"She rides like a Mountie," said Monty proudly. "Sometime soon she shall go out for a full day's ride. If she stands that half as well as today, I'd say she and Beppo could go anywhere."

"Oh, Michael," said Sue, "did you hear what he said? Do you suppose it's true?" As they went into the house she started to tell him of her adventures, but John was at the piano singing and the song had such a lovely lilting air that they stopped to listen.

> "Ottawa's tide, this trembling moon,
> Shall see us float o'er thy green surges soon."

"What's the name of it?" asked Sue.

"Well," said John, "you two should know. It's the *Canadian Boat Song*, written by an Irishman, one Thomas Moore. Sing it, Sue," he said. And with Sue between them on the piano bench the three sang it over and over until Sue knew it by heart.

Michael was in a mood for music, too, and he taught her another song, one that had just come out, with a dancing refrain called "Ta-ra-ra-ra BOOM-de-ay." He taught her to dance to it with him, and when Uncle Dennis opened the door later, it was to the sound of music and dancing.

Sue ran to meet him. He had been away all day and was tired and hungry. Sue helped pour his tea, told him of her ride, danced with Michael for him and sang her songs. When Matilda called her from the hall, Uncle Dennis answered, "Miss Sue is staying up an hour later tonight."

He touched the golden crest on her habit. "I'm glad to see you're wearing it, Sue," he said. "And gladder still to hear nothing but good reports of you. It makes me very happy. Michael," he said. "Is there anything fresh at H.Q.? Should I go over before I tub?"

"Nothing," said Michael. "No news of any kind except a rumor that Joe Labiche is supposed to be headed north again."

"Joe Labiche," thought Sue, "where've I heard that name before?" She looked at her uncle and remembered the dreadful morning when she had been caught putting moustaches on the picture in the Commissioner's office, and how angry Uncle Dennis had been. The man's name had been Joe Labiche, Sue remembered very well. But she thought she had better not remember him out loud now. She didn't want anything to spoil the pleasant time she was having.

12. Sue Rides

What's the matter, Smith?" asked Sue, as she came for a visit at the stables early one morning.

Smith brushed the Commissioner's horse Ginger even harder. "It's Scottie," he said.

"What's the matter with him?" asked Sue.

Smith seemed very put out. "He's been out with a skunk and he smells like nothing on earth," he replied. "What's more, the wild horses are coming this afternoon, which means all afternoon fatigue has to be shoved forward into this morning so that I haven't time to wash him. And," added Smith, "the Missus won't let me come home until Scottie's washed. I can't have him in the stables for he'd smell up even the horses. I can't have him at home, and the poor dog's miserable out there behind the stable."

Sue peered out. True enough Scottie, the collie pup, was sitting out in the prairie grass looking very unhappy.

"He doesn't look as if he liked the smell," said Sue.

"He doesn't," said Smith shortly.

Sue looked at Smith for a few minutes. He seemed very unhappy, and remembering his care of her and the way he found the pony-cart for her, she wished there was something she could do to help him.

"How do you wash a pup?" she asked.

"You put him in a tub with warmish water," answered Smith, "and wash him with carbolic soap. It's good for fleas, too. And then you rinse him in clear water, rub him dry and make him run in the sun."

That shouldn't be hard, thought Sue, and disappeared out the back door of the stable. Smith didn't even notice her go, neither did he see her take a light chain off the door. "Poor Scottie," Sue said. "Come with me; I don't mind skunks." Scottie wagged his fluffy tail and came willingly to have the chain attached to his collar. Sue led him around the Parade. He does smell, she told herself, but perhaps Matilda will help me wash him.

"Sue," a voice called. "Sue!"

She turned. Behind her was Jane, climbing down from the old buckboard. "May Jane spend the morning with you, Sue?" Mr. Holmes asked.

"Oh, how lovely," cried Sue, for with Jane to help her, she knew she could wash Scottie. As Mr. Holmes drove away, she told Jane of her plan.

"Well," said Jane doubtfully, "skunk is very hard to wash out of anything, but we can try. Where can we get the soap?"

"Michael uses carbolic soap," Sue told her. "I'll get it while you find out if the laundry is empty."

The laundry was empty and the two girls filled a tub full of warmish water, rolled up their sleeves and took poor bedraggled Scottie and put him in. He didn't like the carbolic soap, even though it made a lovely lather, and struggled very hard to get out. But Jane held him firmly until he licked his chops and got soap in his mouth. Then with one bound he jumped clear, upsetting the tub over Jane and racing around the laundry as if he were playing a game. By the time they had caught him they could hear Mrs. Schofield and Matilda coming downstairs.

"Quick," said Sue. "He must be rinsed." And quickly they poured the jugs of clear warm water they had ready, over the soapy puppy. A last frantic wriggle joggled Jane's elbow and she emptied the water over Sue.

When Mrs. Schofield opened the door no one could tell who was the wettest—the puppy or the two girls—and the smell of carbolic soap, skunk and wet clothes mixed together was bad enough to make even Sue hold her nose.

For one awful moment Sue thought Mrs. Schofield was going to be cross. Her face had flushed as she saw the tidy laundry in such a mess, but when Sue told the story, she sat on the laundry stairs and laughed until even Matilda joined her.

"Give me a bath towel," she said. "I'll dry the puppy and Matilda'll dry you two. You must lend Miss Jane one of your dresses. Run along now. As soon as the puppy's dry I'll send him up to you."

"Thank you, Mrs. Schofield," said Sue, giving her a very wet embrace.

"Shut the door as you go up," Mrs. Schofield warned. "I don't want the smell of skunk to get into the soup. The captain wouldn't like it."

Quickly Matilda dried Sue and Jane and gave them fresh clothes, but long before Sue's hair satisfied Matilda, the puppy was scratching at the door. Jane opened it and Scottie came racing in, curling himself around in half circles and making short puppy barks.

"Come, Miss Jane," said Matilda.

"I can brush my own hair," said Jane shyly.

"Yes," said Matilda gently, "but I'd like to do it for you this once." And Jane went over to the bureau and stood there while Matilda brushed her dark head vigorously.

"Jane," said Sue. "Do you know this puppy still smells of skunk?"

"Oh, he couldn't," said Jane, "not after all that soap and water."

"Smell," replied Sue, holding out Scottie, who looked like a ball of brown fluff.

"He does," said Jane, lifting her head from the puppy's coat. "Whatever can we do?"

"I know," answered Sue, running into Uncle Dennis's room. She came back with a bottle of Florida water. Jane and she shook it over the puppy's coat.

"Smell," said Jane. Sue did.

"He still smells very queer," said Sue. "Let's take the bottle with us and just before we give Scottie to Smith we'll empty it over him."

They started out around the Parade, all three very clean and tidy. Sue had Scottie on the chain and Jane carried the bottle of Florida water. How nice Jane looks, thought Sue, in a pretty dress and with her hair brushed until it shines. For the first time Sue realized how lucky she was to have a batman, as Matilda was now called by Monty.

Half way round the Parade they met Michael, who stopped and asked them where they were going. But he had no sooner asked them than he sniffed. "What on earth have you got with you?" he asked. "It's simply horrible." And he sniffed again. They told him their story, but they were hardly half way through when he started to laugh, and kept it up until the end.

"Dog-washers-in-chief to the North West Mounted Police,"

he said. "Well, I think you've done a good morning's work. But you ought to go in for it as a business. Now what would you charge for a dog?"

"How would five cents do?" asked Jane.

"Oh, I think I'd make it a quarter," said Michael, "when you're washing a skunky dog." He put his hand in his pocket and brought out two shining silver quarters. "This," he said, "is for you, Jane, and this for you, Sue." Still laughing, he went into H.Q.

On around the Parade they ran, and met Monty just coming out of Block C. They told him their tale and Sue gave him her quarter. "Will you get us sugar sticks at the Canteen?" she said. "We'll be home in a very short while."

Monty promised and went off laughing, too.

"I'm glad they all think it so funny," said Sue. "I'm sure I don't like the smell at all."

Smith thought they had done the nicest thing he had ever heard of anyone doing. They asked him to smell Scottie and give his opinion as to whether all the skunk had been removed. Smith buried his head in the fluffy coat. "I can only smell Florida water," he said. "But it's a nice rich smell, and I'm sure the Missus will be grateful for your help, Miss Sue. Thanks very much."

Just as they left the stable, Jane asked Smith where Scottie found the skunk.

"He's under the Riding School," said Smith. "He's been there for a couple of days."

"Sue," said Jane, as they left the stable. "Do you know if anyone else in the Barracks has a dog?"

"Yes," said Sue. "Mrs. Walsh has a little dog. Why?"

"Well, let's skunk it and wash it and get another quarter," said Jane.

Sue looked at Jane with admiration. "If I catch the dog, will you skunk it?"

Jane nodded, and they crept into the Commissioner's garden through the kitchen gate. Toni, the Pekingese, was asleep on a cushion on the verandah and easy to carry away. Over the prairie they marched until their noses told them they must be very near the skunk. Jane took Toni. "It'll only be just one bad moment," she said to the dog, and, bending down in the grass, she rubbed his hind quarters on the spot where Scottie had plainly met the offending visitor.

"Oh, phew!" said Sue. "Woof, woof," said Toni. But Jane said nothing. She just held her breath and looked very determined. They carried Toni back to the laundry. It hadn't been tidied yet and the noise of getting luncheon was distracting Mrs. Schofield.

They took their dresses off and started in. Toni was so small they could manage him better than Scottie, and they washed him and rubbed him dry. But he still smelt of skunk, just as Scottie had.

"Is there any more Florida water?" asked Jane.

Sue shook her head. "No," she said, "but John Hogarth has some bay rum. It's a hair tonic." They crept upstairs and into John's room, and rubbed the bay rum well into Toni's coat.

Jane held her nose. "It's pretty bad," she said. "Bay rum and skunk makes a queerer mixture than Florida water did."

"Don't let's take Toni to Mrs. Walsh," said Sue. "Let's find Miss Vicky."

Miss Vicky was reading in the garden.

"My goodness," she said, as Sue and Jane came toward her. "Skunk!" and held her pretty nose.

"Yes," said Jane politely. "Toni got mixed up with a skunk, and we just washed him for you."

"But this is more than skunk!" cried Miss Vicky.

"Well, there is a little bay rum, too," said Jane.

But Miss Vicky was laughing like the others, and holding Toni at arm's length.

Jane looked at her. "The last dog we washed," she said, "we were each paid a quarter."

Still laughing, Miss Vicky went into the house and came back with two silver quarters. "Thank you very much," she said. "Toni and I are most grateful."

"We almost missed that quarter," said Jane with a sigh.

Sue agreed. "I wish you lived at the Barracks," she said. "You think of such lovely things to do."

They told Monty the whole story when he brought them the sugar sticks. Sue thought he would never stop laughing, but he made them eat their luncheon out on the back porch, "for," he explained, "you are as bad as skunks yourselves by now."

Afterwards Sue changed into her habit and by the time Matilda had ironed Jane's dress, Mr. Holmes called for her and drove them both over to the Drill Hall.

Miss Vicky was there and Monty and Michael, Sergeant Whiteside and Smith, with Beppo saddled and ready for her to ride.

"I brought him over," said Smith, "in case you wanted to use him after the wild horses have come in."

Sue thanked him. She had seen a grey cloud far off in the west and had heard a mysterious thudding. "Wild horses?" she asked.

Smith listened. "Yes," he said. "It's the wild horses coming."

The cloud grew larger, the thudding sound nearer; and now and then there was a cry, full and round, and a high whinny. Sometimes the cloud seemed to whirl in circles, sometimes stand still; but out of it came horses, wild horses, and hundreds of them, it seemed to Sue. Heads up, tails and manes flying, running, turning, twisting, but always coming nearer. Beppo whinnied and moved restlessly. Sue patted him and rubbed his nose.

"Look, Monty," she said, "there's Little Chief out in front."

Lying low on his horse's neck, waving his arms, Little Chief kept close to the flying wedge of horses, and as they swerved from left to right, drove them back again toward the corral. There were two Indians at the head and two at the rear of the herd. Two others rode freely at the sides, for it seemed as if the horses knew they were headed for the corral and were trying to escape.

"Ho—h, ho—h!" cried the Indians. "Ho—h!" On came the storming herd. The Indians' cries grew louder. "Yah, yah, yah," they yelled. "Ho—h!"

Thundering by them, the wild horses swept into the corral until, their speed checked by the pole barrier, they turned, and kicking, screaming and with flying hoofs, tried to fight their way out. But Laughing Cloud knew more about "blowing in" wild horses than the horses did about getting out, and two young braves quickly ran poles across the entrance as the last horse pounded into the corral.

Sue couldn't have imagined such a sight. Black, grey, brown, pintos, large and small, the wild horses surged up and down the corral. Little by little they quieted down, the dust settled, the whinnying stopped, and Monty took Sue down to the corral. They talked to Little Chief who, along with one other Indian, had been left in charge.

"Aren't you afraid they might get out?" asked Sue.

Little Chief shook his head. "By and by, when they are rested, we will bring them hay and water," he said. "It is only after a long run that they go wild like this. Besides, the Shamoganis will buy many of them."

Sergeant Whiteside looked them over and told Miss Vicky that they were as fine wild horses as he had seen. "In three months' time, they will be as quiet as your Beppo for riding or driving," he said to Sue. "We'll leave them alone today, but tomorrow we'll begin sorting them for purchase."

"Can I come and watch you sort them?" asked Sue.

"Why not?" he answered. "You might as well learn how to buy a horse, now that you can ride one!"

Jane interrupted. "I've got to go now," she said, "but I'll be back soon. Can't you ride with us a little way?"

Sue turned to Monty. "Yes," he replied, "only Sue is to turn back where the road forks and ride straight home." Sue promised.

Mr. Holmes drove slowly so that Sue, riding alongside, could hear his tales of the wild horses he had seen in the hills near the Rockies and hear about the great feasts of the Indian tribes. He taught them both the night call of the wolf, "Yi-yip-yip, he, heeh," and the forks of the trail came all too soon.

Sue sat on her pony, watching the buckboard and her friends disappear. Across the prairies came the faint sound of the bugle. She could see the Barracks, a pile of buildings low against the sky. After the excitements of the morning, the world seemed suddenly very empty. Little Chief couldn't play with her because he was guarding the wild horses, Jane had gone home, and Matilda was cleaning the laundry. Sue smiled as she remembered Scottie running around the laundry floor all wet and soapy. Beppo moved restlessly and turned around.

Against the blue bowl of the sky, Sue suddenly saw the scarlet and gold of the Force, riding eastward. She remembered the day she had been sworn in as a recruit and Michael's answer to her question as to when she should get her red coat: *"Not until you've ridden with the Commissioner."* But every time she had suggested riding with the Commissioner, Monty, Michael or John had put her off. She wished she knew why, and felt that she never would know except by finding out for herself.

Gathering up her reins and digging her heel into Beppo's side, she rode lickety-split over the long grasses, past the badger and gopher holes, around the patches of marshland. Steadily she advanced on the Force. They were walking their horses now and she could see the shining flanks, hear the jangle of bit and spur.

"Come on, Beppo," she said, and with a final burst of speed charged through the open formation toward the Commissioner. She could hear the sudden laughter of the men, but pressed on. Miles above her, it seemed to Sue, the Commissioner astride Ginger looked down at her with complete surprise.

"I've come to join up," she said, "all over again."

The Commissioner looked at her gravely. "I'm sorry, Sue," he said, "but we do not accept recruits until they are eighteen."

Sue looked around. So this was why they had been putting

her off, and after all her hard work, too. Suddenly everyone seemed so tall, their horses so big. Uncle Dennis was looking at her grimly. There wasn't a smile on either Michael's or John's face. She felt if she didn't do something quickly, she would cry.

"Do I have to wait until I'm eighteen to ride with you?" she asked.

Uncle Dennis leant forward in his saddle. Sue heard him say: "May I take her home?"

The Commissioner shook his head. "It won't take you very long to grow to eighteen, Sue," he said. "And today you shall ride home with us."

Slowly they turned back over the prairies, and with Beppo trotting like mad to keep up with the light cavalry mounts of the Force, Sue rode proudly beside the Commissioner. Uncle Dennis still looked grim and Michael and John didn't seem very merry, but all the men smiled. And with the red coats and gleaming boots and shining spurs around her, Sue didn't care whether anyone was cross at her or not. This was the greatest adventure she had ever known!

Nearer and nearer they drew to the Barracks. Sue hoped Little Chief would see her as she rode by. Out of the corner of her eye she saw him standing by the corral, open-mouthed with surprise. Sue tucked her elbows in in the way Sergeant Whiteside had told her and held her head straighter.

Through the gates they rode, with the Commissioner leading and Sue beside him. Behind them a little group of officers and behind them the Force.

Clattering around the Parade the Commissioner drew up in front of Uncle Dennis's house. "Thank you, Sue," he said.

Monty came out of the house and lifted her off Beppo. "What have you been doing?" he asked.

She told him, and told Miss Vicky, too, who called from her garden. They listened to her tale. Sue didn't know whether they were pleased or not. She didn't care. She was too happy to care about anything.

"I've ridden with the Commissioner," she cried. "I've learned to ride and all my bugle calls. I've a good-conduct sheet, and I can salute smartly. WHEN do I get my red coat?"

13. Wild Horses

Sue," called Monty from the stairs, "Miss Vicky wants you to drive her over to the Drill Hall. They are separating the wild horses this morning and she thinks you would like to see them. I've ordered Beppo and the pony-cart."

Sue's eyes shone with excitement as Matilda fastened her dress at the back and tied her sash in a large bow. To drive Miss Vicky was always an adventure.

"Please hurry, Matilda," she said. "Miss Vicky and Beppo will be here right away."

"Now don't get yourself worked up," said Matilda crossly. "You've got to be tidy and look like a lady once in a while. You've hardly worn anything for weeks but your habit. You'd think you were a Mountie."

"Well, I am," said Sue. "I rode with the Commissioner yesterday, and anyway I like my habit better than dresses."

"You do, do you?" replied Matilda. "Well, you're going to wear a dress this morning. Off you go."

Sue giggled as she went down the stairs. She knew why Matilda was cross. She had to stay home and help with the housework while Sue was riding, and she didn't like that. What she preferred was walking Sue slowly around the Parade all afternoon and calling it exercise, or driving into Regina with Beppo.

Monty was talking to Miss Vicky in the doorway but they were soon in the pony-cart and round to the Drill Hall. There they found the band practising in the centre of the hall and going through all kinds of movements. Right turn. Left wheel. Form fours. In front of them the Drum Major marched, twirling his baton and looking very fierce and important. "As if he were the whole band," said Sue to Miss Vicky. "Isn't he funny?" As he passed the Drum Major flung his baton in the air and beamed upon them.

"Do it again," called Sue, and much to her delight he did. Sue laughed and tried to imitate him but Miss Vicky hustled her out of the Drill Hall, scolding a bit. "You mustn't laugh, Sue, and it's rude to imitate," she said. "All military bands have a Drum Major and he always leads his band that way."

"But he looks so funny," answered Sue.

"Hush," answered Miss Vicky. "That's not a nice way to speak of anyone."

Just then Sue noticed Sergeant Whiteside and a number of others crossing over to the corral. "Are they going to separate the wild horses now?" she asked.

"Not just yet," answered Miss Vicky, "but it won't be long now. I wish Monty were here."

Sue looked at Miss Vicky. "You like having Monty with us, don't you?" Miss Vicky didn't answer, but Sue knew she was right for Miss Vicky always asked her to bring Monty when they went on riding picnics.

She remembered the first riding picnic again. How she and Miss Vicky and Monty had ridden all one lovely morning until they came to Pile O' Bones Creek. How Monty had looked after Miss Vicky's horse and his own, and how she had taken off her own saddle and bridle and hobbled Beppo, right front leg to left back leg and turned him loose to nibble at the grass. She remembered, too, the delicious sandwiches and the peppermints that Monty had found for her in his saddle bags. How he and Miss Vicky had made a nest of long grass in which she slept for a time, while the sun was hottest, of the long ride home when the sun was almost down and one star showing over the flag pole. Matilda was waiting at the door to welcome her home that night. "Sure, I thought you were lost," she said, when she was undressing her, "and I couldn't bear to lose you, Miss Sue, for all your naughty ways."

Sue remembered Matilda this morning, looking mournfully out of the window as she drove away with Miss Vicky, and her niceness to Jane and herself yesterday over the washing of Scottie. "Miss Vicky," she said, "could I go and get Matilda? I know she'd like to see the wild horses."

By the time she and Matilda returned, Laughing Cloud and his son-in-law had joined Sergeant Whiteside and were busy separating horses. Sergeant Whiteside would look at the herd for a long time and then point to a particular horse. Laughing Cloud would nod his head and he and Little Chief would ride into the corral on their herd ponies and drive the horse chosen into an extension of the corral.

Sue found it most exciting, for it was like a race to separate one horse from the others. But Laughing Cloud and Little Chief knew their business. They would quietly ride through the horses until they reached the one they wanted. Keeping him between them, they nosed him toward the smaller corral. When they reached this, they would drive furiously. Like a flash, someone would let down the barrier into the extension and as the frightened horse dashed into it, quickly replace the poles. Then they drove him farther down the small corral until he was forced to the very end. New poles were then thrust across, leaving the horse in a narrow stall-like enclosure at the end of the smaller corral, in which the veterinary surgeon and stable men had a chance to examine him.

Sue watched the veterinary very carefully, for she wanted to be able to choose a horse some day and show Little Chief that she could not only ride with the Commissioner, but that she knew something about horses, too.

She found that the teeth were examined, the eyes, the back, the feet, but she was not sure she wanted to be a veterinary surgeon. It seemed to be very hard work, for horses didn't like being examined any more than people and kicked and coughed in just the same way. By the time the bugle-call for dinner sounded, the Sergeant Major had made his choice, but Miss Vicky and Sue waited with Matilda to see Laughing Cloud and his son-in-law start out for Regina with the balance of the herd. By nightfall, Miss Vicky told Sue, Laughing Cloud would have sold them all, for his were the best wild horses on the prairies.

Sue wanted to speak to Little Chief and ran back to the corral. The veterinary surgeon was talking to him and advising him to wash the flank of a silver roan. "This is a nasty cut," said the veterinary. "Wash it with clean water and then rub it with this medicine." He gave Little Chief a bottle.

"Little Chief," said Sue, "let's hunt gophers after luncheon."

He shook his head. "Catching gophers is child's play," he said proudly. "I am in charge of the wild horses now."

"What do you do?" asked Sue.

"I watch to see that no one comes near them," he said.

"Well, I'll come out and help you when my riding lesson's over," called Sue, as she ran back to Miss Vicky and Matilda.

All three drove home in the pony-cart, although it was really too small to hold two grown-ups easily, and Matilda was in danger of falling out every moment.

Uncle Dennis was home for luncheon, and Sue asked him about her red coat. "Now that I've ridden with the Commissioner," she said, "when do I get my red coat?"

"I'm afraid I haven't time to talk about it now, Sue," he answered.

"But, Uncle Dennis, when will you have time?" she asked.

He looked at the clock. "Well, not today, I'm afraid," he replied. "I've a very busy afternoon."

Sue looked at him. She knew he was a busy man and often wasn't home for tea, but he was behaving in exactly the same way they all had over their promise to give her her red coat when she had ridden with the Commissioner. There was something very mysterious about her red coat, it seemed to Sue.

Michael and John came in, and while they were eating their luncheon she told them of her fears. "I think it is very funny," she said, "that no one has given me my red coat. I was to have a red coat as soon as I had a good-conduct sheet and rode with the Commissioner. I've done both. When do I get my coat?"

Michael asked John. John asked Michael. Neither of them seemed to know.

"You're just trying to be funny," said Sue severely. "What's wrong with my getting my red coat."

"Ask your Uncle Dennis," said Michael.

"I did," she answered.

"Ask Monty," suggested John.

"I did," said Sue, "and he told me to ask Uncle Dennis."

"Ask Matilda."

Matilda was sent for and Michael questioned her. "Do you know when Miss Sue gets her red coat?"

"I'm sure I don't," said Matilda in her weak voice, "but I think she ought to have it."

Sue couldn't believe her ears. Here was Matilda sticking up for her instead of complaining. She made up her mind to take her driving oftener.

Michael got up and pushed back his chair. "I think if I were you, Sue," he said, "I'd leave this matter for a few days."

"I won't," said Sue crossly. "When I leave things to you men, you try to fool me."

John bent down and kissed her. "Keep your chin up, Recruit Winston," he said cheerily. "We'll see about this tomorrow."

"That's the way they always talk to me," Sue said to herself, "and they're always trying to fool me, too. Well, this time I'm not going to be fooled."

At her riding lesson Sergeant Whiteside raised the jump a whole notch higher. "I hear you rode with the Commissioner yesterday, Miss Sue, and did me proud," he said. "So I'm going to raise your jump. Can you take it?"

Sue rounded Beppo and flew straight at the barrier in the centre of the Drill Hall. Beppo sailed over it like a bird, but the sergeant stopped her from going around the second time.

"Easy, easy," he said. "No one should ride when they're in a temper. Come now, what's the matter?"

Sue told him. "And I asked them all at luncheon," she said, "and all they did was put me off."

"Perhaps they've ordered your coat as a surprise and are

keeping it a secret," said the sergeant. "Did you ever think of that?" Sue hadn't and said so, and he advised her to see the tailor.

As soon as her lesson was over, Sue rode up to the tailor's. He shook his head when she finished her story.

"No," he said, "I've heard nothing about it but perhaps they'll order it yet." Sue thanked him, but in her heart she knew they were fooling her, in spite of all that everyone told her.

Little Chief was lying on the grass beside the corral, tired and lazy with the heat of the sun.

"Did you know that I rode with the Shamoganis yesterday? At the very front with the Commissioner?" she asked.

"So?" said Little Chief. "I did not know." But he laughed as he spoke and Sue knew that he was teasing, for she had seen him staring at her as she rode in.

"Yes," said Sue, "and I'm now a real Shamoganis."

"So," said Little Chief again. "Then where is your red coat?"

Sue couldn't bear to tell him that Uncle Dennis and the others hadn't given it to her. "Coats take time to make," she said, "and the coats of the Shamoganis have to be very specially made. How would you like to race?"

Little Chief shook his head. "I have to watch the horses," he said.

"Come on," coaxed Sue. "I know I could beat you. Beppo is a much better horse than yours," she added, hoping that such an insult to his horse would get him up.

But Little Chief wouldn't move. "I've got to watch the horses," was all he said. Sue knew that was only partly true and that he was lazy, too. She went over to the corral. In the extension the silver roan was standing, head down, with the cut in his flank irritated with dust and flies.

"Did you wash this horse, Little Chief?" called Sue.

"No," said Little Chief. "Too much bother. He'll get all right."

Sue stamped her foot. "You mean boy, how would you like to have a sore cut on your leg left open for the flies and dust," she stormed. "You come here and fix this horse AT ONCE."

Little Chief didn't move. Sue went over to where he was lying. "Get up," she said. Still Little Chief didn't move, but she saw the bottle of medicine the veterinary surgeon had given him sticking out of his pocket. Bending over, she snatched the bottle and running back to the corral, called to him to come and help her. He didn't move. Angry at his neglect of his horse, Sue determined to doctor the horse herself.

"Shuh, shuh, shuh," she said, deep down in her throat as the Indians did to soothe a frightened horse, and then moved a little can of water over closer. There were no clean rags to bathe the cut, so she took out her handkerchief and dipping it in the water, reached through the bars and dabbed at the wound, talking to the roan in a quiet voice.

At first it trembled and drew as far away as it could from the bars of the corral, but after a time it stood still and let Sue clean the cut as well as she could. She poured some of the medicine on the handkerchief and dabbed it on. It smarted, and the roan drew away from her, just out of her reach.

"Come and help," she called to Little Chief.

"I won't. You're too bossy," he answered sulkily.

This made Sue very cross and even more determined to reach the roan. Remembering how the Indians had moved the poles until they could handle the animals easily, Sue studied which pole to slide back, and then pushed. She found it hard work, but kept on pushing until the pole suddenly dropped with a bang, and on top of it three others.

"My goodness," said Sue, for she had pushed upon the wrong pole and made an opening.

Frightened at the noise, the wild horses huddled together in one corner, but the roan, seeing the poles were down, started running. Out on the prairie he galloped and in less time than Sue could think, the rest of the horses were streaming from the corral. They moved aimlessly, as if they were without a leader.

"Ho—h! Ho—h!" called Little Chief. He was on his pony and racing across the prairie, rounding the horses back. Sue had never mounted herself before but she managed to scramble on Beppo, and obeying Little Chief's pointing arm, raced up the other side of the herd. The horses were scattered now and running wild. Sue had never known anything as exciting as trying to drive them back. Beppo seemed to know just what to do, for he turned and twisted and chased, just like Little Chief's horse.

"Yah! Yah!" Sue shouted, and after a few moments of mad racing the horses turned and trotted back into the corral, all except a few who had made off toward the Barrack's stables. Little Chief flung himself off his horse and ran the poles back in again, and was off like a flash toward the Barracks. Sue followed, but they were too late. Five wild horses were in the road leading into the Parade, and the faster Sue and Little Chief rode, the faster the wild horses ran before them. But the thud of hoofs had raised an alarm in the stables and Smith and some recruits were soon mounted and helping to turn them back, though not before they had trampled the Parade and raised much alarm within the Barracks.

Smith shook his head, as the last horse was rounded into the corral. "You'll be in hot water for this," he said to Sue. "It's lucky for you that the Commissioner is in Regina this afternoon."

Little Chief comforted her. "You are a very good rider," he said. "You ride like an Indian and a Shamoganis. Don't you mind what they say. Great chiefs forget the mistakes of the young. I got you into this trouble. I should have washed the horse and fixed him like the medicine man told me to do."

"Still, I was cross and bossy," said Sue.

Little Chief waved his arm. "It is forgotten," he said.

But when Sue rode home, she found it wasn't forgotten. There was a crowd of recruits on the Parade, raking and spading the earth where the wild horses' hoofs had torn great holes. Mrs. Schofield told her that Monty had just gone off to hunt for her. "You're in for a proper wigging, Miss Sue, when he finds you," she said, "and the captain will be very annoyed as well."

"Well, I feel pretty bad myself," Sue admitted. "I was promised a red coat and I haven't got it. I didn't mean to let the horses out. All I wanted to do was to fix the roan's cut."

Leading Beppo, she went down to the Commissioner's house to see Miss Vicky and found her in the garden. Throwing the reins over the gate post, she went in and told her the story.

"Never mind, dear," Miss Vicky said. "The Parade will all be tidy by the time Father returns. He'll never even know it happened."

Sue wasn't so sure. Smith had told her once that the Commissioner had eyes in the back of his head and ears that could hear around the world. But if that were so, he would know that she hadn't been given her red coat and could tell her why. No one else would explain. She resolved to ask him, but when he and Uncle Dennis came in for tea a little later, she wondered if she hadn't better wait until she made certain about the wild horses and whether the Commissioner knew about them. However, both officers smiled pleasantly at her, and when Miss Vicky sent her in for forgotten sugar tongs, Sue skipped along the back verandah, happy that her afternoon's adventures had not reached their ears.

But when she opened the pantry door, Sue stopped and held her breath with terror. Through the window she could see the Commissioner's flower garden and in the exact middle of it Beppo, hungrily cropping the flowers, nibbling the shrubs and digging his feet into the soft earth. Sue remembered: instead of tying her horse, she had thrown the reins loosely over the fence post and left the gate open.

Quietly she stole off the verandah and led Beppo outside the gate and tied him tightly. Racing back, she went down on her hands and knees and tried to cover the damage done by the pony's feet. Patting and pushing the earth, straightening bruised and crushed plants, she worked as fast as she could, but not fast enough, for the Commissioner had gone in the house to hunt for a favorite pipe and had seen his wrecked garden from another window.

Sue heard him coming. She knew now why everyone was scared of him. His eyes flashed blue fire like lightning, and his voice was sharp and cold like a piece of ice. She couldn't make out what he said. She was too frightened, but she knew that he was very, very angry and that she was to blame. The others, hearing his voice, had joined him; and when Sue looked up at the house, there seemed to be faces everywhere, and each one of them anxious.

Sue scrambled to her feet. "I left Beppo untied. I left the gate open. I'm very sorry. I don't think he hurt things very much," she told the Commissioner.

Uncle Dennis took her arm. "Come along with me, Sue," he said quietly, in the polite tone he used when he was really very angry. At the gate he turned her over to Monty who took her home and listened to her gravely. "Tell me, Sue," he said. "What made you so naughty? I understand how the wild horses got out, but what made you forget to tie Beppo and why did you leave the gate open?"

"I was so mad," answered Sue. "I was so mad at everybody that I couldn't remember anything."

"What were you mad at?" asked Monty.

"At everybody," replied Sue. "I rode with the Commissioner and I had my good-conduct sheet, and nobody gave me my red coat, and I couldn't find out why."

"Crying won't help," said Monty, with a shake of his head. "Think of the Commissioner's garden. Think of how your uncle must have felt when he saw what had happened."

"You don't know how *I* felt," answered Sue, "when no one would give me my red coat."

Michael and John came in. They were very grave, too, for they had heard of the afternoon's troubles from Miss Vicky. Uncle Dennis followed them. By this time he had learned about the wild horses and that, added to her leaving Beppo untied, had made him angrier than ever.

"What excuse can you have for behaving so badly, Sue?" he asked. "Quick, out with it."

"I wanted my red coat," said Sue, "and you never gave it to me."

. "That will do, Sue," answered her uncle. "I don't want to hear another word about your red coat. I'm thoroughly ashamed of the way you have behaved, and this time, you'll have to be punished."

Sue waited. She wondered what would happen next. But just then a pleasant voice sounded in the hall. Mrs. Schofield lifted the heavy portière over the door as Mr. Holmes entered. Sue thought she had never been so glad to see anyone in her whole life before.

"How do you do, Captain Lyons," said the missionary. "I'm driving over to Qu'Appelle tomorrow to spend a few days. Jane is coming with me, and I wondered if I might take Sue along. She would be company for both of us."

Sue held her breath. Qu'Appelle, she knew, was about forty miles away across the prairies. Her Uncle Dennis looked down at her thoughtfully. "That's very good of you, Mr. Holmes," he said. "As a matter of fact, it might be an excellent idea if Sue went away for a few days. But have you room for her? You're sure she won't be a nuisance?"

Mr. Holmes laughed. "We'll have plenty of room. We'll spend one night on the way with the Bishop and the remainder of the week at the Indian Mission School in Qu'Appelle. The nuns will take good care of Sue and Jane, and they'll both learn how young Indians are trained to become Canadians."

14. Qu'appelle

Can I drive now?" asked Sue.

Mr. Holmes smiled and gave her the reins. They had left the Barracks early, in a big buckboard that held the three of them easily. Everyone in the house had come down to see them off, and as a parting gift Uncle Dennis had given Jane and herself each a lovely round fifty-cent piece and warned Sue to be a good girl and to behave like a little lady and not a hoyden. But Mr. Holmes was so friendly and kind. "Don't worry," he said. "Sue is always good when she is with us, aren't you, Sue?"

Sue had not answered. Jane had given her a warning pinch, and she realized that Mr. Holmes had not heard about the skunk. If he had, he might not think she was so good.

As they passed the Commissioner's house, Miss Vicky ran out with two sunbonnets in her hand. "Stop!" she cried. "Mother thinks they both should wear these. It's so hot driving all day in the sun and she doesn't want them to come back looking like turkey eggs."

Although neither liked wearing hats of any kind, the two girls tied them on their heads.

"What's a turkey egg look like?" Sue asked Jane.

169

"All covered with little brown spots," Jane answered, "just like freckles."

"My goodness, I don't want anyone to mistake me for a turkey egg," said Sue, and tied the sunbonnet tighter.

When they passed the stables, Smith ran out with Scottie at his heels, carrying a tin box. "Some cookies my Missus baked last night when she heard Miss Sue was going on a visit with you," he said. "She can't forget how kind Miss Sue was to Scottie."

Sue thanked him and asked him to take special care of Beppo, and they drove on.

"What did you do for Scottie?" asked Mr. Holmes.

"Oh, he was sort of dirty," said Sue, "and we washed him one day when Smith was busy. It was nothing very much!"

Jane snickered beside her and Sue gave her a pinch in turn.

Sergeant Whiteside, on his way to the Drill Hall, waved to them and ran over with a small parcel in his hand. "They're sugar sticks," he said to Mr. Holmes, "for the two young ladies. We shall miss Miss Sue. She has livened us up since she came!"

Sue could hardly believe her ears. She was not used to having her adventures referred to in such pleasant terms.

Everyone smiled and waved so gaily as they passed that Sue was glad when they left the Barracks and all of yesterday's misdeeds were behind her. She was afraid that if she stayed there much longer some fresh crime would be discovered and all this pleasantness pass.

The corral was gone. The wild horses were now in the stables, learning to stand quietly in a stall and learning too that when men touched them, their hands were those of friends.

"We will see Little Chief at Qu'Appelle," Mr. Holmes told them. "Laughing Cloud started for there at dawn this morning with the balance of the herd."

All through the lovely day they drove over the prairies. Sometimes they sang, sometimes Mr. Holmes told them tales of the Indians, and each in turn drove the fat bay ponies that pattered so busily over the dusty trail. No one passed them. It seemed as if they were the only people in all the world.

"Look, Sue," cried Jane. "Trees!"

Ahead of them a few scraggly trees and a barn broke the monotony of the prairies. But before they reached the trees they passed great stretches of wheat, golden as the sun. The farm was owned by a Russian immigrant who could speak very little English, but who worked early and late in the vast acreage with his wife and children. There was no one in the house, but a droning sound in the east told them that the reapers were cutting wheat.

They unharnessed the horses and after giving them hay and water ate their picnic luncheon in the shade of the poplar trees. Afterward they slept awhile and then started out again over the trail. A little breeze rustled the grass and swayed the first tufts of golden rod. Black-eyed daisies lay in great drifts of color, but beyond a gopher or the call of a prairie hen they heard no sound, saw no one pass. The world seemed so very big and with so few familiar things in it.

But just as the shadows were growing long they reached Indian Head, the tiniest town Sue had ever seen. Tinier than Regina, but nicely planted with very young trees that bent over in the wind. The largest building was the church and beside it the Bishop's house. Sue had never seen a Bishop before and was very much interested in him. He wore gai-

ters, long and black and buttoned up the side like those she wore
with her habit, and a short black pinafore under his coat. His
collar was turned around like Mr. Holmes' and he had a beard
as long as Santa Claus. His wife put the two girls in a room
together, and helped them tidy up before supper.

"You'd better wash extra clean," said Jane. "Mrs. Grisdale's
very strict about washing."

She told Sue of how once she hadn't washed and Mrs. Grisdale had cried and told her father that he was bringing her up
like an Indian child. "Ever after," said Jane, "Daddy's examined me night and morning to see if I'm scrubbed."

Sue went back and scrubbed again. She didn't want any complaints to spoil the good time she was having.

Both girls were too tired and sleepy after their supper to
listen to the Bishop and Mr. Holmes talk about their travels
in the Northwest before either Sue or Jane were born. To
Sue there was something very strange about Indian Head.
She couldn't think what it was until Mrs. Grisdale took them
up to bed and turned out the light. Then she remembered.
No bugles. She was waiting for First Post to blow. She wondered how Monty was and Minnie-Pooh-Pooh, and fell asleep
wondering.

They were away again early in the morning, but not before
Sue had asked the Bishop about his beard.

"What do you want to know about it?" he said, smiling at
her.

"I want to know if you must have a beard as long as yours
to be a Bishop."

"No," he said, with a twinkle in his eye, "but I'll tell you
why we bishops out here have beards, Sue. They're to keep
us warm in winter!"

Sue stared at him for a moment. "Truly?" she asked. "Like a fur coat?"

"Well, almost truly. When I first came to the Northwest, I was in the Far North, and you couldn't shave in that cold, and there were no barbers to shave you, so I got used to wearing a beard, and now I feel cold without it."

Sue laughed. "I think you're fooling me," she said. "If it's as cold as that in the winter, why don't all the Force grow beards?"

The idea amused everyone, but Sue did find that all the bishops wore beards and that they had worn them first because of the extra warmth they gave.

The prairies were changing now. Every little while they would pass a cluster of small scrub poplars, a low-growing bush, and there were other travelers on the trail, too, who would turn out to let them pass and wave a cheery greeting. Now and then an Indian rode gravely by. The whirr of a reaper sounded in their ears. More trees, and a sharp turn in the road. Sue caught her breath. Far below them lay a wide valley, green with young poplars and bushes, the earth laid out in patterned squares of farm land, and the buildings of the Mission School looking like fairy castles in the sunset.

"Qu'Appelle," said Mr. Holmes. A bell rang steadily, and between the buildings they saw tiny figures running toward the church.

"We shall just be in time for supper," said Mr. Holmes, and shook his reins. Quickly the ponies clattered down the valley and into the grounds of the Mission.

Father Hugenard, the head of the Mission, had seen them coming and was waiting at the steps for them. "How are you, Padré Holmes," he said. "We are glad to welcome you, and you too, Jane. And who is this?" he asked, as Sue climbed out of the buckboard.

Sue curtseyed. "I'm Susannah Elizabeth Fairfield Winston," she said, for she thought Sue wasn't much of a name to give to such an important looking person as Father Hugenard.

He smiled at her. "What a splendid name," he said, "but what shall I call you? Will Sue be all right?"

"*Oui, mon père,*" she answered, for she could tell by his accent that he was French.

The priest broke into the jolliest laugh Sue had heard since her own father went to India. "So you speak French," he said.

"Only a very little," she replied. "*J' suis une 'tite rascalle.*"

Again the priest laughed, and calling a nun who was passing along the hall, asked her to take them all to rooms on the guest floor. "Supper will be ready in a very few moments," he said. "Come down as soon as you can. Be good, little rascal."

Sue had never seen so large a dining room. There were several hundred boys and girls waiting to sit down to supper. She and Jane sat at Father Hugenard's table, which was on a platform raised above the rest of the room. There were other guests from various parts of Canada, and the priest talked long and earnestly of the Mission.

Sue learned that Indian children were taken into the school at the age of six and that besides learning to read and write the boys were taught to be good farmers, the girls to be nurses, maids and cooks. "When they leave us," he explained, "it is to go into a household that we know about and where we are sure that they will be well taken care of."

Mr. Holmes leaned forward to Jane and Sue. "Little Chief

is here for nine months every year," he said. "That is why he speaks English so well. You will see him in the morning."

After supper a gentle nun took them up to bed. "Your father will talk late tonight," she said to Jane. "He and Father Hugenard work together a great deal for the education of our young Indians. Your father is a very good man, Jane," she added.

"I know," said Jane, who was struggling with the catch of a traveling bag. "But look, Sister Mary Monica." Sue looked, too. Jane was holding up Madame La Tour. "Isn't she beautiful?"

With a little cry of joy, the soft voiced nun took Madame La Tour in her arms, cradling her, and then busily examined the clothes. "Will you lend her to me in the morning," she asked, "so that my children may copy her clothes for their own dolls? They have never seen anything so beautiful."

Jane nodded shyly. Madame La Tour had made everyone happy, Sue thought, and wished she had a hundred of her to give away. It made the doll seem extra precious just now, and the two girls tucked her in between them in the big bed for safety when Sister Mary Monica blew out the light.

In the morning there was the ringing of bells for church services, followed by drills for the older boys, and much cleaning and polishing by the older girls. Jane and Sue were shown the school rooms, the hospital and church, the great barns and stables, the kitchens where the Indian girls were making bread, pie and cakes, the great dormitories with their wide-open windows, and from the verandah of the main house they watched Father Hugenard receive and talk to the parents of the various children. He knew them all by name.

An Indian would arrive with his family and perhaps one or two horses and a wagon. He would unharness his horses, lay robes upon the grass or put up a tiny tepee and prepare to spend the day. Sometimes there would be ten to twelve families camped in front of the main house. As soon as they had made themselves comfortable, the father and mother would call upon the priest and ask to see their child, who would immediately be sent out to his parents.

"See," said Father Hugenard. "There is Black Hawk's youngest son going out now." A little Indian boy of seven ran across to his people. "He has only been here a month and his mother is suspicious of us," the priest continued. "We wash him too much, she thinks. The child's hair was full of bear grease when he arrived. We *had* to wash him!"

Sue and Jane watched. True enough, Little Badger was turned upside down by his mother, and from her angry mutterings it was clear that she thought he was far too clean. Little Badger himself chattered like a monkey and apparently thought himself quite happy, but Black Hawk looked very glum.

Mr. Holmes called the children. "Sister Mary Monica wants you to show Madame La Tour to the girls," he said to Jane. "Come along."

They went over to the sewing room, and there the Indian girls examined the red velvet cloak, the cashmere dress, the underclothes, and laughed over the toque and spotted veil, the tiny buttoned boots. Sue liked watching them. Their skins were brown and their shining black eyes narrow, and they laughed as if they were happy all the time.

Leaving Madame La Tour with them for the day, Sue and Jane visited the gardens, the dairy and the laundry, and then,

tired and warm, came home to luncheon as the deep toned
bell rang through the valley.

During luncheon one of the older boys came up to the table
and spoke to Father Hugenard who left hastily. Mr. Holmes
followed, and Sue and Jane, full of curiosity, ran after him.
They found the priest in his cassock and high silk hat climbing into a buckboard along with two Indian boys of nineteen,
and learned that Black Hawk, in the priest's absence, had taken
Little Badger away with him.

"We can't allow that," said the priest, as one of the boys adjusted a broken harness strap. "These prairie lands are all right
for the Indians now, but in time they will be covered with
wheat and great ranches. There will be no room for the Red
Man to roam or deal in wild horses. We must educate the
young Indian for the new life that lies ahead of him. That is
our mission." Picking up the reins, he drove rapidly away.

Sitting on the steps, Sue and Jane talked to the Indian children and their parents, and waited for the priest's return. Mr.
Holmes laughed at them. "He may be away until night," he
said, "and he may be back within an hour."

"Why did Father Hugenard go?" asked Sue. "Why didn't
he just send one of the Indian boys?"

"Because he wants the Indians to know that he is never too
busy to look after the smallest child."

"Why does he wear that high silk hat?" asked Sue.

"That is the hat his Order wore in France," answered Mr.
Holmes. "There has been no change in their clothing, and so
he must wear it here."

"It looks very funny," said Sue. "Couldn't he change it if he
wanted to?"

"He could," said Mr. Holmes, "but the Indians wouldn't know him now without it. It's like a crown to them. I doubt if he will ever change it."

Up the Mission drive an hour later, came a buckboard, and above the horses' heads they could see the high silk hat. On the priest's knee, Little Badger sat contentedly.

"Black Hawk had not gone far," the priest explained, "and my horses were better than his. He gave the boy up without too much argument and will be back next week to pay us a visit."

But at supper time there was fresh news of Little Badger. He had been playing lacrosse in the ball field and an Indian had called to him from the road. He had not been seen since. Father Hugenard sighed and sent off a note by one of the boys. In a short time, to Sue's delight, a Mountie rode up, red-coated and smiling. Without getting off his horse, he listened to the tale.

"All right, Father," he said. "I won't be back until I've found him." He saluted and rode away.

Long after bedtime, Sue and Jane sat on the verandah steps, wondering about Little Badger. They were going home in the morning, for Mr. Holmes had to be back before the Gymkhana and it was only a week away. A gymkhana, Sue learned, was an athletic display put on every year by the Force, in which the Indians took part. Prizes were given to the winners, and it was a day of much ceremony and feasting.

"You see, Sue," Mr. Holmes explained, "the Indians used to hold yearly war and sun dances. These left them so excited and wild, they would forget that the prairies were theirs no longer and do cruel and savage things. Often months passed before the Force could quiet them and restore law and order again. So the police tried the Gymkhana, and now it takes the place of the sun dances and is the great event of the Indian year. There are no longer troubles—just feasting and good will."

"Will I go to it?" asked Sue.

"I think so," he said, "but just now you must both go to bed. And don't worry about Little Badger. Your Mountie will bring him back."

It seemed to Sue that she had hardly crept into bed before the sun wakened her. Jane was asleep beside her, with an arm around Madame La Tour. In the distance Sue could hear a horse's feet. Sleepily she wondered who it could be and then suddenly remembered. Over to the window she ran. Far down the drive there was a flash of scarlet.

Wrapping a shawl around herself, Sue tiptoed over to the door, opened it quietly and pattered down the stairs. The front door was open and the scarlet coat was coming nearer as she ran out on the steps. As if in answer to her wish, the horse broke into a trot and in a moment Sue saw Little Badger's head against the red coat. Smiling and chattering happily, he was sitting in front of the constable, who held him with one arm.

"Well done!" said a voice behind her.

Sue turned. It was Father Hugenard himself. He, too, had heard the horse's feet and come down. As the constable rode up to the steps the priest lifted Little Badger off the horse, and carried him into the dining room. Sue and the constable followed. The Indian night watchman brought in some breakfast and the four of them ate together.

Black Hawk had picked up his son while he was playing lacrosse, and on a swift horse had ridden him far off and in among the brush of the valley. It had taken the constable some little time to find his trail, and when he found the Indians Black Hawk refused to give up his son.

"I argued with him," the constable said, "I told him how much education would mean to his child. I was stern but I could make no headway. All this while Little Badger was lying asleep in front of the fire, so I got off my horse and asked the squaw to make me some tea. She did, and I argued some more. Finally I just bent down and picked up Little Badger and jumped on my horse. 'Black Hawk,' I said, 'you will find your son at the Mission' and I rode away."

He turned to Little Badger. "We had a nice ride, didn't we, son?"

The small Indian smiled happily. The constable rose. "That's all, Father. Is there anything more I can do for you?"

"No, my son," said the priest. Whatever else Father Hugenard might have said was interrupted by Sue.

"Were you scared when you rode away?" she asked the Mountie.

He looked down at her. "Scared of what?"

"Scared of what Black Hawk might do to you when you turned your back and rode away," Sue answered.

"Sure I was," he replied. "But what could I do? When you're in a jam, you've got to show a bold front. I bluffed Black Hawk into thinking I wasn't scared, and I won. See?" The next minute he had said goodbye and was riding down the drive.

"What are you thinking of?" asked Father Hugenard, as he poured out another glass of milk for Little Badger.

"I was wondering about Little Badger," said Sue. "Do you hide him now so that his father can't find him?"

"No," he answered. "Nothing is changed, and Black Hawk won't try stealing his son again. The fathers are like that at first, but the children are happy here and they soon learn it is best to leave them with us. You know Laughing Cloud's son, Little Chief?" Sue nodded. "Well, Laughing Cloud stole his son five times." The priest smiled. "Now, when his grand-children are two years old 'he brings them to us. Run along now, my child, and get dressed or I'll be in trouble for keeping you down here."

Just before they left the Mission, Sister Mary Monica beckoned to Jane and Sue from the hallway. There were two girls with her from the sewing room, and they shyly handed Jane two tiny garments. A nightgown of cotton with dainty tucks and frills, and a dressing jacket of mull, delicately em-broidered with feather stitching. "For Madame La Tour," they said together.

What a LOVELY adventure, thought Sue, as she and Jane waved farewells until they turned out of the Mission drive.

15. The Gymkhana

They spent that night at Indian Head and early the following morning were on their way to Regina. Mr. Holmes had found a letter waiting for him at the Bishop's house from his sister at Duck Lake. She was leaving for England in a few weeks and wanted him to bring Jane and pay her a farewell visit.

"That means that we must go at once," said Mr. Holmes. "We'll just leave our things in the tent at Laughing Cloud's camp and take the train."

"But you'll miss the Gymkhana," said Sue. "Won't you mind?"

Jane shook her head. "Not much," she replied. "I can see it any time and I do love Aunt Nancy."

So they were up early the next morning and left just as the sun began to rise. Long shadows stretched before them as they started along the trail. Before mid-day, they passed the wheat farm and when the ponies slackened their pace, Mr. Holmes unhitched them and lifted out two canvas water buckets full of water. A large piece of sailcloth hooked onto the back of the buckboard gave the little party shelter from the sun, and they ate their sandwiches and dozed awhile, with no sound save the horses cropping the prairie wool to disturb them.

Sue was wondering what the Gymkhana would be like when

Mr. Holmes touched her shoulder and pointed to the west. A constable rode steadily toward them. He was doing a prairie patrol, he explained, after he had dismounted and sat down with them. He expected to spend the night in Indian Head. He had no news except that the Indians were already beginning to come into Regina for the Gymkhana, and a rumor that Joe Labiche had been seen again. "He's traveling by freight," he told Mr. Holmes. "He moves at night and then disappears. A few days later he catches another train. It was an Indian runner who warned us."

"Do you suppose you'll ever find him?" asked Mr. Holmes.

"You never know," said the constable with a shrug of his shoulders. "He's been across the border for a couple of years but he's a sly one and the American police haven't been able to lay hands on him either."

"Do the Americans help you hunt for men you want?" asked Mr. Holmes.

"Yes," answered the constable. "The relations between the U. S. and Canada are very friendly and we both help each other as much as we can."

He helped Mr. Holmes harness the horses, and while the two men talked, Sue told Jane of the day she had put moustaches on the picture of Joe Labiche, in the Commissioner's office. "He looked quite nice by the time I'd fixed him up with large moustaches," Sue confided, "but wasn't Uncle Dennis mad!"

It was lovely coming home with the sentry calling out, "Pass, Mr. Holmes and party, and welcome home, Miss Sue." Everyone at the Guard House smiled and waved, but Mr. Holmes drove right on. He and Jane had to go out to the camp and then catch the train to Duck Lake and could only stop long enough at Uncle Dennis's to drop Sue off.

Uncle Dennis was having a tea party. Mrs. Walsh and Miss Vicky were there, and several others. Sue's crimes all seemed to have been forgotten. Monty swung her as high as his head. Mrs. Schofield had baked a little cake especially for her return, and every dress she had was washed and ironed. Even her habit had been cleaned and was hanging in the cupboard. Matilda was all smiles as she brushed her hair and changed her dress, and Sue felt more than ever that the Barracks was the only place in the world to live.

Before Mrs. Walsh and Miss Vicky left, Uncle Dennis told Sue he had had a long letter from her mother. "You are to stay here with me all winter, Sue," he said. "Your father's murals are so well liked that the Maharajah has ordered others, and neither your father or mother can come back until they are finished."

Sue looked at him. Not see her mother for another whole year? She couldn't bear it, and knew she was going to cry. "Don't they want me any longer, Uncle Dennis?" she asked.

"Of course they do," cried Miss Vicky, "but India is a very long way off—too far for you and Matilda to travel to alone."

Uncle Dennis lifted her to his knees. "See, Sue," he said, "here is what your mother writes:

"And tell my darling little Sue to be a good girl and not to fret, that the winter will not be long and when we meet her in London, Daddy will have earned a lot of money and we can all be happy together. I am sure she will not mind the long wait when she knows that she will be crossing to London with the Jubilee Contingent."

"Truly?" broke in Sue, before anyone could speak. And Miss Vicky answered, "TRULY!"

"Oh, lovely," said Sue, "and will I get my . . ." She stopped. If she was going to spend the winter here, it might be just as well not to make any references to the red coat, for a little while anyway.

"And tomorrow," continued Miss Vicky, "you are going to the Gymkhana and are to ride in the children's race."

"I don't mind spending the winter here a bit," said Sue. "What time do we start for the Gymkhana?"

"Not until the morning," laughed Miss Vicky, "and not until ten o'clock. You are to drive with me, and Smith will take Beppo down early so that he will be rested and ready for the race. Now tell us all about your visit to the Mission."

But long before Sue had told them the tale of Little Badger, Matilda called her, and for once Sue was glad to go to bed, glad to hold Minnie-Pooh-Pooh close again, and very glad to hear Lights Out across the Parade.

She was up at Reveille, examining the day. There wasn't a cloud in the sky; in fact, Sue thought the sun was shining extra brightly. By the time Matilda came in to her, she had laid her habit out on the bed, found her shoes and a clean hankie and had tidied her room. Parade was over quickly that morning. Monty declared he had never seen her so prompt, as he fastened her crest on her left shoulder.

Miss Vicky was early, too, and they started out in the high dogcart—she and Miss Vicky and Monty, as they had the day they went to choose Beppo. Out along the dusty road they trotted, passing slow-plodding, two-wheeled Red River carts, constables riding to and from the Barracks, Indian families in bright Hudson Bay blankets, with travois dragging out behind the ponies' feet. As they swung off the road toward the Fair

Grounds, they passed Laughing Cloud and his family, with Little Chief riding his own paint pony.

Sue was delighted to see him again. "I'm in the horse race," she called, "and I'm going to beat you!"

Little Chief grinned up at her. "You mean you try," he said. "My horse is like the wind. You'll see!"

"There'll be ice cream, too," she cried, "AND cake!" But some cowboys rode past at a fast trot and she couldn't hear his answer.

Sue thought the Gymkhana most exciting. There was a grandstand for the Government and Barracks Officials, with a square box in which the Commissioner and the Lieutenant Governor sat, and a large red and white striped tent with tables full of glass and china, and behind them ice-cream freezers. There were smaller tents where one could buy pink lemonade and popcorn; and there were Indians of every size and age. At stations around the racetrack the red coats of the Force could be seen, and just opposite the Lieutenant Governor's box there was the starters' stand. Ranchers, Indians, Red Coats, ponies, people arriving, horses being taken back to the lines, lost Indian children crying for their mothers, and a band playing gaily. Sue did not believe the Jubilee could be any nicer.

Miss Vicky was very much the centre of attraction and she introduced Sue to all the important people and then took her over to where Mrs. Walsh was sitting. A constable rode rapidly down the racetrack, clearing children and stragglers from it. And then to the strains of *God Save the Queen,* the Lieutenant Governor and his wife drove around the track. They had outriders and drove in an open Victoria. Sue thought the Lieutenant Governor very grand. He wore a pale grey frock coat and trousers, and had a pale grey topper on his head. He bowed to everyone as if he were a king. All the officers were presented to him. But grand as he was, Sue thought Michael and John even grander. They were perfect in their scarlet and gold and white helmets. The band played a march; the Lieutenant Governor and his wife moved slowly into their box and the Gymkhana began.

There was tent-pegging by the Force and a musical ride, with the constables carrying lances with fluttering pennons; some trotting races and exhibitions of broncho busting; and in all these the white men and Indians entered freely and won about equally. Everywhere and in everything there was high good humor.

But it was the sack race that pleased Sue most. About twenty young braves stepped into sacks which were drawn up over their arms and tied around their necks, leaving them unable to do anything but jump like frogs from the starting line to the big gate and back. They leaped into the air and turned and twisted, and in their frantic haste to win often knocked each other down. When they fell, they were funnier than ever, for the only way they could get up was by bunting against each other.

Sue had never laughed so much. There was a three-legged race, and throwing the hammer, and lassooing wild horses, and then the children's race. The Indian children ran beautifully, and it didn't matter much whether you came in first or not, for you got a prize just for running. It was all so gay, with bugles starting and ending each race, and the Red Coats helping winners and losers alike.

"It's your turn, Sue," said Miss Vicky. "After the men's foot race is over, there'll be the children's horse race. Shall we go down and get Beppo?"

If Miss Vicky hadn't held on to her Sue would have slid down the railing, she was so eager to start. But Miss Vicky held on tightly and Sue found herself walking slowly across the grounds and behind the grandstand to where Smith was standing with Beppo, brushed and shining like the Commissioner's own horse.

It was the first time she had seen Beppo since she left for Qu'Appelle and she thought him more beautiful than ever. He nuzzled at her for sugar and while Sue rubbed his head, Smith gave her advice about racing. "When the other fellow passes you, don't rush your horse. Ride steady and you'll creep up on him like a thief and steal the race from under his very nose."

"Yes, Smith, thank you," said Sue, for she was in a fever to be mounted. Finally she was up and Smith adjusted her skirt and tried her stirrup. "Off you go, Miss Sue," he said, "and I hope you win!"

Waving to Miss Vicky and feeling very important, Sue rode forward to the track. Monty met her and led Beppo over to where Michael was in charge of the race.

Sue counted. There were fifteen of them racing and hers was the smallest pony, but by this time she knew a little about horses and could tell that at least half a dozen of them wouldn't stand up under the strain of the race. Little Chief came over. He was riding Natose, his own pony, and Sue could see that he was as excited as she was. Michael tried to get them all to keep their horses in a straight line, but soon gave up. Everyone was too eager to be off, so he and John decided it should be a handicap race.

Little Chief had the best and largest horse. They put him at the starting line, and a few feet ahead the next best horse and so on, until Sue found herself out in front and almost half way around the track. She didn't like that. She really wanted to be back with Little Chief, but Michael explained that this was the only sporting way of running the race. "Now mind, Sue," he said. "You must listen for the starting gun and when you hear it, ride as fast as you can."

Sue listened so hard that she never knew whether she heard the starting gun or not, but she saw the other horses start, and lickety-split she was off. For the first time in his life with Sue, Beppo felt her crop on his fat sides.

"My goodness," thought Sue, "this race is leaving me behind." For as hard as Beppo ran, the others ran past him. But she remembered Smith's advice to ride steady and crept up on some of those who had passed her. "Ho . . . h! Yah! Yah! Yah!" called the young Indian riders. "Yoh! Yoh! Yoh!" answered Sue, forgetting to keep her elbows in, and looking everywhere but between her horse's ears.

"Hi . . . ee . . . eeh!" cried Little Chief, riding by. That was too much. Sue forgot every rule that the sergeant had taught her. She just remembered to stick on and ride as fast as she could. "Run, Beppo," she screamed. "Run!" And Beppo did run. He ran so fast that he didn't know that he had passed the winning post a full minute behind everyone else.

"Who won?" Sue cried. But Little Chief was already beside her. "I did," he said proudly. "I knew I'd win. Natose is the best pony in the prairie. But you get a prize, too," he added.

"What kind of a prize?" asked Sue. "A booby prize?"

"No," he said. "You listen and you'll see."

"First boy's prize to Little Chief Laughing Cloud," announced Michael. "First girl's prize to Miss Susannah Winston."

Sue thought she'd never stop laughing. "I was the only girl riding," she said.

"You stop laughing," said Little Chief. "Big ceremony now."

Monty took Beppo by the rein. "Well done, Sue," he said softly. "Hitch up your skirt and follow Little Chief."

Sue followed him to where the Governor's wife was presenting prizes at a table. Uncle Dennis stood beside her, and to Sue's delight she found she had won a little velvet bag with a brush and comb inside.

But as she curtseyed her thanks, Little Chief touched her on the arm, and turning Sue found Laughing Cloud standing before her. In his hand he held a white doeskin shirt and trousers, beautifully beaded and ornamented with ermine tails, and on top of all, a small feathered Indian headdress. "For me?" asked Sue.

"For Little Golden Hawk," said Laughing Cloud. "She rides like an Indian."

Sue held the headdress out to him. "You put it on for me," she said, and the brown fingers took it back and placed it on her shining head. "Do I look nice?" Sue asked her uncle. "I feel *very* nice."

Miss Vicky carried her off to the refreshment tent for there was to be a two-hour wait before the next events. Everyone complimented her on her headdress and admired the doe-skin outfit and told her how well she had ridden, and what a beautiful pony she had, until Sue really began to think she was as nice as they said she was. It was Michael who came in and found she was still without the promised ice cream.

"Never mind, Sue," he said. "I'll get you an extra large helping; and don't believe everything you're told."

But being with Miss Vicky still kept her in the centre of everything, and even Sue grew tired of compliments after awhile; besides, she was very tired of curtseying. It was so difficult to curtsey and hold a large plate of slippery ice cream and a piece of cake at the same time. "I know I'm a first-rate rider," she told herself, "now I wish there was something else to do." She wondered where she could find Little Chief. She hadn't long to wonder for as she moved toward the tent door, there was a hissing sound, and through a tear in the canvas Sue saw Little Chief.

"What is it?" she asked.

"Where's the ice cream?" he whispered.

"You wait," answered Sue, and going back to Miss Vicky she interrupted to ask if she might see whether Beppo had been fed and watered.

Miss Vicky gave her a gay nod of approval, and Sue stormed the ice-cream table. "I want four helpings of ice cream in a bowl," she asked, "*AND* lots of cake, please." When the maid hesitated, she explained, "They are for a friend of mine," and added, "if there are any sandwiches left, I should like a few."

A few minutes later she wriggled herself out under the flap of the tent, having first handed out the supplies she had gathered to Little Chief. "If I'd gone out the front way, they'd never have let me out," she confided, "with all this. We'd better find some place where we can enjoy it in peace and quiet."

Little Chief saw an Indian friend looking enviously at the ice cream and moved Sue away. "I know," he said. "Let's go to where the horses are."

"Yes," said Sue. "Let's find Smith."

16. Not Wanted

Smith welcomed them with open arms. "I saw you ride, Miss Sue. You didn't come in first, but you ran a good race, and next time you'll do better."

"Did you see my prize?" Sue asked.

"I did," he answered. "I was standing right behind you when Laughing Cloud gave you the doeskin suit. My, my, Miss Sue, that's the prettiest suit I've ever seen. Where did you leave it?"

"Miss Vicky has it," she replied. "She was afraid I might drop it. I'm going to have my photograph taken in it to send to Mummy in India."

Little Chief was interested only in the ice cream which was melting rapidly. "Where can we eat?" he asked.

Smith fixed them up a grand seat among the bales of hay by the horse lines and promised not to tell where they were. "We want to eat our ice cream in peace and quiet," Sue explained.

But there was no peace and quiet for anyone at the Gymkhana, and less for Sue and Little Chief. All around them the sleek cavalry horses were being groomed for the military review, the great event of the day. Mr. Holmes had told them that this review impressed the Indians more than any other single event. It showed the strength of the Force and kept any troublesome members of a tribe from becoming active.

"Hello, Miss Sue! How are you, Little Chief!" called the red-coated constables as they came to get their mounts. Some of them asked why she was not riding with the Force, others why she wasn't marching in the review. Two buglers stopped and spoke to her.

"Aren't you going to march with the band, Miss Sue?" one asked. Sue shook her head. "Too bad, I thought you were a member of the Force." But the second bugler smiled understandingly. "She is," he said, "but she hasn't a uniform."

"Could I march if I had a uniform?" asked Sue.

"Of course! You rode with the Commissioner, didn't you?"

The bandmaster stopped. He looked simply magnificent, and twirled his moustaches and pulled down his tunic as he told her he thought it would be a good thing to have her in the band. "You might be the drummer boy," he said, "only in your case I'm afraid you'd have to be drummer girl." Laughing at his own joke, he too marched away.

"That's a silly joke," said Sue to Little Chief. "Drummer girl, when I'm already a member of the Force. He must think we're babies."

Sergeant Whiteside passed. "How are you, Sue?" he called. "Not marching with us today?" Sue shook her head. "Next year then," he said, and was gone.

Smith came out to join them. "Have you kids finished your ice cream? Well, then, hop up on top of these hay bales. You can see the March Past from there."

When they clambered up, the sight made Sue catch her breath, so lovely did it seem. Spread out below her were men, horses, officers and bandsmen, getting ready for the review.

Pennants fluttering in the breeze, band instruments glistening like gold, horses tossing their heads and the jangle of chains and bits, the calls of the buglers, the shouted commands and the flaming red of the Mounties' tunics made a picture Sue knew she would never forget. One by one the squadrons moved off to the far end of the field where the Force re-formed, for the march past the reviewing stand. Nearer to them the band began to play.

"I MUST march with them," cried Sue to Little Chief. "I MUST! If I only had a uniform!"

Little Chief looked at her and then at Smith's tunic lying on the hay at his feet. Smith being the only small man in the Force, had the only tunic she could have worn. Quickly, taking off Sue's Indian headdress, he reached down and picked up the orderly's red tunic. "Put it on. Hurry!" he said. The tunic fitted her like a frock coat and came almost to her feet but she could wear it.

"Do I look all right?" she asked. Little Chief nodded.

"You look like a real Shamoganis."

Close to them the band was playing gaily. "But I must have a hat," cried Sue.

"There's one," Little Chief pointed to Smith's hat, hanging on a nearby tent pole. Jumping down, Sue grabbed the hat, jammed it over her curls and ran as fast as her legs could carry her after the band. It was hard running, with the skirt of her habit and the tail of the coat bunching as she ran, and the hat sliding over her eyes, but she knew she could fix them after she fell in line.

Slowly the band moved across the grounds toward the reviewing stand. Beside it Sue could see the Commissioner and her Uncle Dennis mounted, ready for the review, with their orderlies behind them.

"I'll have to hurry," she said to herself, and as the band wheeled she put on a final burst of speed, and breaking through the ranks of marching bandsmen, fell in behind the drum major. Pushing her hat back and pulling down the red tunic, she watched him carefully and then threw out her chest and lengthened her steps as far as she could. At last she felt completely happy.

In a quiet part of the military march a drummer called to her out of the corner of his mouth, "Go to it, Miss Sue. You're dandy." But on the other side another drummer advised her to run along home before it was too late.

As the band wheeled, she heard a burst of laughter from the crowd and wondered what it was about. On marched the drum major. On marched Sue. But at the sharp command, "Left Wheel," something quite unexpected happened. Monty and a horse appeared from nowhere and she suddenly felt herself swept off her feet and was conscious only of being held very tightly and feeling a horse under her again—not Beppo, but a very big horse, ridden by a very cross Monty.

Sue wondered what was the matter. "What are you doing?" she gasped.

"I'm picking you up," he snapped. "From the middle of the band where you had no right to be. What do you mean by such antics, Sue?"

"Let me down," she answered. "I want to march with the band." But Monty rode rapidly around the race course and out behind the horse lines where Smith and Miss Vicky were already waiting with the dog-cart. He lifted her into the seat of the cart, and before Sue quite knew what was happening she was out on the dusty trail and driving toward the Barracks beside a very silent Miss Vicky. She wondered again what she had done that was so wrong. Miss Vicky had never been angry at her before. Everyone else had, including Smith, but never Miss Vicky.

"Don't you think I marched very well?" she asked.

"Yes," said Miss Vicky, "for the sort of marching you were doing, you marched very well, *only* you shouldn't have been marching."

Sue couldn't see how that could be. "I rode with the Commissioner," she said, "and I got my good-conduct sheet and wore my crest and I wasn't given my red coat, so I just took the first one I saw. I knew I couldn't march without a red coat. Anyway Smith didn't need his. I only borrowed it."

"That's not the point, Sue," said Miss Vicky impatiently. "You were not asked to march, and you behaved like a showoff. You spoiled the review and you made father and your uncle very angry."

"But, Miss Vicky. I didn't mean to do anything wrong."

"Perhaps you didn't, Sue, but you succeeded very well," replied Miss Vicky sharply.

When they drove into the Barracks, Miss Vicky took Sue home with her, then up in her own room where she tried to make Sue understand how badly she had behaved.

"Don't you see, Sue? The Indians are a very dignified and ceremonious people. Father tries to conduct the Gymkhana with all possible ceremony, so that it will impress the Indians with the dignity and importance of the Force. Do you understand?"

Sue nodded.

"And when they see anyone behave as you have today," continued Miss Vicky, "they interpret such behavior as an insult to themselves. They argue that they would never have allowed any of their children to spoil a great tribal meeting, and that if the Shamoganis can do so, it is because they do not consider the Indians important."

Now Sue realized that she had behaved badly and that in the eyes of everyone she had disgraced the Force and been a bad, bold, little girl.

Miss Vicky called down the stairs to Dawson. "Send over to Captain Lyons' house," she said, "and ask them to bring over a complete outfit for Miss Sue. She will change her habit here."

"Could I apologize to the Commissioner?" Sue asked. "I never meant to be bad, and I'll tell Uncle Dennis how sorry I am."

"No, Sue," said Miss Vicky firmly. "The best thing you can do now is to keep absolutely quiet. Everybody has had as much as they can stand from you today. You are to stay up here in my room for the rest of the afternoon and not leave it."

"Yes, Miss Vicky," murmured Sue meekly.

"Mother holds a reception each year after the Gymkhana," Miss Vicky continued, "and with everyone so indignant over what you've done, Sue, it is best that you're out of sight. If I were you, I'd try and have a nap."

After her clothes were changed Sue was left to herself. She was much too unhappy for any nap and the sound of carriages arriving and of voices downstairs drew her to the window, where she watched all the notables arrive. The Lieutenant Governor and his wife and aides, the Bishop of Saskatchewan and Calgary, Mrs. Gordon, who had the largest house in Regina, the

Premier of the North West Territories, and at last the Force, swinging in through the gates. The Commissioner and Uncle Dennis dismounted and crossed the Parade together, and as they came up the path the Commissioner seemed to be as angry as her uncle was anxious.

Sue felt that she must see the Commissioner herself and tell him exactly what had happened. When he understood and knew how really sorry she was, all would be well again, she felt sure, for the Commissioner was always fair, even if he did become so angry at times. Opening the bedroom door and leaning out over the banisters, she listened. She could hear the Commissioner thanking people and acknowledging congratulations on the success of the Gymkhana, and Mrs. Walsh protesting when he told her he couldn't stay.

"But, John," Sue heard her say, "you can't leave our guests."

"I'm sorry, Eliza," he answered crisply, "you'll have to manage without me. I have to go back to the office. Dennis and I have something to talk over."

"My goodness," said Sue to herself. "This *is* bad." She started down the back stairs and managed to escape through the side door without being seen by anyone.

Entering the office at H.Q., she told the constable on duty that she wanted to see the Commissioner.

He shook his head. "You're not supposed to be in here, baby. I couldn't even tell him you are waiting."

"I'm not a baby," answered Sue stormily, "and I'm going to wait until I see him. I've disgraced the Force and I've got to apologize."

"You've disgraced the Force?" repeated the constable. "How?"

"I ran out and marched with the band in the review."

"My word!" exclaimed the constable. "Why, the old man will skin you alive for that."

"Not if I apologize?" Sue asked.

The constable shook his head doubtfully. "You can't tell. It might help. You'd better sit over there and wait."

"Will he be long?" she asked.

"I can't say. He's in there with Captain Lyons and he has some letters to sign before the mail cart leaves for the station. You'd better sit down. I'll call you when he's free."

Sue sat down on a long bench outside of the Commissioner's door. She wished now that she'd thought a bit before she grabbed Smith's coat. She wished she had stayed upstairs in Miss Vicky's room, but most of all she wished that she had her apology over. She hoped the Commissioner wouldn't be very angry. Sue felt very small and unimportant.

But there were sounds in the office. A chair was pushed back and there was the jangle of spurred boots. The constable heard them, too. A buzzer rang. "Here's where you catch it," he said cheerfully. "Shall I tell him you're here, now?"

"No, thank you," Sue replied. "I'll go in myself."

Lifting her hand to knock, she heard the Commissioner's voice as clearly as if she were in the room with him. "It's no use, Lyons," he was saying. "This little niece of yours is undisciplined, disobedient and a hopeless little showoff . . . and she's getting worse. Look at her behavior this afternoon. It was outrageous, and you know it . . ."

Sue's hand dropped from the knocker. Her uncle was speaking now, pleading for her. "She is so young, sir. I know she's badly behaved, but I'll see to it that this does not happen again. . . . There is so little I can do. Her people are in India. I can't send her out to them."

The Commissioner interrupted. "I've listened to these excuses before, Lyons. I've heard you all pleading for her and Sue has promised to mend her ways time and time again. She only gets worse. She came here, didn't she, with that helpless nurse? Well, then, she can leave the same way. Ship her back to Montreal, put her in a school or a convent until you can send her to her people. . . ."

"Sir, I beg of you," her uncle began, but once more the Commissioner interrupted, and this time he spoke so slowly that Sue knew some awful thing was coming.

"Lyons, this is no longer a request. This is an order. That child has to go. I no longer want her here."

"I'm not wanted," said Sue to herself, and again as if she couldn't believe it, "I'm not wanted."

She turned from the door. Everything seemed blurred and queer in front of her, and her throat hurt. Outside on the steps she stood still, wondering what to do, where to go in this strange world that no longer wanted her.

"Sue!" It was Miss Vicky's voice from the verandah. "Sue, where have you been?" Michael and John were with her. Sue didn't answer. She couldn't.

Miss Vicky ran down the steps. "Come here, Sue, what's the matter? What's happened?"

The tears spilled over, but Sue couldn't help it. "I've got to go away," she said. "I'm no longer wanted."

Miss Vicky bent over her, and while Michael mopped up her tears with his handkerchief, Sue told of the Commissioner's decision. "I won't let you go, sweetness," said Miss Vicky, all sternness gone now. "I'm going straight to Father!"

"It's no use, Vicky," said Uncle Dennis, coming out of the office in time to hear her words. "The Commissioner's decision is final," and with an arm around Sue's shoulders he led her out across the garden and home. "You'd better go upstairs and get ready for supper, Sue," he said gently, as they came in.

Without a word Sue went upstairs, but at the turn of the stair she heard him talking to Matilda. "I want you to get Miss Sue's things washed and ironed and in complete order. You'll be going east as soon as she is ready."

If he'd only scolded her, she could have stood it all better, thought Sue, as she remembered that her uncle had not said one cross, unkind word to her. Her habit was lying on the bed, and suddenly she realized that she was going away from all this loveliness, from Beppo and Monty and Smith, from Mrs. Schofield and Michael, that she would never get up again to Reveille, never go to bed with the notes of the Last Post in her ears.

She flung herself down on the bed. "I can't bear it," she whispered brokenly, over and over. But no one came up to her room, not even the kindly John. Sue didn't know that Matilda was in tears in the kitchen and that John and Michael were trying to persuade Uncle Dennis to go and see the Commissioner again. "Not wanted"—the words turned over and over in her mind. Not wanted by anyone.

Sue looked at her habit again, with its golden crest on the shoulder. *"Maintiens le Droit!"* Well, she hadn't maintained the right, but touching it reminded her of the night Monty had given it to her, of Beppo and Laughing Cloud and Little Chief. Sue's tears stopped, and a look of determination crossed her face. Moving quickly, she pulled off her dress and buttoned herself into her habit. The golden crest on her shoulder stared at her from the mirror. Holding back a sob, she unpinned it and placed it on the bulletin board.

Then picking up Minnie-Pooh-Pooh, she opened the door softly and, hearing no sounds, crept down the stairs, out the door and across the back way to the stables. Smith was away at his supper. There was no one to watch her; her saddle hadn't even been taken off Beppo.

Slipping the bridle over Beppo's head, Sue scrambled up on his back and, holding Minnie-Pooh-Pooh as she had seen the constable hold Little Badger, started out across the prairies.

17. Man Wanted

"Miss Sue," called Matilda from the foot of the stairs. "Miss Sue!"

There was no answer, and thinking Sue might be asleep, Matilda opened the bedroom door very gently. But there was no one on the bed and no sign of Sue, except a heap of clothes upon the floor.

"Now don't get yourself worked up," said Mrs. Schofield when Matilda rushed into the kitchen. "Miss Sue has climbed into her habit before this. You'll find she's with Beppo. Wait until Mr. Monty comes in, he'll go fetch her for you."

But it was Michael who came home first, and the news disturbed him. "I don't like it," he said. "There's no telling what she might do after all that's happened to her this afternoon. Where's Monty?"

Monty and John came in together and were equally disturbed. "Does the captain know?" asked Monty. Mrs. Schofield shook her head.

"I think I'll go over to the stable and see where Beppo is," Monty said, "and while I'm gone, it might be a good plan to get hold of the captain."

It seemed a long time before he returned. He shook his head as he entered the hall. "Beppo is gone," he said, "but I think I know where Sue is. I've got a horse outside and I'll go and look for her. Don't worry. I'll probably bring her back with me. Have you found Captain Lyons?"

"Yes, he was in Regina," said John Hogarth. "He's on his way back now. We telephoned the Guard House, but Sue didn't go through the gates and she hasn't been seen on the road to town."

The sunset light was almost gone as Monty rode along the trail to Laughing Cloud's camp. The old chief and six young braves had just returned from the Gymkhana and were taking the bridles off their horses. The camp was almost deserted. The wild horses had all been sold, and the squaws and their children had left for Qu'Appelle right after the Gymkhana. Four tepees, two wagons, the missionary's tent and a pile of poles were all that was left of the big Indian encampment. Monty told Laughing Cloud of his worry and asked him if he had seen Miss Sue.

"Not since she marched with the band," replied Laughing Cloud.

"Little Golden Hawk lost?" asked Little Chief.

"Well, not lost," answered Monty, "but, for the moment, missing."

Wheeling his horse, he rode rapidly back to the stables, only to find Beppo riderless in his stall but still saddled and bridled. Smith and he held a hasty conference and agreed that Beppo had been ridden. Monty's horse went around the Parade faster than it had ever been ridden before. Jumping off, he ran into the little study in Bachelor Hall where the group of anxious officers were waiting.

"I think you had better advise the Commissioner, sir," said

Monty, after telling of his ride. "It will need a general alarm to find a child on the prairies after dark."

But the Commissioner was dining at Government House and it took a little while to reach him on the telephone. Uncle Dennis reported Sue's disappearance.

"I'll be back at once," said the Commissioner. "Meanwhile, turn out enough men to scour the immediate country thoroughly." Before the Commissioner returned with Vicky, mounted men were riding hard, trying to make use of the last few rays of daylight.

Miss Vicky was in tears by the time the little group of officers and friends gathered in the Commissioner's office. "I don't think you have anything to worry over, really, Lyons," said the Commissioner. "After all, nothing very serious can happen to her on the prairie."

"But you don't understand, Father," said Miss Vicky. "The poor little thing was heartbroken over your order to send her away. She may have done anything, gone anywhere, climbed aboard a freight car . . ." Miss Vicky wept again.

But the Commissioner wasn't listening. He was busy putting the whole Force in motion. Orderlies were dashing to and fro, commands being given, bugles sounding. "Is there anything else, Lyons?" he asked, "that you can suggest."

"Yes, sir," the Captain replied. "I should like to enlist Laughing Cloud's help. He has six young braves there and all of them know Sue and like her. They know every Indian encampment within thirty miles of here. If they'll search for her, too, I feel it would be a help."

"An excellent idea," said the Commissioner. "How about sending your own batman to them?" and he looked over at Monty.

Monty saluted. "I should like nothing better," he said, and in a moment was on his horse and riding back to the Indian camp.

The camp was a peaceful place. Around the fire the seven Indians sat, with Little Chief wide-eyed beside his father. The horses were hobbled nearby, and the flames cast long shadows on the tepees. The Indians started to their feet as Monty rode in and listened with anxiety to the tale he told.

"Too bad. Too bad," they said. "Little Golden Hawk flies fast, but we move like wind. Tell the Chief of the Shamoganis we will bring her back." And rapidly Laughing Cloud gave his orders. The six braves were to ride to the nearby Indian camps. If they found Little Golden Hawk they were to ride to the Barracks with her. If they didn't find her, they were to ride to the Barracks anyway and report.

"If she is found," Laughing Cloud said, "we will rejoice with the Great Chief. If she is lost, we will take council together and go out again."

Bidding Little Chief stay on guard, Laughing Cloud and Monty returned to the Barracks, while the braves started out in different directions.

Little Chief watched them disappear. In only a few minutes the sounds of the horses' feet died away, and nothing remained but the firelight dancing on the tepees and throwing long eerie shadows on the ground. In his pocket he found some sugar, and standing at the edge of the camp, whinnied softly. There was no answering sound, but quietly Natose nuzzled her head against him and with gentle lips found the boy's hands. There was the sharp crunch of sugar, and the contented huh, huh, huh of the petted pony.

The fire died down until only a flicker of light was left. Little

Chief sat there motionless, listening, watching. Suddenly he bent, and picking up a pan, scooped up a few glowing embers and slipped along the row of tepees until he came to the missionary's tent. Here, dumping the coals on the ashes of an old fire, he found some chips and boiled a pannikin of tea. Returning to the big tepee again he brought back some bread, sugar, a pot of jam. Arranging these in front of the tent, he drew back the flap and poked his head inside.

"All right. You come out now. Get tea. No one here."

There was a slight upheaval in one side of the tent, and then cautiously stealing out into the glow of the fire, sleepy, rumpled and tear-stained, came Sue.

"I slept so hard," she said, "and I feel so queer."

Little Chief nodded. "Lots of men come looking."

"I heard them," replied Sue.

"You still want to be an Indian?" inquired the boy.

She nodded emphatically. "But I'm *very* hungry."

"Yes," said Little Chief. "You get food. Have sleep. Go home tomorrow." And he poured her a mug of hot tea.

Sue shook her tousled head. "No, I won't go home. I'm not wanted."

Little Chief spread some jam on the bread and watched her quietly while she ate it and drank the strong sweet tea. She had ridden into the camp just as he returned from the Gymkhana ahead of all the others, and in a storm of tears told him of how she had no home. "I've come to be an Indian," she had cried. "I won't go away on a train, and they don't want me any longer."

Little Chief had been frightened. It was all very well to race with her, to tease her and help her catch gophers, but to keep her in the camp, to hide her as she suggested, was, he knew, very bad business. Any way Little Chief looked at it, the keeping of Sue Winston was a crime in the eyes of the Shamoganis and his tribe. Later he had explained this to her, and she had answered by getting off Beppo and giving him a smack on the side that sent the startled pony galloping toward the Barracks. "Now," Sue had said, "I'm here forever."

On top of that remark he had heard the braves returning. Little Chief had lost his head and pushed her into the missionary's tent, bidding her not even to breathe out loud. He didn't know which he was most frightened of—Sue, Laughing Cloud, or the Commissioner.

Sitting on his haunches in front of the dying fire, he wondered what he would do with her in the morning. Sue wondered about the morning, too, but only vaguely.

Little Chief poured her more tea and cut her another slice of bread. But as he reached across the fire to hand it to her, his arm froze and Sue saw that he was listening with the same intensity with which he watched for gophers. She started to speak, but he lifted his hand in warning. "SH!" he said, and then quickly, "someone coming. Get in there."

Swiftly he kicked earth across the fire and taking Sue by the shoulder, shoved her into the tent, pulled the flap across and again listened. Picking up the blanket Sue had been sitting on, he rolled himself in it and lay down before the tent door and pretended to be asleep.

Inside the tent, Sue lay on Jane's little cot and covered herself with blankets. She wondered what it had all been about, whether it was Monty coming back or whether there were bad Indians around, or whether Little Chief had heard anything at all. Sprawled in front of the tent, Little Chief wondered the

same thing. He was sure he had heard a man's low voice somewhere near, and yet there hadn't been a sound since.

A tiny flame burst through the earth he had kicked over the
fire, dimly lighting two shadowy figures crouching by the nearest tepee. One was a man of medium height, the other tall and
thin. Both carried rifles and both were shabby and travel-worn.
They began to argue in the broken English of the French Canadian.

"But where is the old Indian? You tole me he would have
money, and we must have money, my fren' . . ."

"Dat's all right," the short man answered. "The old Indian'll
be back. He's been selling horses and has plenty money."

But the tall man was nervous. "Let's go 'way," he said. "The
Red Coats are everywhere tonight. How do we know they
won't come back here?"

His companion laughed. "All right. Fix up that fire. We
make some tea, and then we go." But in lighting the fire, the
tall man came on Little Chief and kicked him awake.

Angrily he asked why the camp was empty, why the Red
Coats were on the prairies. Little Chief explained that all the
Indians were out hunting for a baby child that was lost from
the Barracks. The Shamoganis had come down and taken all
the braves away for the search.

The short man laughed. "Dat's what I tole you, ole scared-
face. See, the Red Coat won't be back tonight. We will eat,
sleep a bit, and go on early in the morning." He opened a small
bundle he was carrying and brought out bread and a bit of pemmican. Secure now in the thought that the police would not
be back that night, the two men stirred up the fire a bit, laid
their rifles at their sides and relaxed, ready to enjoy their meal.

Inside the tent, Sue wriggled off the cot, and crawling over to the entrance, raised a corner of the flap and watched the two men eat their meal. She couldn't see them very well in the shadows but she didn't like their looks. There was something frightening about them. They were very dirty and ate like hungry wolves, but their voices were soft and they spoke with the French Canadian accent she remembered in Montreal. She wished she could see them more clearly.

At that instant a leaping flame lit up both their faces. Sue thought she had seen one of them before; the shorter man. There was something about his face she remembered. She wondered where she had seen him. And then she knew! The short man had the same face that she had once decorated with moustaches. Although she could hardly believe it herself, it was Joe Labiche, wearing the very moustaches she had drawn on the picture in the "Men Wanted" book. Sue didn't know whether she would giggle or scream. She held her breath. For one awful moment she was afraid she was going to scream. There was Joe Labiche and back across the prairies at the Barracks he *was wanted*. Somehow she must get word to the Force.

Very carefully she slipped her hand under the tent and pulled the blanket that Little Chief had around him, ever so little. He made no sign. She pulled again. He nodded his head sleepily and Sue waited.

"You want something?" he asked the two men.

"No, we doan want a t'ing," the tall man answered.

"All right. I go sleep then," said Little Chief.

Sue heard him get up and move toward the back of the missionary's tent. Very cautiously she crawled over to the other side of her tent. Little Chief was there, lying flat on the ground with the back canvas raised enough for them to speak in whispers.

"Go get Monty," she said. "Those men are bad men. They are wanted by the Force. Run quickly."

But Little Chief refused. If they were bad men, then it was clear he should stay with her, and he told her so.

"No," said Sue, "I'll hide under the cot. I'll keep quiet. I won't move. These men are *wanted*. Little Chief, you must go."

"No," he answered. "My place is here."

"If you don't go," declared Sue, "I'll scream and scream and start awful trouble."

Little Chief knew her well enough to know that she was as good as her word, and that even one little scream would bring worse than trouble on them both. "All right," he whispered. "I go. I take Natose. You pretend sleep. I'll see Red Coat Monty."

Little Chief squirmed away and when she was sure he was gone, Sue crept back to the front of the tent and through the same hole in the flap watched the two men. Suddenly the tall man moved and lifted his rifle.

"By Joe, dat's funny. I thought I heard a horse."

His companion laughed. "All dat hiding on freight cars is on your nerves, my fren'. Look at your hand dere, how she shake. Dere was no horse." He laughed and rolled a cigarette.

Back at the Barracks the Sentry paced to and fro, wondering what could have happened to Sue. There was still much going and coming, but no one had reported news of her. From beyond the gates came the sound of thudding hooves. Someone was riding a horse almost beyond its strength. The Sentry

peered out. Without saddle or bridle, Natose dashed through
to the Guard House with Little Chief hanging onto his mane.

The Indian boy pulled up and asked for "Red Coat Monty."
He would give no explanation. He would talk to no one. He
wanted Red Coat Monty. The Sergeant took him over to Headquarters.

Monty came out and listened to him for a moment. "Why
didn't you tell me this before!" he demanded sharply. "I've
been at your camp twice. Why did you hide her?"

Little Chief shrugged his shoulders. "Little Golden Hawk
say the Shamoganis tired of her, she not wanted."

Monty stepped forward. "That was no excuse. How
DARED you hide her?"

But Little Chief was the son of Laughing Cloud. He was
engaged on a man's work and he would permit no one, not
even the Shamoganis, to rebuke him at such a moment. "Stay,"
he said, lifting his hand, "listen to what I, son of Laughing
Cloud, have to say."

Monty listened and without a word jumped on his horse.
"Ride my stirrup," he said. "How did you get here?"

"Pony by gate."

But Monty rode straight through the gate. "There'll be no
time to pick up your pony," he said. "We can't ride all the way
in or they'll hear us. We'll hobble my horse and creep up on
them."

Back at the camp, Sue watched the two men fearfully. They
smoked many cigarettes and drank more tea, but the tall one
was restless. "Joe, I t'ink we better move," he said, "and where's
that money you tole me Laughing Cloud would have?"

Labiche shrugged his shoulders. "No Laughing Cloud, no money," he said.

The tall man sneered. "How do you know the ole Chief will give it to you?" he said.

Labiche chuckled softly. "Ole Chief doan like me," he said, "but my brother married his niece. He pay me to go away. I know." And he chuckled again.

But the anxiety of the tall man was so great that Labiche finally agreed to move on. "Widout monie, we can't cross dat line into the States," he warned, "but we come back later if you wish. Three, four hours maybe. Perhaps that keep you quiet."

Sue caught her breath. If they left before Monty got back, the Force would lose a wanted man, a man they had waited two years to catch. That would be dreadful, but what frightened her even more was the sight of their guns. If they came upon Monty and Little Chief riding out to her they would shoot. She put her hands up to her eyes in terror. Into her mind the picture of the morning breakfast at Qu'Appelle returned. What was it the constable had said? "When you're in a jam, you've got to show a bold front. I bluffed them into thinking I wasn't scared and I won."

A moment later she pushed the flap of the tent aside and walked out into the firelight, rubbing her eyes as if she had just wakened.

"By Joe, look, a white kid! What she doing in dis place!"

Labiche laughed. "Doan you see that cross on dat tent? She's the Padre's little one, dat's what. Where's your papa, *ma petite?*"

"Gone away," answered Sue in a very small voice, for now that she faced the men, she was scared, dreadfully scared.

"Have you got anything to eat?" she continued. "I'm very hungry."

"Let's go," said the tall man, but Labiche sank back on the ground. "Well, now, maybe we can find somet'ing. Dere is some tea here and some bread and maybe wan leetle piece of pemmican. How would you like dat?"

"I'd like it very much," said Sue, accepting a tinful of tea and a hunk of bread.

Labiche looked at her. "By Joe, you are one pretty child," he said, "and your curls, dey are pretty, too."

"Are you French?" asked Sue, biting into the hard bread.

"Maybe, maybe not."

"Comment ça va?" said Sue.

"Well, by Joe, you speak French, eh?"

"I can sing in French, too," she answered, "and I can dance an Irish jig and sing the *Canadian Boat Song*." Sue sang but they didn't care much for the *Canadian Boat Song*, and the tall man kept urging Labiche to move on.

"So! Is dat all you can sing?" Labiche asked.

"No," said Sue, smiling at him. "If you are French, you can sing this one, too." And before either of them could speak, she began:

> "Alouette, Gentille Alouette
> Alouette, je te plumerai."

She saw at once that Labiche liked the song and when he marked time for her with his hand, she felt she might be able to keep them there until Monty came. When she looped up her habit and, putting her hands on her hips, both sang and danced the *Pretty Maid Milking Her Cow*, they laid their rifles down and, leaning forward, watched her with delight.

"Encore! Encore!" they laughed. She sang it again.

Sue wondered now if Monty would ever come. She was nearly at the end of her songs. The fire was dying out. Some carefully gathered birch bark lay in strips already cut for basket weaving. Throwing them on the coals, she made a mock curtsey, and as the flames burned high, started her last song.

> "Ta-ra-ra-ra BOOM-de-ay
> I saw someone YES-terday."

The blaze shone brightly on the men's faces and for the first time Sue saw how very evil they were.

"Ta-ra-ra-ra BOOM-de-ay" she sang on bravely, and lifting her head, looked out across the fire. In the shadows beyond the fire light, she could see the blur of a red coat and Monty's anxious face. "Sing," cried Sue, "SING with me."

"Ta-ra-ra-ra BOOM-de-ay" . . . and she danced from one side of the fire to the other, curtseying, gesturing as Michael had taught her. In the darkness she could just see Monty's arm, motioning her further away from the fire. Finally he waved her right away. As fast as she could run, Sue raced back into the darkness between the tepees.

At the Barracks a group of silent men sat in the Commissioner's office. Mrs. Walsh was in the corner, red-eyed and worn, with Miss Vicky beside her. It was long after midnight. The Indian runners were all in but one, and there was no word of Sue. Soft-moccasined feet ran past the window and in the outer room the heavy breathing of an excited Indian could be heard.

"Bring him in," ordered the Commissioner. Rapidly the interpreter questioned the young brave. Coming in, he had just seen against the sky the figure of a constable riding slowly toward the Barracks with a child before him on his horse. Behind him walked a boy; in front of him two men.

"It's Monty," cried Vicky. "He's found her!"

"Not so fast, my dear," said the Commissioner. "We don't want any false hopes raised now. This is a large party. A boy, two men, a constable and a child on horse back. That might mean anything."

"Oh, Father, never mind!" begged Vicky. "Let's go and see." And she ran out across the Parade. Worn with watching and glad of any break in their anxious waiting, they all followed.

Just as they came opposite the Guard House, the Sentry's challenge rang out. "Who goes there?"

"Constable Montague and party," was the reply, as Monty rode through the gates and up to the Guard House. Before him in the saddle sat Sue, almost asleep, and in front marched two prisoners. Behind him strode Little Chief.

Monty saluted. "Two prisoners to book, Sergeant," he said.

The sergeant returned his salute.

"Name of prisoners?" he asked.

"Pierre Duval and Joe Labiche!"

For one breathless second the sergeant paused. He took another look at the prisoners. "Great snakes!" he said. "It IS. It's JOE LABICHE." And then in his most official voice: "Name of Constable booking prisoners?"

Monty paused a moment.

"Susannah Elizabeth Fairfield Winston," he answered, in a ringing voice. Lifting Sue, he held her out to the Commissioner's waiting arms.

18. The Red Coat

Through the window a long shaft of sunlight turned to brighter gold the crest on the top of the bulletin board at the foot of Sue's bed. She stirred sleepily, yawned and stretched. She couldn't quite remember what was going to happen today, except that it was something pleasant. Last night so much had happened that it was all a blur. What *HAD* happened? Lying there in the sleepy, shadowy warmth, she tried again to remember, but it was too confused. All she was sure of was that everyone liked her very much. Burrowing her head into the pillow she slept again.

"Miss Sue!" The room was lighter. It must be Matilda calling. Sue wriggled her toes and drew the covers up further.

"MISS SUE!"

Sue heard Matilda drawing the curtains, and then her voice close beside her. "Look, Miss Sue."

Sue opened her eyes. Matilda held Minnie-Pooh-Pooh in her hands. "Little Chief just brought this to you," she said. "You left her behind you in the tent last night."

"Oh, Matilda—thank you. Wasn't that nice of Little Chief?" cried Sue, giving Minnie-Pooh-Pooh a hug. "I remember everything now. *Wasn't* it an adventure?"

"An adventure for all of us," answered Matilda. "But the

219

captain says you're to get up now and come and have breakfast
with him in your dressing gown."

Sue hopped out of bed. Breakfast in her dressing gown was
always a treat and, as if Matilda understood, there wasn't too
much bother about washing. Her uncle, John and Michael
were waiting for her in the dining room. Everyone seemed very
gay and happy. When Sue heaped brown sugar on her oatmeal
and drowned it with cream, no one seemed to notice, although
usually Uncle Dennis was very crabby over too much sugar.

Before breakfast was over, Monty came in with a letter.
Uncle Dennis read it and handed it back to him. "Read that,"
he said, "and act upon its contents."

"Yes, sir," said Monty, smiling.

"At half past ten, Sue," her uncle continued, "you and Monty
are to go to the Commissioner's office together. He is very proud
of your actions last night and wants to tell you so himself."

Sue wasn't so sure that she wanted to go to the Commissioner's office, but she thought she had better not disturb the
pleasant atmosphere around her by starting any argument.
And anyway Monty would be with her.

"Yes, Uncle Dennis," she said meekly.

"And we'll cut inspection this morning," he continued, "but
you'd better go up to Matilda now, so that she'll have you nice
and tidy when Monty calls for you."

"By the time you're bathed," Matilda said, as she brushed
Sue's hair one hundred strokes, "your habit will be back from
the tailor's for you to wear. I sent it over before you were awake
this morning to get it cleaned and pressed. It was very soiled
and crumpled."

Before they left for the Commissioner's office, Mrs. Schofield
and Matilda inspected both Monty and Sue and found them

perfect. Sue agreed. "I can see my face in your boots, Monty," she said, "and if my boots were big enough, you could see yourself in mine, too."

The constable in the outer office of H.Q. said immediately, "The Commissioner is waiting for you, Miss Sue," and opened the door.

Monty gave her a little push and she marched in ahead of him. The Commissioner was seated at his desk, but he stood up at once. Uncle Dennis was standing beside him. Sue returned their salutes.

"Come over here, Sue," said the Commissioner. "I want to tell you how proud we were last night of your bravery and how much we admire the way you kept your head in the face of danger."

He spoke very slowly and took Sue on his knee. "You and I haven't understood each other, Sue," he continued, "as well as we should have. I thought you were only a mischievous little girl and therefore a nuisance. Last night I found I was wrong. I realize now that it was your admiration for the Force that led you to do many of the things I thought only mischievous. When the chance came to do something worth while, you did it, and the Force is very proud of you."

Sue thought this all sounded very grand. The Commissioner went on, "Yesterday you overheard me say you were not wanted. I was wrong, Sue. You *are* wanted."

"Oh, Commissioner," cried Sue, "I do love you," and flinging her arms around his neck, kissed him soundly on the cheek. Behind her she could hear happy laughter, and disentangling herself, saw Miss Vicky and Mrs. Walsh in the door.

"Have you told her, Father?" asked Miss Vicky. He shook his head.

"Told me what?" asked Sue.

"Shut your eyes, Sue," Miss Vicky replied. "I've got a surprise for you." She had her hands behind her back. "Are they tight shut?" asked Miss Vicky.

"Tight," answered Sue. What could they be doing, she wondered. They had unbuttoned her jacket and were taking it off. That was more than she could bear.

"What are you doing?" she asked, opening her eyes the tiniest bit. In front of her, over Monty's arm, was a red coat, and by its size Sue knew it was for her.

"Oh," said Sue, opening her eyes wide. "Oh!"

"Oh!" said the Commissioner in his deep voice.

"Oh!" said Uncle Dennis in a deeper voice.

"Oh! Oh! Oh!" said everybody, in every kind of a voice.

The Commissioner took the red coat and held it out. Sue slipped her arms into it, and Uncle Dennis buttoned it. It had brass buttons on it, like those on Monty's tunic, and the tailor had stayed up all night to make it. And it was red, gloriously, beautifully, triumphantly red.

"How does it look?" asked Sue, who was so happy she felt she might burst.

"Grand," said Uncle Dennis. "But come along, Sue. You and I have something else to do with the Commissioner."

They followed him through the outer office. The young constable was standing at the salute as they passed. Sue stopped. She had no pill-box, and the constable had. She couldn't go out of doors without a pill-box, too, she felt. Her uniform wouldn't be complete.

"PLEASE, will you lend me your pill-box?" she asked. The young constable looked nervously at the Commissioner who nodded approval. And with the pill-box crowded down on her curls, Sue marched out of the office.

But the glories of the morning were not ended. There beside the Commissioner's horse stood another almost as large and with Sue's saddle on his back. The Commissioner mounted, and they lifted Sue to the other horse. In spite of her red jacket, she felt a bit frightened, for on Beppo she was so near the ground and on this horse so far away from it.

Monty was very comforting. "Don't be frightened," he whispered, as he put the reins between her fingers. "You ride this horse just the same way you do Beppo, but more slowly."

They started out, Sue beside the Commissioner; on his right, Uncle Dennis, and behind Sue and to her left, Monty. Slowly they started off around the Parade. There seemed to be an extra lot of Red Coats about, but Sue was too busy managing her horse to pay much attention. "Riding a big horse is a bumpier business than riding a little one," she told the Commissioner. He smiled at her and then turned into the Parade Ground where Little Chief joined them.

"My goodness," said Sue, for the entire Parade was lined with red-coated police and the band burst into the *British Grenadiers* as they slowly rode past them. Everyone was smiling, and when the music stopped, the Commissioner made a speech. Sue tried to listen, but she felt so uncertain on the big horse that she couldn't pay much attention to anything but sticking on. The Commissioner's words came dimly to her; something about:

". . . by her courage and resourcefulness brought us a criminal long wanted by the Force. . . . We are grateful, too, for the bravery of Little Chief, son of Laughing Cloud . . . and Constable Montague. . . ."

Across the Parade, Sue could see Sergeant Whiteside. As the Commissioner's voice ceased, the sergeant stepped forward. "Three cheers for Miss Sue," he cried. Everybody cheered then and the horses jangled their bits and stamped their feet, and then, wonder of wonders, all the men threw their pill-boxes in the air. Taking her horse's rein, Smith led Sue along in the centre of the Parade. The ranks broke then, and they all crowded around her in a swirl of red coats.

"Thank you! Thank you!" cried Sue. "Thank you all a million times!" and added, "I'll be a very good Mountie!" There were more cheers as she left the Parade and Monty carried her shoulder high into Bachelor Hall.

There she found all her friends, as well as the Lieutenant Governor and his wife, and Bishop Grisdale of Indian Head, who happened to be in Regina for the day. There was chicken and salad and trifle and wine jelly, and little sponge cakes and coffee; and no one sat down, but just held their plates in the left hand and used a fork only. This, Sue found, was what was called a buffet luncheon and she liked it much better than any other kind. They drank her health, too, and made her little speeches, and when they all left Uncle Dennis poured sherry into glasses on a tray and had her carry it out to the kitchen where he thanked Mrs. Schofield for an "excellent luncheon" and they in turn lifted their glasses and wished "the captain, and yourself, Miss Sue, long life and happiness."

"And now, Susannah," said her uncle, "let's go into the study. We have a lot of planning to do." He spread a map out on his desk before him. "This," he said, pointing, "is Regina and from here we have to go to London next May with our Jubilee Contingent."

Sue watched him draw a line from Regina across the map to Quebec where, he explained, they would go aboard a ship and cross the ocean to Southampton, in England, and from there take trains to London.

"And I'll be with you all the way?" Sue asked.

"All the way," he answered. "But, Sue, I don't speak French very well and in Quebec one needs French. Do you think you could learn to speak French this winter if I found someone to teach you? Then you could act as an interpreter for me."

"Like Mr. Holmes does for the Indians?" asked Sue.

"Yes," her uncle answered, "and besides French, Sue, I think you should get on with your reading and writing. Sergeant Whiteside's wife was a school teacher in eastern Canada, and I think we could get her to come in to you for a couple of hours every day. How's that?"

She remembered the Sergeant's wife. She had sent her toffee once when she was going on a picnic. "She's very jolly," said Sue, "I'd like her."

"You see, Sue," her uncle continued. "Now that you have been accepted and honored by the Commissioner and the Force as you have been today, you'll have to work hard. If you find things that you don't understand, come and tell me. Is that a bargain?"

"Yes," said Sue, and they shook hands on it.

But even then the day of great adventure was not at an end. That night Sue, for the first time, saw the Northern Lights. Silvery green, pale rose and mauve, they flashed and crackled across the sky, lighting the great dome overhead with shimmering color and bathing the ground and buildings in a strange soft light.

A few days later sunflowers turned the prairies into drifts of gold before they faded and died. The long grasses were bluish grey and the Indian camps vanished to the foothills for winter shelter. A smoky haze was in the air, a tingle of cold.

"It's Indian summer," said Michael, "and there are wild ducks and prairie chickens down by Pile O' Bones Creek."

19. Winter

Sue found that preparation for winter in the prairies was a serious matter. Prairie chickens, wild ducks and geese were brought in and hung in long rows in a little storehouse; choice portions of beef and pork, two sheep, domestic chickens and half a dozen turkeys were added, and butter in great crocks. It was so cold now that everything in the storehouse was frozen stiff. Double windows were put on and earth banked around the foundations of the house. Two large barrels were brought into the kitchen.

"They're for snow," Mrs. Schofield told Sue. "Sometimes in the winter the well doesn't give enough water for laundry purposes. Then we fill these barrels with snow and when it melts, we have the loveliest soft water in the world."

One night when Uncle Dennis came in, he stamped his feet and shivered, "There's a smell of snow in the air," he said, "and the glass is falling. We'll have a blizzard before morning."

When Sue awoke the next day, the world was white with snow and remained white until the end of March.

New clothes came from Winnipeg, from the Hudson Bay Company. A navy blue coat for Sue with hood lined with scarlet, and a scarlet sash and toque to wear with it. The toque

had a bobbly woolen tassel on top and was worn pulled low down on the forehead, Mrs. Schofield explained, so that her ears wouldn't freeze. And there were felt boots with mother-of-pearl buttons, and white and blue cashmere dresses, and woolen stockings and underwear, mittens and scarves.

One day the Commissioner came with Miss Vicky and gave her a sleigh and two Irish setters. "I thought you'd miss your riding, Sue," he said, "so I've brought you these dogs, Rocket and Romper. Smith will show you how to drive them."

Sue thought them the most perfect dogs in the world, dark russet red, with long soft ears and brown eyes. They were gay, restless dogs, and their grooming was Sue's special care. Every day they had to be brushed and combed and then wiped down with an old piece of velvet. Mrs. Schofield gave her the velvet.

"It's a bit of my Mother's best black velvet dress," she said. "She wore it for forty years that I remember and even yet it's good. There's nothing like a bit of velvet for gloss," she added, "whether it's furniture or silver, or dogs' coats." Mrs. Schofield was such an interesting woman, Sue thought. She knew so many different ways of keeping things nice that you never tired of listening to her.

Rocket was the largest and strongest dog of the two and Romper the prettiest, with a large white ·star on his chest. He was the lead dog in the tandem and to see him trotting toward you over the snow with tail and ears flying in the wind was thrilling. Smith showed her how to put on the black leather harness, and how to sit on the red, white and blue sleigh with its high curved front, later how to kneel in the sleigh and drive, and finally how to stand with moccasined feet wide apart and keep her balance with the cold wind rushing against her face.

Each morning when her lessons were over, she would harness

the two dogs and drive Mrs. Whiteside home over the hard white prairie snow. The runners of the sleigh were like sharp skates, the dogs strong, and with black harness outlined against their dark red coats, tails waving and Sue shouting, they often raced the mail sleigh home. The mail sleigh was full of buffalo robes, and the two constables driving it almost looked like buffaloes themselves, they were so covered with fur coats and caps and felt boots and fur gauntlets. The mail ponies grew thick coats and their eyelashes were frosty and little icicles hung from their soft lips.

But of all her lessons, it was French that Sue liked best of all. Miss Vicky was her teacher, and Monty used to help her. Verbs with these two laughing, gay people were great fun. Sometimes she thought they were teaching each other French. They used to forget about her almost altogether, but she had Rocket and Romper to talk to and didn't care.

Mrs. Schofield, too, had many mysterious things to do in the winter time. There was beef to spice, and that in itself was a business. Every day at two o'clock, you went down with a candle into the cellar, and taking a large piece of beef out of a crock, rubbed both sides of it with a powder smelling of rich spices and peppers that made you sneeze. Mrs. Schofield's hand was large and red and she could wallop the beef grandly, but after watching Sue imitate her a couple of times, she told her she had an equally good hand at walloping, and they lifted the beef back in the crock again until the next day. It was to be cooked just before Christmas and was called "Spiced Christmas Beef—Grandmother's Recipe."

Afterward there were the raisins to stone for the plum puddings. Wrapped up in a large apron, Sue didn't mind staying in at all when the weather was stormy as long as she could sit on a high stool at the kitchen table and stone raisins and blanch almonds, and nibble at both when no one was looking.

Christmas Eve they all hung their stockings around the fireplace. Sue had to lend the three men stockings, for their socks would never hold enough, she told them. She was right, for when Michael came bouncing into her room on Christmas morning and carried her downstairs with the two dogs barking and John at the piano playing and singing *God Rest You Merrie Gentlemen* the stockings were all full of knobby bundles. In the centre of the drawing-room floor was an enormous wooden box addressed to Miss Sue Winston, and inside, on top of the silver paper, was a card, "For our darling Sue, from Mommy and Daddy."

Inside the box, Sue thought, there was everything wonderful in the world, with a little card on each parcel. A silk dressing gown for Uncle Dennis, smoking jackets of brocade for Michael and John, dress lengths of silk, blue and rose, for Mrs. Schofield and Matilda, an exquisitely carved ivory fan for Miss Vicky and one of peacock feathers for Mrs. Walsh, cuff links for the Commissioner. And scarfs and sandalwood boxes and little bottles of perfume, and small jewel boxes of filigree silver and turquoise. Jangling bangles of silver for Miss Vicky's pretty arms; a long chain of blue turquoise matrix for Mrs. Whiteside. In a little box among Sue's own presents, which were on the bottom layer, there was a really lovely little silver frame. Across it a card read "For Monty, with the ever grateful thanks of Sue's Mother." Sue lifted the paper. "Uncle Dennis, look," she said. "It's a picture of me."

"Yes," Uncle Dennis said, "it's what is called a miniature, Sue, and it's one your clever father did before he went to India. I'm glad he sent it to Monty."

For Sue there was a white silk dress, a little dressing gown of palest yellow crepe, a lovely shawl with a deep fringe, puzzles and games, a set of jewelry for Madame La Tour, a frock of blue for Jane, and then from the last box, Sue drew a doll of India. She was about the size of Minnie-Pooh-Pooh, and was elegantly dressed in golden silk, with a veil over her head and with many necklaces and bangles. She was Princess Sunda Singh.

When Monty came, he found them still in their dressing gowns, having a leisurely breakfast. He was delighted with his gift and helped tidy things away, for "After church," said Uncle Dennis, "we'll ask everyone to come in and collect their presents."

Shortly afterwards, over the snow covered Parade, the entire household went to church. The little Chapel was crowded to the doors, and when they all stood up and sang, *Hark, the Herald Angels Sing,* Sue felt that this was a perfect Christmas.

All day long, at Bachelor Hall, people came and went, and there was Christmas dinner at the Commissioner's house. It was the first time that Sue had ever been allowed to stay up for a late dinner and she wondered if all late dinners could be as nice. There were decorations of holly and mistletoe and in the dining room the·red curtains were drawn; extra leaves had been added to the table until it almost filled the room. Red and gold china and much sparkling glass held fruit and nuts and there were candles in silver holders, deep red wine in glasses.

The room was full of people in evening clothes—Miss Vicky, in white, wearing red roses, and Mrs. Walsh, gorgeous in violet silk, with lace and passementerie trimming. There were others too—a pretty woman in geranium pink, a vivacious one in black who kept everyone around her laughing. But it was the Force that delighted Sue the most. The officers wore short red scarlet mess jackets with gold lace, long blue trousers and shining silver spurs, and when they went in to dinner each man offered a lady his arm, just as she had been taught at dancing school in Montreal when she danced Sir Roger de Coverly.

The turkey was wonderful and the plum pudding even better, but for Sue the high point of the dinner was when the table was cleared and only the candles on the sideboard left alight. Then Dawson carried in a silver platter heaped high with raisins. The Commissioner pured brandy over them; a place was cleared in the centre of the table and the brandy lit. A blue flame ran across the platter and everyone stood up and, leaning across the table, snatched at the raisins.

Sue found she had the fastest fingers and soon had more raisins on her plate than anyone else. You didn't really burn your fingers she found, if you were quick. It only just made you feel you might, and that was why it was so exciting a game. Uncle Monty explained it was called Snap Dragon and was only played on Christmas night.

After the New Year, there were lessons again and long sleigh rides over the snow, deeper now, with blue shadows where the sun touched the drifts.

St. Valentine's Day came, and Sue took her valentines across to show them to Miss Vicky. She found her in the Commissioner's study, opening a huge box. Around it were two kinds of brown paper and then thick wads of newspapers, cotton batting and waxed paper. "So many papers," said Sue, "will they ever end?" Miss Vicky wondered, too. But finally they came to a box covered with white moiré paper and inscribed in gilt letters, "To my Valentine."

Inside was an armful of red roses, but there was no card tell-

ing who had sent them. Miss Vicky shook out every piece of
paper and separated each rose, but still there was no card. Bury-
ing her face in the roses, she said, "Never mind, Sue, just tidy
the papers while I put the flowers in water."

Sue picked up all the papers and rolled the string around her
fingers. She wanted some stout string to mend Romper's
harness, and this was just right. Rummaging for more, she
found a card with a man's writing on it:

> "I could not love thee, dear, so much
> Loved I not honour more . . ."

She put the card in her pocket, meaning to give it to Miss Vicky,
and then forgot it until it tumbled out on the floor as she was
undressing.

Uncle Dennis was giving a dinner party that night and Miss
Vicky would be there. Running downstairs, she found Monty
and her uncle in the study.

"Look, Uncle Dennis," she said, holding out the card. "I
found this with Miss Vicky's flowers and forgot it. Will you
give it to her when she comes tonight?" She looked at the card
again. "Why, Monty," she exclaimed, "it's your handwriting!
Did you send Miss Vicky the flowers?"

Monty looked very angry, and Uncle Dennis stood up. "Perhaps you'd like to talk to Sue alone for a moment," he said.

But before Monty had finished explaining that messages
written on cards were personal and therefore never read by
people for whom they were not intended, Uncle Dennis had
opened the door again. "Susannah is in here, waiting to say
good night to you," he said, and Miss Vicky came in, lovely in a
soft blue dress. There were red roses in her hair, red roses at
her breast. Sue had never seen her look so lovely. But neither

Monty nor Miss Vicky spoke. They just stood looking at each other.

Sue touched Miss Vicky's hand. "Look," she said. "I found this card after you'd gone this afternoon. I was just giving it to Uncle Dennis to give to you."

"Read it," said Miss Vicky. Slowly Sue read the words out loud:

> "I could not love thee, dear, so much,
>   Loved I not honour more . . ."

"What's it mean?" she asked Monty.

"Long ago, Sue," said Monty, speaking very slowly, "an English poet wrote those words to the lady he loved because he hadn't any money and couldn't ask her to marry him. You see, it's always been considered rather dishonorable to ask a woman to marry you if you can't afford to take good care of her, which is why he says, 'loved I not honour more.' Understand?"

"I think so," said Sue, doubtfully, "but if I loved anyone I'd tell them so, money or no money."

"I would, too," said Miss Vicky.

She loosened a rose and held it out to Monty, who took it for all the world as if one red rose were a jewelled crown. "I knew you sent them," said Miss Vicky. "I didn't need the card."

"Then why did you bother so much hunting for it?" asked Sue. Sometimes she wondered if she would ever understand grownups and their strange way of saying one thing and meaning just the opposite.

20. Strange Letters

Sue," said the Commissioner. "I have a mystery here and I need your help." He leaned across the desk. "The English mail arrived this morning and there is a letter from a firm of lawyers in London asking about a man called James Douglas. Have you ever known anyone by the name of Douglas, Sue?"

Sue shook her head. "I don't think so. Where does he live?"

"That's the point," answered the Commissioner. "No one seems to know where he lives."

"Is he a 'Man Wanted'?" asked Sue. She and the Commissioner were very good friends now and she felt the importance of being called to his office to help him.

"No," he answered. "He's not another Labiche. This man Douglas is wanted for something very nice."

The Commissioner picked up the sheaf of papers lying on his desk. "The London lawyers are trying to find the whereabouts of the Earl of Falkney and Dunleith. It seems that the new Earl, Sue, is a bad boy. He ran away from home at the age of twenty-one and they traced him as far as India. After that, he vanished completely until three years ago, when they got word that he had been in Japan. Again he disappeared. Now, it seems, someone has seen him in Canada. They don't want to advertise for him and admit they know nothing about him, so they have written asking me whether he is in the Force."

"Perhaps he is," said Sue. "Wouldn't it be exciting to have a real Earl in the Force?"

"Yes, but he's only been an earl for the past six months," said the Commissioner, "and probably doesn't know a thing about it."

"Why did you think I could help?" asked Sue.

"It seemed to me, Sue, that you once told me of a man in the Force who had an aunt in Scotland. Now this man Douglas has an aunt and Falkney and Dunleith is a Scottish title."

Sue thought for a moment. "Hasn't he any more names than just James Douglas?"

"That's all," answered the Commissioner.

Sue asked another question. "Well, doesn't it give his aunt's name?"

"I think it does," said the Commissioner, looking again at the letter. "Yes—her name is Lady Charlotte Dawkins."

"Monty has an Aunt Charlotte," said Sue, thoughtfully, and suddenly she remembered something else: the day on the train coming to Regina and Monty telling her all his names. She didn't remember them at all clearly now but she was sure some had sounded like "James Douglas."

"It's MONTY," she shouted. "That's who it is, MONTY!"

"Are you positive, Sue?" asked the Commissioner.

Sue nodded her head and explained to the Commissioner how she and Monty had told each other their names on the train.

"But that was almost a year ago, Sue."

"Yes, but he's often told me about his home in Scotland," went on Sue, "and how bad he was when he was a little boy and how his Aunt Charlotte wouldn't give him any pocket money and so he ran away and joined the Force."

The Commissioner sat looking at Sue for a long time. "Do you know anything more about him?" he asked.

"Well," said Sue, "he must have been in India, for at Christmas time he showed me how to put the veil back on Princess Sunda Singh when I'd taken it off to see how her hair was fixed." She paused for an instant. "He never gets any letters," she added.

"How do you know?" asked the Commissioner.

"I know, because he told me it must be nice to have a letter from your family every week, like I get from Mummy."

"Well, Sue, I don't like questioning the men of the Force. It is not my business. If a man joins under the name of John Smith and does his work well, it's his own business, even if his real name is something else. But in this case, the title is one of Scotland's oldest. I feel I must do something, but I must be sure before I move. Look, I'll tell you what I want you to do." The Commissioner leaned across the table, and he and Sue laid their plans.

At three o'clock, Miss Vicky came into Bachelor Hall, and Monty, who was waiting with Sue for the French lesson, helped Miss Vicky take off her high overshoes and fur coat, her little cap and warm gloves.

Sue wondered why Monty always took such a long time now to help Miss Vicky in and out of her wraps.

"What shall we talk about today, Sue?" Miss Vicky asked. "Playing ball with your little French friends, Arlette and Colette, or shall we pretend we are going shopping in the French market?"

"I don't like Arlette and Colette very much. They're dull. I'd like to go somewhere else for a change," said Sue, remembering what the Commissioner had told her.

"All right," agreed Miss Vicky. "You choose a place."

"How would Japan do?" asked Sue.

"As good as any," answered Miss Vicky. "How do you spell Japan?"

"J . . A . . P . . A . . N," spelled Sue carefully.

"Wrong," said Monty. "In French it's J . . A . . P . . O . . N. I've been there so I ought to know."

"Please tell me about it," Sue asked innocently. She and Miss Vicky sat there listening to his tales of Japan and the cherry blossoms, which was exactly what Sue hoped to hear. When the lesson was over, Sue walked home with Miss Vicky and left her with the excuse that she was going to take Rocket and Romper out. The Commissioner was still in his office.

"Name, please," said the constable on duty smilingly.

"Constable Winston," said Sue, "and please say it's URGENT." Urgent was a new word she had learned, meaning very quickly, immediately and at once.

Sue waited until the door closed behind her, and then ran around the Commissioner's big desk. "He knows all about Japan," she said.

"Congratulations, Constable Winston," said the Commissioner. "Tell me how you did it."

Sue told him and the Commissioner touched the bell on his desk. "Ask Constable Montague to report to me immediately," he said.

They could hear Monty in the outer room, removing his winter coat and cap, stamping snow off his boots.

"You sent for me, sir?" he said, stepping up to the desk.

"Have you ever heard of a firm of solicitors in London called Fraser, Macdonald and Fraser?" asked the Commissioner.

For one second only, Sue and the Commissioner saw him hesitate.

"Yes, sir," Monty said.

"Is your name James Douglas?"

"That's part of my name, sir. My full name is James Andrew Patrick Angus Montague Douglas."

"Then it would seem," said the Commissioner, "that I am the first to congratulate the new Earl of Falkney and Dunleith." He pushed the papers in front of him toward Monty.

All the color faded from Monty's cheeks. "I don't understand," he said.

"Your uncle and his son were killed nearly six months ago, mountain climbing in Switzerland. An aunt, Lady Charlotte Dawkins, has been hunting for you ever since." The Commissioner looked at Monty keenly. "It seems," he said, "that you and your aunt quarreled before you parted. You'd better sit down and tell me whatever you care to."

Monty sat down, and the Commissioner and Sue heard of how, when his parents died, an aunt of Monty's, Lady Charlotte Dawkins, had taken him into her home, educated him and given him every opportunity. "She was a crusty old lady," he said, "and as obstinate as a mule. I was her heir and she was determined I should marry my cousin, Agatha. I didn't want Agatha as a wife and said so. She insisted and one day we had a fine flare-up. 'Either you marry as I wish,' she said, 'or I'll disown you.' Well, I told her to go ahead and disown me, that I'd look after myself in future and also marry a girl of my own choosing.

"I had a little money of my own. I went to India, Japan,

Russia, and finally came out here. When I was down to about
my last fifty dollars, I joined the Force in Winnipeg and came to
Regina first class, lunched Susannah on the train, and slept
that night in Barracks. I have never written home nor heard
from there and so I knew nothing of my uncle's death."

"Were you fond of your uncle?" the Commissioner asked.

"I hardly knew him, sir. I don't think I saw him more
than half a dozen times in my life."

"What are you going to do now?" the Commissioner asked.

"I don't know, sir."

"Well, I have to answer these letters immediately," said the
Commissioner, "so you will have to make up your mind to
something."

Monty rose. "May I come back in an hour, sir?"

The Commissioner nodded, and as the door closed behind
him Sue ran over to the window. "I wonder where he's going,"
she said, "and what he's going to do."

"Come here, Susannah," said the Commissioner. "We'll
wait and see."

Sue thought that Monty would never come back and had
almost come to the end of her patience when he returned, walking like a conquering king. He wasted no time.

"With your approval, sir," he said, "I shall buy myself out
of the Force, and then I should like permission to marry your
daughter."

"You'd WHAT?" demanded the astonished Commissioner.

"Marry your daughter, sir," said Monty briskly. "She has
just told me she would marry me whether you gave me your
permission or not . . . but I thought it more mannerly to ask
you." Monty laughed. "I've been in love with her for a long

time, sir. Now I am in a position to marry her, I hope you will say I may."

After that everything moved so fast that Sue wasn't sure whether she was on her head or her heels. Cables were sent to England and Scotland. Mrs. Walsh was told and Miss Vicky, all smiles and blushes, asked Sue to be her bridesmaid.

"We've got it all settled," she told Sue when it was time to say good night. "Monty will go back to Scotland immediately and tidy things up there. The Jubilee Contingent leaves for London about the first of June. Before they leave we will be married here and go on ahead to London."

"Do you mean Monty will go away now?" inquired Sue. Miss Vicky nodded.

"But why?" asked Sue.

"He's a very important person now and has all sorts of things to look after in Scotland," said Miss Vicky, "and he wants to go home and get Dunleith Castle ready for me. You are to be my bridesmaid, Sue, and when you come over with the Contingent, we shall all meet in London and see the Queen drive by."

"My goodness," said Sue. "That will be a very new kind of adventure."

"The nicest one of all," said Miss Vicky.

In the morning, cables came for Monty and there was great excitement in the house. Monty wouldn't leave until he had trained someone to take his place, someone who would know how to take care of them all, the way they liked to be looked after. But Sue solved that problem. "Let's send for Hawkins," she said. "He'll come back if the Commissioner says so. He'll have to, and besides, Matilda is different now. She doesn't bother anyone—not even me."

The Commissioner was amused when Sue and Vicky made their request, but in a couple of days Hawkins reported for duty. He seemed really glad to be back at Bachelor Hall once more.

"I've missed the captain and the young gentlemen frightful, Miss Sue," he said, "and when I learned of all your pranks, I often wished I was back with you."

One night not long after, Monty and Miss Vicky came up to say good night to Sue. Sue knew he was leaving the following day and that never again would he come in the scarlet of the Force to wish her happy dreams.

"Please go away, Miss Vicky," Sue said. "From all I hear you're going to have him always, and I want him now." And Sue wept.

"I shall miss you dreadfully," she said. "You are the kindest friend I've ever had, Monty, and I never would have got my red coat without your help."

Monty comforted her. "I shan't be away long," he said, "and while I am away, you're to take care of Vicky for me. And when you start your riding in the spring, remember to keep your chin in. And, Sue, keep an eye on Matilda. She's really a good sort, and her silliness is just on top."

"I know," said Sue.

"And don't let Hawkins be uppish with her."

"Yes, Monty," promised Sue, wondering if she could remember all the things he was telling her.

"And most of all, take care of your uncle. He has so much to do between now and the Jubilee."

"Yes, Monty."

"Where's Minnie-Pooh-Pooh?" Monty asked.

"Here," said Sue. "She's beside me on the pillow."

"Then you'll be all right," said Monty. "Happy dreams, Sue." And the door shut behind him.

But Sue couldn't sleep. She tossed and turned and fretted. Matilda came in and turned her pillows and sponged her face and hands, but still Sue didn't sleep.

Finally a brisk knock came at the door and Hawkins appeared. "I can't quite fill Mr. Monty's place," he said, "but I've brought you a glass of warm black currant tea. It's good for colds and for almost anything that needs comfort."

Sue sat up and drank the warm, spicy drink, and Hawkins told her about his mother's garden in Somersetshire where the gooseberries grew as big as thimbles, where cherries were the size of plovers' eggs, and where the bees bumbled and bumbled and bumbled . . . and Sue drifted off to sleep.

The morning was unexpectedly busy. Mrs. Whiteside appeared right after breakfast and suggested that they start early with the dogs and go into Regina and see Lord Dunleith off.

"Who?" asked Sue.

"He was Mr. Monty yesterday," said Mrs. Whiteside, "but today he's Lord Dunleith and if we start now we can be in Regina early enough to wish a happy journey and a quick return."

Rocket and Romper raced over the snow, and taking turns at driving, Sue and Mrs. Whiteside got into Regina in time to see Monty's bags put aboard the train, for Sue to kiss him again and wish him luck, and to wave until the train was only a black spot on the snow.

It was very cold coming home, so the dog sleigh was tied to the back of the double cutter and Mrs. Whiteside put Sue in the middle of the back seat, with Romper and Rocket on either side of her. Then she and Hawkins piled buffalo robes around them until only the three red heads peered out above the dark robes. Mrs. Whiteside climbed into the front seat with Hawkins, and they set off for the Barracks.

The sleigh bells jingled and the steel runners on the cutter sang, but there was no music in the sounds for Sue. Her best friend had gone away and she felt forlorn. As if they understood and wished to comfort her, Rocket and Romper snuggled closer to her and rolled their deep brown eyes in sympathy.

After luncheon, Sue went over to Miss Vicky. She and Mrs. Walsh were in the middle of much planning. Vicky's trousseau was to be sent for from London, and as the wedding was to be a large one, it was not too soon to start preparations.

Everything had to be brought to Regina. The town was too small to supply any of the things that a young lady of fashion and position required for her marriage. When the Commissioner came in for a cup of tea, he declared that it took less time and trouble to look after the whole Force than it did to prepare one girl for her wedding. But Sue thought he looked very pleased all the same.

There was much discussion, too, as to whether white satin or ivory brocade would best become Miss Vicky's fair loveliness. Mrs. Walsh argued for ivory, her daughter for white.

And now, Sue found that there were things for her to do, too, for a bridesmaid, it seemed, was a most important person. She must precede the bride up the aisle in a formal, stately way and her carriage and deportment set the pace for the wedding procession. While Miss Vicky was giving her a first lesson before the long mirror, Mrs. Walsh appeared, rather breathless, carrying a long black tin box.

"Eliza, my dear," said the Commissioner, "why didn't you call me?"

"I hardly knew where to look for it, John," Mrs. Walsh replied. "I wasn't quite sure whether it was still there."

"What's in it?" asked Sue, curiously.

"Wait and you'll see," said Mrs. Walsh, while the Commissioner was trying to force back the catch which had grown rusty.

"There you are, my dear," he said at last, lifting back the lid.

There were piles of soft blue tissue paper on the top. Mrs. Walsh lifted them out. Inside lay an ivory brocade dress with much lace on it, a veil and tiny coronet of waxlike flowers. A faintly bitter perfume hung about it.

"Sandalwood," said Miss Vicky, sniffing.

"Whatever is it?" asked Sue.

"It's Mother's wedding dress," answered Miss Vicky. "I've never seen it before. Isn't it sweet?"

"Put it on, Vicky," said her mother, "and then we'll know whether it is to be ivory or white that you wear on your wedding day."

The dress was much too small for Miss Vicky, but she pinned it around her and fastened the veil and tiny coronet in her hair, and came down stairs.

Her mother smiled. "You are right," she said. "White is more becoming to you. Don't you think so, John?"

But the Commissioner was looking at his wife. "She'll be all right," he said, "but she'll never be the lovely bride you were on your wedding day, Eliza."

Sue thought Miss Vicky would be lovely, no matter what she wore.

21. The Wedding

The days grew longer, the sun climbed higher in the sky and the shadows on the snow shortened. Spring was in the air, the snow was going fast and the prairies were turning a dun color. Once again the bugles sang across the Parade; crocus buds showed on the south side of the buildings and there was a vague restlessness in the air.

Sue tried to explain this restlessness to Matilda. One day she thought it must be because they were all waiting so anxiously for Miss Vicky's trousseau to arrive from England; another day because they were expecting Monty; and again because Uncle Dennis was so busy getting ready for the Jubilee. But Matilda only shook her head.

"It's just the spring feeling," she said. "We all get it, Miss Sue, young or old; and young or old, a dose of sulphur and molasses is the best cure." And every morning afterwards, Matilda gave her a spoonful of the sticky stuff.

The invitations to the wedding had come and were being addressed. They were printed in silver on heavy ivory paper, and were very elegant, Sue thought. The drawing room at the Commissioner's house was being freshly papered and painted, and every day they watched for letters from Scotland and London. Finally word came that great boxes from England were at the station, and that afternoon, with Matilda and Mrs. Schofield in attendance, Sue helped Miss Vicky and her mother unpack the trousseau. Huge cartons covered with waterproof paper held dozens of boxes, and the whole world seemed to be filled with tissue paper, as dresses, hats, shoes, cloaks were shaken out of their wrappings. The last box was made of tin and so tightly sealed that a mechanic had to come and open it. Inside they found satin, pearls, lace, opalescent embroideries, little shoes and over all clouds and clouds of tulle.

"I shall unpack this myself," said Miss Vicky, "with only Sue to help me. It's my wedding dress."

There were letters that day, too, from Monty. Letters that threw everyone into a fresh state of excitement. His aunt, Lady Charlotte Dawkins, he wrote, had decided to come out for the wedding. Could Uncle Dennis find room for her in Bachelor Hall and would Uncle Dennis act as Monty's best man?

"The wedding is hardly a month away," said the Commissioner. "If I were you, Lyons, I'd cable Monty and tell him you'll be delighted."

Michael and John doubled up to make way for Lady Charlotte, and Sue helped in fixing over the room for the guest, for it was too muddy to ride. At times she thought that April would never end.

But when May came, the old excitement over the Jubilee took first place again, and one day Sue donned her red coat and with Hawkins rode over the crocuses to see the horses entrained for the Jubilee Contingent.

"Ours will be the only contingent from Canada to take their own mounts," said Hawkins proudly. "And won't we give them a thrill in London!"

Monty came a few days later. Sue wanted to wear her red coat to the station to welcome him, but Uncle Dennis shook his head. "Put on your blue dress and the hat with the ribbons," he said. "Lady Charlotte might like you better that way."

It was just a year ago, Sue remembered as she waited on the station platform with her uncle, that she and Monty had come out there together. In the east a plume of smoke appeared, the tracks began to hum, and down the long strips of metal the Transcontinental thundered in with shrieking brakes.

Monty was on the last car, laughing and waving to them as the train stopped. The porter placed the carpeted steps and Monty ran down, hastily shook hands with Uncle Dennis, kissed Sue, and turned to the Pullman again.

"My Aunt Charlotte," he said, as he held out his hand to Lady Charlotte Dawkins, carefully descending the steps to the crowded platform. She was almost as tall as Monty, and what little she lacked in height was more than made up for by her hat, a deerstalker with a ribbon quill sticking up at the back. She wore a tweed suit, an Inverness cape, and carried a rug over her arm, as well as an umbrella. My goodness, thought Sue, what a lot of her there is; she'd make a lovely Mountie.

"How do you do, Captain Lyons," said Lady Charlotte in a deep voice. "Shall I call you Dennis, at once. You have been so good to my boy, that I can't think of you except as an old friend."

Uncle Dennis bowed and muttered something pleasant. "And this," she said, raising a lorgnette and smiling at Sue, "must be the little girl, Susannah. How are you, my child?"

"I'm very well, thank you," said Sue, curtseying. But if there was one thing Sue disliked more than another it was being called *little,* and she had almost decided she was not going to like Lady Charlotte when she heard the visitor draw in her breath.

"Oh, Monty," cried Lady Charlotte, "you didn't tell me they wore scarlet! Why, they're astonishing, simply astonishing!" She was standing with her head thrown back, gazing in admiration, exactly as Sue had done a year before, at a detachment of the Force which had just arrived at the station. Sue changed her mind then and knew that she was going to like Aunt Charlotte almost as much as she did Monty.

"May I take your rug, Lady Charlotte?" she asked. "It's so warm."

"Thank you, child," said Lady Charlotte.

It seemed to Sue that they would never get through the crowd to the victoria. Monty had been popular while he was with the Force, she knew, but she hadn't known that he had so many friends and when they drove away, cowboys waved their lariats and ranchers their hats, and everyone wished him joy.

"I think that I am going to like your Canada very much," said Lady Charlotte, leaning back. "Your voices are too high pitched, of course, but your welcome is most kindly." She prodded Sue with her umbrella. "Well, young one, I hear you're to be bridesmaid," and before Sue could answer she was asking questions of Uncle Dennis about the Jubilee Contingent, about how long it took to get a farm ready for wheat, whether the Indians still massacred people and what kind of ploughs were used. Often before they could answer her questions she asked more, so that it was a breathless sort of drive home to Bachelor Hall. Before Uncle Dennis had taken off Lady Charlotte's coat, Monty had disappeared.

"Don't bother about him," said his aunt. "He's gone to see his fiancée. Let us have tea without him."

But before tea was over, Commissioner and Mrs. Walsh arrived to call on Lady Charlotte, and later Monty came in with Miss Vicky on his arm. There was a little pause as Lady Charlotte crossed the room to greet her.

"So you are Victoria!" she said, in her deep voice. "And you are going to marry my nephew?" She examined Miss Vicky in the frankest way imaginable, Sue thought, but then bent and kissed her warmly. "I'm glad he's marrying you, my child," continued Lady Charlotte in an even deeper voice, "for I've never seen a prettier face. Nor one I've liked half so much."

Vicky held out her left hand. A great ruby glowed upon it. "It's the engagement ring of the eldest son of the family," said Lady Charlotte.

But when the others crowded around Vicky to look at her ring, Sue caught Monty's arm. "Matilda and Mrs. Schofield are in the kitchen," she said, "and the dogs are in the laundry. Please come and see them all." Monty followed her out to see his old friends who welcomed him warmly.

"You're to share Captain Lyons' room, sir, and I've unpacked and laid out your things," said Hawkins. "Between them, Matilda and Mrs. Schofield will be able to maid her Ladyship while she is here. They have already unpacked her boxes."

"Come on," said Sue. But before Monty could hear the good points of Rocket and Romper, there was the sound of more people arriving and after that the house seemed to be more like a circus than Bachelor Hall. The Commissioner was giving a dinner party in honor of Lady Charlotte, and Hawkins had to help the four men dress, and the two maids helped Lady Charlotte, and everyone used Sue as a messenger. And altogether, Sue hoped that weddings would happen every day.

Just before they left for the Commissioner's house, she inspected them. Lady Charlotte seemed taller than ever with her hat off and a diamond tiara in her grey hair. Her long black dress had a train, and there were diamonds at her throat, and wrists. A feather boa fell from her neck to the ground, and she carried a fan and a gold lorgnette, which Sue noticed she used more for emphasis than to look through.

"My word," said Hawkins, as he helped Sue and Matilda tidy up. "If it takes all this excitement to get ready for a dinner, just think what the wedding day will be like."

But he need never have worried, for by that time the wonder of having Monty back and of getting used to his aunt was over. Besides, Lady Charlotte took entire charge of the household, suggested new desserts to Mrs. Schofield, arranged Sue's rides, helped Miss Vicky with her wedding presents, and held conferences with Mrs. Walsh over the church arrangements.

The night before the wedding Laughing Cloud and Little Chief arrived with Mr. Holmes and Jane. Nothing would satisfy Miss Vicky but that Mr. Holmes should stay and help the Bishop marry her. "You helped christen me," she said, "and now you've got to help marry me."

Mr. Holmes flushed. "You see, it's Jane," he said. "She came dressed for a summer of camp life and not for a fashionable wedding."

But Miss Vicky quickly arranged that. Jane stayed with Mrs. Whiteside, and it was Lady Charlotte herself who trimmed her dark hair and helped alter Sue's white silk dress for Jane's sturdier build.

Laughing Cloud's present was a great buffalo robe which occupied the place of honor among the wedding gifts, along with the silver tray from the Force, and Little Chief brought the bride a small bag of doeskin, embroidered with ermine tails and beads. Sue had never seen so many lovely presents or so many happy people.

But remembering one dark moment in all the happiness, she hopped out of bed as soon as Reveille sounded on the wedding day, and stole into her uncle's room and stood beside Monty's bed. There was no need to inspect the weather. It was gloriously, riotously sunny.

"Wake up. It's your wedding day," she whispered, careful not to wake her Uncle Dennis, who was still sleeping soundly.

"I know it is, Sue," said Monty softly, "but why the mystery? Shouldn't anyone know about it? I thought all the world knew!"

"It's about Lady Charlotte," confided Sue. "I found her crying last night, and I offered her my hankie, but she said it was too dirty, and I asked her what was wrong, and she showed me a picture of you in a sailor suit. My, you looked funny!"

"Sort of like a rumpled monkey?" asked Monty.

"Yes," agreed Sue delightedly. "But, Monty, I thought if I waked you and we went down stairs and got the morning tea together and took it up to Lady Charlotte that she might be happy all day. She'd know you really liked her then, and had forgiven her about the pocket money."

Tiptoeing down stairs, they made their way to the kitchen and, by the time Mrs. Schofield arrived, were leaving with the largest tin kitchen tray with cups on it for six, the big brown teapot and large thick slices of bread and butter. Sue preceded

the tray and knocking at Lady Charlotte's door, asked if she
could come in and bring with her a little boy named Monty.
There was a moment's pause, and then Lady Charlotte's deep
rumbling voice called "COME IN."

They found her sitting up in bed with a lace cap over her
kid curlers, and pretending to be very annoyed. Sue and
Monty only laughed at her, for they knew that she was really
delighted. Before long the others joined them, and they all
had tea together, including Rocket and Romper who kept
swishing their long happy tails around the cups.

Afterwards Hawkins laid out all the uniforms, Matilda
brushed Sue's hair until her arms ached, and Uncle Dennis
went over to H.Q. He came back to tell them that the chapel
had been decorated by the men with flags and bunting, and
from the Mission gardens at Qu'Appelle had come masses of
flowers to make the setting for the wedding even more perfect.

There was so much to do, so much hurrying up and down
the stairs and along the halls, that Sue thought they could
never all be dressed for the wedding in time. But finally, one
after another, they went down to the drawing room in all the
magnificence of their wedding finery, Sue last, for she wanted
to see herself in the long glass in her uncle's room and had to
wait until he and Monty had dressed.

"There now!" boomed Lady Charlotte. "What do you think
of yourself?"

Sue looked at herself in the tall mirror, and thought there
never could be anything half so pretty as her bridesmaid's
frock. It was stiff, blush rose satin, hanging from a high waist
garlanded with rosebuds. Tiny puffed sleeves left her arms
bare; silver sandals covered her feet, and to crown everything,
Mrs. Schofield put a tiny wreath of rosebuds on her head to

hold her curls in place. Running down the stairs she stopped just inside the drawing-room door. "Will I do?" she asked. "Do I look beautiful enough for Miss Vicky?"

"You're beautiful enough to eat," said Monty. "Come here and be kissed by the bridegroom."

"Don't crumple me," she cried, "any of you. I mustn't sit down or hardly move. I've simply got to be perfect for the wedding."

"Well, then, you inspect us," said Uncle Dennis, and they drew up in a line in front of her. They were quite perfect, Sue thought, in their scarlet dress tunics, gold lace, shining swords and spurs. But she was very disappointed in Monty.

"I liked you better in your red coat," she said, looking disapprovingly at his black frock coat, striped trousers and puffed ascot tie. And she thought the pill-box much better than his high silk hat.

Soon afterwards they left for the chapel, the men first and Sue with Lady Charlotte in gleaming grey satin and plumed hat following. At the entrance Michael took Lady Charlotte to a front pew and Sue waited in the porch for the bride.

Mrs. Walsh arrived, and more guests from Regina hurried in. There was such a breathless air of suspense that Sue could feel her heart beating. Around the Parade the clippity-clop of the horses' hooves sounded, and four dashing greys swept up to the church steps, drawing an open victoria in which sat the lovely Vicky, clad in shimmering satin, her tulle veil lifting in the breeze and on her head, like a Princess, a coronet of orange blossoms. The Commissioner stepped out of the carriage and gave her his hand, and in a moment she was standing in the porch with her long satin train trailing out behind her.

Sue had rehearsed the day before and knew just what to do.

"Are you ready, Miss Vicky?" she asked. The bride nodded. "Then watch me and walk slowly, and you'll be all right." Sue listened a moment. The organ was playing the same tune it had played yesterday—tum, tum, tee, tee; tum, tum, tee, tee. "Remember, Miss Vicky," she continued. "Left, right; left, right." And the slow, formal march up the aisle began. At every pew a constable stood, holding a shining lance.

There was more music, and Bishop Grisdale and Mr. Holmes talking very softly. Sue and Uncle Dennis followed the bride and groom into the vestry where they all signed their names in a big book. The Bishop lifted Sue up so that she could sign her name with ink opposite Monty's. That, Sue found, was called being witness to the wedding.

The music rang out joyously again, and the chapel bells pealed as they followed the bride and groom down the chancel steps. A bugle blew and the shining lances lifted high to form an arch above the floating veil and orange blossoms as the new Countess of Falkney and Dunleith passed down the aisle of the chapel on her husband's arm.

Outside on the steps again, it seemed to Sue as if the whole Force were waiting to see Monty hand his bride into the low open carriage. As he took his place beside her, there was a sudden cheer, a rush of laughing men, the four horses were unhitched, a hundred men grasped the pole, the sides, the back, the wheels, and the short journey to the Commissioner's house began.

"What are they doing? What *ARE* they doing?" asked Sue. For a second, she stood there, unable to believe her eyes. Monty and Vicky had gone off without her, and she was their bridesmaid. Had they gone crazy, she asked herself, or had they forgotten her. Shoving her bouquet into her uncle's hands, she picked up her full satin skirts and started after the cheering men as fast as she could run.

"Wait!" she called. "*Wait!* You've forgotten me." The crowd of men ahead of her gained in speed, and fast as she ran, Sue couldn't catch up until they reached the Commissioner's gate. "You forgot me," she cried reproachfully, but her voice was lost in the cheers of the men as the first bride of the Force passed into the house.

"Smith," Sue said. "They forgot me."

"Sure they did," said Smith cheerfully. "They've forgotten everyone in the world but themselves by now. Wait until you're married, Miss Sue."

Sue smoothed her dress and watched the laughing, cheering crowd of men move off with the empty carriage. Weddings were very strange adventures, she decided. Entering the house, she found Dawson, the old butler, in the hall. "What do we do now?" she asked.

"Well," he said, "first the friends of the family come and there are speeches and toasts and the bride cuts the cake with her father's sword, and there is champagne and everyone lives happily afterwards."

"Isn't there any ice cream?" asked Sue.

"Oceans of it," said the butler, nodding his head mysteriously in the direction of the pantry. Sue stole off to the pantry. There were rows upon rows of plates with little sandwiches, cakes, and not only one kind of ice cream but three: white, yellow and pink!

While she was busying herself with a large dish of pink ice cream, she looked up and saw Jane peeking through the swinging door. "Come in quickly," whispered Sue. A whistle sounded behind her, and she turned to see Little Chief looking in the window.

"Which kind of ice cream would you like?" asked Sue. "Pink, yellow or white?"

"Perhaps he'd like all three," said the practical Jane.

Sue thought that a good idea and just had time to heap a plate with ice cream, sandwiches and cake before Hawkins appeared to take her back into the drawing room. She hastily pushed the plate through the window to Little Chief.

In the drawing room they were toasting the bride and groom and wishing them happiness. Monty made a speech which Sue didn't listen to particularly until she heard her own name mentioned and discovered he was toasting the "Happy Bridesmaid" and wishing her luck, love and laughter all her days.

"Come, Sue," said the bride. "I'm going to change my dress." Carrying the long train, Sue followed her up the stairs. She took off her veil and handed it to Sue. "Take it to Mother's room, dear," she said.

It seemed only a moment then before Miss Vicky and Monty were running down the stairs and out to the carriage where the four grey horses waited to take them to Regina and the train that would carry them across Canada on their way to England.

A long time later, Sue opened the door of Mrs. Walsh's bedroom. She had danced with the Lieutenant Governor and the Commissioner and had been complimented until she was so tired she could hardly stand. The wedding veil seemed very empty hanging there over a chair. She wondered how she would look in it. Carefully she placed the coronet on her head and stepped forward to the long mirror.

"My goodness," said Sue. "I do look grand," and she walked

to and fro, liking the feeling of very special importance the trailing tulle gave her. She thought she would like to try on the wedding dress, too. Sitting down on the bed, she wondered how she could get into it alone and wondering, laid her head on the pillow. She liked the feel of the satin sleeve next to her cheek. "I'll close my eyes for just a minute," Sue murmured to herself.

It was dark when she heard Lady Charlotte's voice. "Lift her gently, Dennis. She is so very sweet." And Sue knew that the wedding day was over and that Uncle Dennis was carrying her home to her own bed where Minnie-Pooh-Pooh, the little brown Indian doll, awaited her.

22. *Almighty Voice*

I disagree with you, Dennis," said Lady Charlotte. "On any other occasion but this, I should say that Susannah should be in bed by nine o'clock."

"But you don't understand," said Uncle Dennis patiently. "Sue has had every opportunity to see the Force at work and play since she came out here a year ago, and I do not think a military ball is any place for a child."

"I agree heartily, Dennis, but this is not an ordinary ball. If it were, I shouldn't dream of taking her."

"Then what do you mean?" asked Sue's uncle.

"Just this. This is the last big festivity of the Force before the Jubilee. There can never be another First Contingent Ball and I want Sue to be able to remember it as long as she lives."

"Don't you think she has enough to remember?" smiled the Captain.

"No," answered Lady Charlotte. "No one can ever have enough to remember, and I want her to see this ball."

Captain Lyons turned to Sue. "Well, what do you think about this?" he asked.

"I'd like to go," answered Sue. "I've never been to a ball."

"If Sue went to bed early and slept until nine," continued Lady Charlotte, "Matilda could dress her, and she and Hawkins take her over to the gallery of the ballroom. She could watch for a half dozen dances and then go home. You will promise not to leave the gallery, won't you, Sue?"

"Oh, *yes*," said Sue, who could hardly believe her ears. It had seemed so dull and quiet all week since Miss Vicky left, and the parties ceased, that the thought of going to a ball was thrilling. "Do say I can go, Uncle Dennis," she pleaded. "I can wear my bridesmaid's dress and I promise to leave the minute I'm told."

"Well, I don't approve of it," said Captain Dennis. "But you and Lady Charlotte shall have your way."

The Barracks seemed very empty without Miss Vicky and Monty, and Sue had been glad of Lady Charlotte's company. She had tried to drive her out to Laughing Cloud's camp in her pony-cart, but Lady Charlotte couldn't double herself up small enough for the pony-cart, and Sue found that she too was getting pretty big for it. But she had ridden Beppo every day, with Rocket and Romper racing through the grasses beside her.

The Force was ready to leave now. They were going to Quebec first and after a few days there, set out for London on the good ship *Vancouver*. Uncle Dennis was going, and Lady Charlotte, Matilda and Sue were sailing on the same ship. Sue's father and mother were to meet her in London, and already plans had been made to see the Jubilee Procession from Lady Charlotte's town house. But the wedding seemed a long way past, and the Jubilee a long way ahead, so the promise of the ball was a real excitement.

Matilda and she examined the bridesmaid's dress; it was pressed and the flowers in the wreath freshened, and Sue went off to bed after an early supper, happy in the prospect of her first ball.

It was much lovelier than Sue could have imagined. Hawkins had carried her across the Parade for fear her silver sandals might be touched with dew, and then, with Matilda, they joined other members of the various staffs in the ballroom gallery. The ballroom was gay with bunting, flags, and greenery, and the band played on a raised platform at the end of the room. All the officers were in scarlet uniforms with much gold lace, and the ladies bowed and curtseyed in the lancers in a way that showed off their lovely gowns. It was almost as good as a wedding, Sue believed. The schottische followed and a polka and then a waltz. "I wish I could stay all night," said Sue, "but I see I've only two more dances left. I hope they're long ones."

The band began another waltz. It was one that Michael and John sang sometimes, with a refrain that was very popular.

> "Still I'm called Buttercup,
> Sweet Little Buttercup,
> Though I can never tell why . . ."

The music swelled and gay voices joined in the refrain. Uncle Dennis smiled up at her and from across the ballroom the drummer raised his stick in salute.

Then the most surprising thing happened! The music stopped suddenly in the middle of a bar, a bugle called attention, and upon Sue's astonished ears broke the strains of *God Save the Queen*. Everyone on the ballroom floor seemed as surprised as Sue was. Commissioner Walsh stepped forward. He looked very solemn.

"Grave news has just been received from the North Country. All available mounted policemen are to start north at once," he said. "The departure of the Jubilee Contingent to England has been cancelled."

"Stay where you are until sent for," cried Hawkins to Matilda, and almost fell over them to get down stairs. It seemed only a moment before the ballroom was empty of every red coat. Civilians from Regina and their ladies stood in little groups and then they, too, began to move slowly out. Lady Charlotte called: "Come, Sue. Come, Matilda."

Outside Lady Charlotte wrapped her cloak around Sue and held her up on the rail that ran around the Parade. "Can you see?" she asked. Sue nodded. "Then watch everything carefully, Sue," Lady Charlotte said. "Tonight history is being made."

Carriages with visitors came and went, flares were lit, guns rumbled out of the Barracks, and down to the siding where a train waited. Men, ammunition and horses passed rapidly out the gates. There was little noise considering the amount of activity.

"What's it all about?" Sue asked.

Her Uncle Dennis stopped by them. "We're off, Lady Charlotte," he said. "Take care of Sue until I come back," and he was gone. Hawkins came back to them. "The Captain's orders are that I am to take you home," he said. "I find I am not to go." As they reached the house, a long windy whistle told them that the special train with its Mounted Police was on its way.

"What's happened, Hawkins?" asked Lady Charlotte.

"It's an Indian," he said, "called Almighty Voice. He's a bad one, your Ladyship. He has killed members of the Force and wounded others, and he and two companions have been surrounded. It looks like a bad business."

Lady Charlotte looked very tired, Sue thought, and evidently

Hawkins thought so, too, for he made them both a milk punch and brought it into the drawing room.

"Get some for yourself, Hawkins, and for Matilda," said Lady Charlotte. "When do you expect Mr. O'Dare?"

Michael came in before they had finished their punch, and Lady Charlotte asked him to tell them more about Almighty Voice. "His story is a long one," said O'Dare. "Do you think you want to hear it now?"

"My people have all been in the army," answered Lady Charlotte. "I am used to border risings and all kinds of petty warfare in India. And it won't hurt Sue to learn of the troubles you have. She already knows the good times."

"Two years ago," said Michael, "Almighty Voice, son of Sounding Sky, was arrested for killing a range steer belonging to the Government. He was taken to Duck Lake and placed in the Guard House of the Mounted Police Post. He was a famous runner and an Indian of great strength, a crack shot, known never to miss his aim, and a man with tremendous courage. That night the Constable on duty, Corporal Dickson, chained Almighty Voice to a large iron ball and told him he could sleep in the Guard Room if he wished. Almighty Voice curled himself up in his blanket and soon was sound asleep.

"At midnight the relief police constable came down. He had been on a long trek that day and was very tired, but he walked over and looked at Almighty Voice lying there so quietly and satisfied himself that he was asleep. Placing the keys on the table in front of him, the constable yawned and then little by little his head dropped forward and he was asleep . . ."

"But that's dreadful," broke in Sue. "He was asleep at his post."

"He thought it dreadful, too, in the morning," said Michael, "when he wakened and found that Almighty Voice had lifted the heavy ball and, creeping forward to the table, had taken the keys and unlocked the iron manacle and freed himself. There wasn't a sign of him when morning came.

"Very soon we heard that he had visited his mother, Spotted Calf, and then with two horses, his young wife and a muzzle loader, he disappeared into the brush. We sent out a man immediately, Sergeant C. C. Colebrook, with a half-breed scout to find him and bring him in. Nothing was heard of him for a while, and then one morning, in a very lonely part of the North Country, the sergeant heard a shot. Through the bush he saw Almighty Voice picking up a prairie chicken. His young wife stood nearby, holding their horses. When he saw the sergeant, Almighty Voice loaded his gun and stood waiting. 'Stop or I'll shoot,' he cried. But the sergeant rode forward. Again Almighty Voice commanded him to stop. The sergeant rode on. There was the crack of a shot and he fell forward over his horse, dead.

"From that day until tonight, Sue, two years in all, we have been hunting for Almighty Voice. We have never seen him. We have never seen his wife, and yet we were sure that he visited his father and mother once in a while. Two days ago the Duck Lake Post sent out a party of three to check up on a tale that Almighty Voice had been seen near there.

"They rode over to One Arrow Reserve where Chief Sounding Sky, the father of Almighty Voice, lived. Getting off his horse on the trail in front of the Indian camp, on the pretense of lighting a cigarette, one of the half-breed scouts heard a sound in the brush. He turned to see what it was. A bullet clipped his shoulder. That told the scout that Almighty Voice was near and that he was on the war path. Later we learned that he and two young braves had disappeared into the woods just outside Duck Lake.

"Yesterday the Prince Albert Post sent out a detachment. Captain Allen's arm was smashed with a bullet, and Sergeant Raven's hip broken. Corporal Hockin took over the command, and when the detachment from Duck Lake arrived, charged the Indians. Corporal Hockin was killed, Constable Kerr went down a few minutes later. Immediately a call was sent out for all available men. And that's the story of Almighty Voice up till now."

"But what will happen?" asked Sue. "Uncle Dennis won't get killed, will he?"

"What will happen?" asked Michael. "Why, Sue, there's only one thing can happen. Alive or dead, we'll catch Almighty Voice."

"He must be a very bad man," said Sue.

"Yes," said Michael, "he's as bad an Indian as they come and there is more in this fight than you realize. If he should escape, we might have another rebellion on our hands."

"Come along, Sue," said Lady Charlotte. "Let us get to bed. The Commissioner might need all three of us tomorrow."

Four days and nights they sat at home waiting for news. Saturday night the Commissioner told them that the field guns were in place and the first shells were sent thundering into the bluff. Late on Sunday afternoon they learned that Almighty Voice and his two companions were dead.

"The Jubilee Contingent will leave in June, after all," said Hawkins. "There'll be no more trouble in the North."

It was good to see them all come home, to plan for England and the Jubilee again, to pinch Uncle Dennis and tell him she wanted to be sure he was really there.

That night after dinner, Lady Charlotte sent up for Sue. "I am sure I am spoiling you," she said, "but I think you should hear the story of the capture of Almighty Voice from a man who was there, and your uncle is going to tell us about it."

"Was he a very bad man, Uncle Dennis?" asked Sue.

"Yes and no," said her uncle. "By the laws of the land he was a bad man. He killed four white men, wounded three others and caused the death of his two friends and himself. Yet he was a good son, a fine husband and a brave man. When I think of the cold-blooded way in which he shot down some of our finest men, I am glad he is dead; and yet he was so brave, I regret his going."

"Tell us about it," interrupted Lady Charlotte. "Sue and I would like to know just what happened."

"He dug himself a pit in the middle of a small woods, and with his two companions took refuge there whenever the shooting got too hot. He had no food, beyond a crow he shot Friday and bark which he and his companions tore off the trees to satisfy their hunger. They had no water, but he called out to us in Cree through the darkness. 'Have no fears, Shamoganis! I am hungry, almost starving. I have dug into the ground as far as my arm can reach, but can get no water. But have no fears, I shall hold out to the end.' Earlier he had asked for food, crying out in his ringing voice, 'We have fought hard today. Send some of your food and tomorrow we'll finish the fight.' *That*," said Uncle Dennis, "was the Indian's code, practised by his forebears: Fairness in battle, fairness in games, generosity in the heart.

"Friday night," he continued, "Almighty Voice's old mother, Spotted Calf, climbed the little hill near the thicket and sang her son a song of hope and encouragement. It was cold, but she never moved. She had her song to sing, and all night she stayed there. We stopped firing, for we were afraid of hitting her, and every little while we would hunt for her and try to persuade her to go home, but she refused. 'Not while my son lies there,' she would say, and begin her song again.

"Late Saturday afternoon, we shelled the thicket. She must have realized that the end was approaching, for early in the evening we saw her figure on the hill again. As darkness came, her voice rang out deep and full throated. It was her son's death song, the interpreter told me, and her voice was triumphant.

" 'Don't weaken, die fighting,' she cried. 'Die, son of mine, die with your heart on fire. Die with the sweet wind in your nostrils and the blood of freedom in your veins. Not for you cramped spaces and the white man's toil. Here where the buffalo ran and sweet grass scented the summer breeze, here will the glory of the Red Man fade, the Indian be forgotten. But to you, Almighty Voice, is given the death of a brave. Let your voice sound then to the stars and the clouds. Die, my son, die with your heart on fire!'

"Out of the thicket a voice of thunder came. It was Almighty Voice answering his mother's death song." Uncle Dennis paused. "That," he said, "was the last time his voice was heard. In the morning we turned the big guns loose on the thicket, and by noon we knew that no living thing was left. We found the body of Almighty Voice in a deep brush-covered pit. Near the spot where the three constables had been killed, a tree bore some crude carvings. The interpreter told me it was Cree writing, and meant HERE HAVE DIED THREE BRAVES. It referred to the Police who had been killed. He thought Almighty Voice had carved the tree himself. He admired courage in friend or foe."

Uncle Dennis leant forward and put his hand on Sue's head. "Don't look so unhappy," he said. "Good or bad, Almighty Voice played his part. There had to be a final, last stand against the White Man. We are glad it has come and is over. There will be no more trouble with the Indian."

23. The Jubilee

Sue had felt very sad at leaving Rocket and Romper until Mrs. Whiteside promised to take special care of them. Beppo she left with Smith; but Minnie-Pooh-Pooh was under her arm as she boarded the train at Regina, along wth Lady Charlotte and Matilda. There had been a meadow lark singing outside her window that morning, but not even its song nor the joyous music of the band kept back Sue's tears as they left the station.

A week later she was on board the Dominion liner, *Vancouver,* standing with Lady Charlotte on the Captain's bridge.

High above the river, the grey walls of the Citadel of Quebec were bright with flags and bunting, and on Dufferin Terrace gay frocks and frilled parasols added colour to another of the gay scenes in Sue's life. From the bridge, she watched Jubilee units from regiments all over Canada come on board. There were four bands playing—one high up on the Terrace, one on the ship, and two others on the dock. They made a lovely din, Sue thought, as she joined the crowd in cheering lustily as the units came marching up the gangway.

But the cheers were growing even louder; there was a note of fresh excitement on shore. Swinging down the narrow crooked streets, rounding the corners, on through the gloom of wharf sheds and out into the sun of the great docks, came the scarlet and gold of the North West Mounted Police, blazing a new trail toward an old Empire. The crowds went wild. They waved and cheered and stamped and whistled and cheered and cheered again.

Smartly the Mounties marched on board and fell into position on the deck.

> God save our gracious Queen,
> Long live our noble Queen,
> God save our Queen.
> Send her victorious,
> Happy and glorious,
> Long to reign over us,
> God save our Queen.

Bands and voices ceased, the gangplank was hauled aboard. Her Majesty's Canadian Jubilee Contingent was on its way. Down the St. Lawrence River the *Vancouver* steamed, and out to sea.

There followed ten happy ocean days for Sue, playing games, loafing on a deck chair beside Lady Charlotte; visiting her Mounties. And then Liverpool, where the Jubilee began in earnest. The dock was lined with British soldiers, and behind them cheering people. Speeches were made and bands played and they went down to London on a special train. At London there were more welcomes, and then from the top of a pile of boxes where Lady Charlotte lifted her, Sue saw her beloved Force march away through the old grey streets to Chelsea Barracks.

"The welcome the Canadian troops receive is astonishing," said a friend to Lady Charlotte.

"It's not astonishing if you've seen the Force," she replied tartly.

"You sound as if you were a Canadian, Charlotte," smiled her friend.

"I wish I were," said Lady Charlotte, "and I wish I were a strong young man and I'd go out and join the Force."

The streets were lined with bunting and flags, and large signs on the National Gallery steps warned people that no parasols could be raised the day of the Jubilee. "So that no one can interfere with the sight of others as Her Majesty drives by," explained Lady Charlotte.

London was the greyest place, thought Sue, and yet the gayest, with soldiers everywhere and everyone in a festive mood. They drove every afternoon in the Park, and Lady Charlotte's London house was so large that when she gave a party, it almost seemed as if very few were there. The Queen was to pass by her windows on Jubilee Day and many people were coming to watch.

Sue's father and mother were to arrive from India the morning of the Procession. Uncle Dennis came in every day, and Monty and Vicky came from Scotland to spend the week— Vicky looking very lovely and proud, and Monty gayer than Sue had ever known him.

There was much talk about the Queen's health—could she stand the strain of the service at St. Paul's, the long drive? Many thought she couldn't, and Sue asked Lady Charlotte about it. "Silly busybodies," said Lady Charlotte. "Of course her Majesty can stand the drive. You don't rule a vast Empire for sixty years without being able to stand a day in an open carriage."

Sue felt comforted. She thought it would have been too dreadful if anything had prevented the Procession, or the Queen seeing her beloved Force.

The weather was a worry, too. Would it rain, and if it rained, what would happen? But Lady Charlotte dismissed the weather in the way she had the Queen's health. "There will be Queen's weather," she said. "This is the first Diamond Jubilee of a British Sovereign. It wouldn't *dare* to rain." And Lady Charlotte looked so angry that Sue felt sure there would be no rain.

June twenty-first seemed an endless day to Sue. If it ever ended then it would be the twenty-second and the day of the Diamond Jubilee. She had heard so much about the Queen now that she felt she couldn't wait another day to see her. Wondering if she would wear her crown and all her jewels, whether her own father and mother would arrive in time and whether the Queen would really know how perfect the Force was, Sue turned over in the high canopied bed and went to sleep.

There was very little sound in the room, just a murmur from the streets outside, but there seemed to be a delicious perfume, faint at first and then stronger, nearer. Sue tried to remember where she had smelt it before. She remembered the train in Montreal and her pretty mother kissing her goodbye.

"Mummy," she murmured sleepily.

"Sue, my little darling. It *is* Mummy and Daddy," and there were arms around her, and Matilda pulling up the blinds and Lady Charlotte coming in in a dressing gown and Monty arriving with Vicky, and tears and smiles and laughter—and there they all were at their journey's end, in time for the Jubilee!

Before breakfast there were crowds outside on the streets. Some of the people had stood there all night. Guests of Lady Charlotte began arriving early to take their places at the windows of Dunleith House. Vicky and Monty took Sue to the gallery of the Great Hall window and with her father and mother beside her she leaned out over the stone balustrade and watched the gathering crowds.

An old man stood beneath them on the steps leading to the house.

"I think it is General Colegrave," Monty said in astonishment to Lady Charlotte.

She lifted her lorgnette. "It *is*," she said, "and he's over eighty. Go down, Monty, and bring him up here." She was plainly disturbed and when Sue ran after him and asked if she could go, too, Monty took her without a word. He introduced himself to the General and gave him Lady Charlotte's message.

The old General smiled. "It is just like Charlotte," he said, "so kind always. But tell her that sixty years ago as a young subaltern, I stood on this very spot and watched the young Queen ride to her Coronation. It was here I saw her drive past as fifty years a Queen, and now today I am watching her celebrate her Diamond Jubilee, and I'd like to see it from the same spot. Sentimental, I'm afraid, but there is no race as sentimental as the British. Thank your aunt for me, but I shall stand here, and come in later." Sue and Monty went back indoors and took up their post again at the great window.

"They're coming!" someone cried in the crowd below. "They're coming!" other voices cried. "They're coming!" cried Lady Charlotte in her deep voice. And the procession started to pass by.

Music, color, rhythm, men, horses, carriages. "There," Monty said, "is Wilfred Laurier, the Canadian Prime Minister, Sue. See, in that open carriage."

Sue looked down. In an open landau sat a grey-haired aristocrat, bowing and smiling, delighting everyone with his charm. Other Colonial Premiers followed; lancers from New South Wales sped by with fluttering pennons and white plumes; troops from Australia and Tasmania; dark-skinned dyaks from North Borneo; Straits Settlements Police; solemn Sikhs from India; Chinese police from Hong Kong with their pigtails and mushroom-shaped hats; mighty Maoris. The British army, too, resplendent with scarlet, blue and gold and flashing steel; guards, lancers, dragoons, hussars, artillery, naval brigades. Court personages passed; richly robed and turbaned native Indian officers; Imperial Service Corps. Envoys from foreign lands, the flaming robes of the Chinese Ambassador, the quiet black dress of the American representatives.

"Here is the Royal Family," said Monty. Sue leaned far forward. There were sixteen carriages, and in each sat members of the Royal Family. They were not at all what she expected them to be. No one wore a crown or an ermine cape like they did in the pictures in the *Graphic*, but in spite of that Sue thought they looked royal, and quite friendly.

More soldiers, and then Princes riding three by three, Indian Cavalry . . . Lord Wolseley, Commander in Chief of the British Army, glittering with medals and decorations. And over all the music of Regimental bands . . . the Life Guards . . . Silver trumpets shattering the air. . . .

And then a low open carriage drawn by six cream-colored horses, a man in uniform astride each horse, men in uniform walking beside them. A tall, stout man riding close to the carriage.

"It's the Prince of Wales," said Monty.

More silver trumpets . . . the carriage passing now. A

little old lady in black and silver with an aigrette bobbing in her bonnet as she bowed right and left, right and left.

"The Queen! The Queen! . . ." voices called. "The Queen!" "God *save* your Majesty," cried everyone.

The little old lady bowed and bowed. The crowds cheered. Lady Charlotte wept.

"Is that really the Queen?" Sue asked. "But where's her crown?"

Lady Charlotte waved her hand magnificently. "There's her crown," she said. "There! Her loyal, happy people."

The silver trumpets sounded again, the cheering grew stronger, swelling out louder and louder.

"It's the Mounties," Sue heard voices cry in the crowd below. "The Canadian Mounties." "It's the MOUNTIES, CANADIAN MOUNTIES!"

Slim, bronzed, erect in their scarlet and gold, Her Majesty's North West Mounted Police rode by. Sue's cup of happiness overflowed.

*   *   *

"And what is your name, my dear," asked General Colegrave, later.

Before Sue could answer, Lady Charlotte's deep voice interrupted:

"Her name is Susannah," she boomed, "and from today on, SUSANNAH OF THE MOUNTIES."